It's late summer in  of August pressing down on Charmaine ~~~~~~~~~~~~~~ Winder. Charmaine and her mother ~~~~~~~~~~~~~~~~~~~~~ between them, but they've been forced by ~~~~~~~~~~~~~~~~~ in a tiny trailer by the river. The last of a line of local holy men, Charmaine's father has turned from prophet to patient, his revelation lost in the clarifying haze of medication. Her sure-minded grandmother has suffered a stroke. At church, where she has always felt most certain, Charmaine is tested when she finds out that her archrival, a sanctimonious missionary kid, carries a dark, confusing secret. Suddenly her life can be sorted into what she wishes she knew and what she wishes she didn't.

A moving, hilarious portrait of mothers and daughters, *Lay It on My Heart* brings us into the center of a family weathering the toughest patch of their lives. But most of all, it marks out the seemingly unbearable realities of growing up, the strength that comes from finding real friendship, and the power of discovering — and accepting — who you are.

❖ ❖ ❖ ❖ ❖ ❖ ❖ ❖ ❖ ❖ ❖

ANGELA PNEUMAN, raised in Kentucky, is a former Stegner Fellow and teaches fiction writing at Stanford University. Her work has been included in *The Best American Short Stories*, the *Virginia Quarterly Review*, *Ploughshares*, and elsewhere. Her widely praised story collection, *Home Remedies,* was hailed as "call[ing] to mind Alice Munro" by the *San Francisco Chronicle*. She lives in Chicago and in the Bay Area of California.

Early praise for

LAY IT ON MY HEART

"You will stay up all night reading this brilliant and devastating novel the way you might have with a new best friend in junior high—one whose revelations thrilled and terrified you, and whose raw, hard-earned wisdom remade the way you saw the world. It evokes the genius of Angela Pneuman's canonical progenitors: Flannery O'Connor, Katherine Anne Porter, Walker Percy. *Lay It on My Heart* is a gorgeous, riveting, and unforgettable book."

— JULIE ORRINGER, best-selling author of *The Invisible Bridge* &
How to Breathe Underwater

"At stake in this must-read novel is the sanity of a modern-day prophet, the state of his God-ordained marriage, and, most of all, the painful coming-of-age of his daughter—our wise, perceptive narrator—in the evangelical territory of the rural South. Angela Pneuman brings searing psychological insight to the conflicts that draw people to extreme faith, keep them there, or force them to emerge—dazed, blinking, and giving thanks. A profoundly moving, deeply compassionate, wickedly funny book."

— ADAM JOHNSON, best-selling author of *The Orphan Master's Son*

"Angela Pneuman has the voice I have been waiting for: sure and graceful, earthy and edgy, heartbreaking and hopeful. It is this wholly unique voice, bolstered by wicked humor and a keen sense of character, that drives so deep into Flannery O'Connor's Christ-haunted South. I feel nothing short of evangelical about this powerful debut; you'll want *Lay It on My Heart* on your 'keep forever' shelf."

— JOSHILYN JACKSON, best-selling author of *Gods in Alabama*,
Someone Else's Love Story & others

"I loved *Lay It on My Heart*. Angela Pneuman has written a funny and moving coming-of-age novel that explores the mysteries of faith and family with uncommon grace and wry wisdom." —TOM PERROTTA, best-selling author of *The Leftovers*, *Little Children* & others

"*Lay It on My Heart* is a lovely book fully steeped in the quirks and growing pains of the changing South. With the biting humor of Flannery O'Connor and the empathic ear of Ellen Gilchrist, Pneuman creates characters who come alive off the page to fully pull you into their lives. A subtle, absorbing, funny portrait of the faith it takes to come of age and to love with grace, from a masterful young writer." —KATIE CROUCH, best-selling author of *Girls in Trucks*, *Abroad* & others

"At the center of this stunning first novel is a family in crisis, a story that in Angela Pneuman's incredibly capable hands is both utterly original and nearly mythic in its powerful universality. A girl on the brink of adolescence, the only child of evangelists living in a small Kentucky town, watches the unraveling of her father's faith and her parents' marriage and discovers, in her necessary efforts to escape the attentions of her troubled mother, the dangers and promises of the secular world." —ANN PACKER, best-selling author of *Songs Without Words*, *The Dive from Clausen's Pier* & others

"I know the voices of southern girls, and when they sing true, my heart expands. Angela Pneuman is a flute. She's let the Big Breath blow through her to create a force of nature named Charmaine Peake, who then lets the spirit blow through her to tell a story about mothers and daughters and fathers, and how we all get lost, and how we might get found—or found-out, and how, ultimately, it's the courage to bear one another's vulnerability that can save us. When I finished this book, I wanted to fold the narrator and the novelist into my arms, and tell them: what stellar gifts you are!" —REBECCA WELLS, #1 *NYT* Best-selling author, *Divine Secrets of the Ya-Ya Sisterhood*; *Little Altars Everywhere*; *Ya-Yas in Bloom*; *The Crowning Glory of Calla Lily Ponder*

Praise for

HOME REMEDIES

"Pitch-perfect ... With her dark sense of humor and almost eerie apprehension of what people are too clenched to say, Pneuman is a stunning new talent to watch."

— *O, The Oprah Magazine*

"Darkly hilarious ... [Pneuman's] real subject is the complexity of female relationships, the ways that women depend on each other in a world where men often make themselves scarce ... The depth of characterization and emotional reach of Pneuman's stories calls to mind Alice Munro ... Pneuman is the master of the disquieting ending ... [like] Flannery O'Connor—another of her literary ancestors."

— *San Francisco Chronicle*

"Pneuman shrewdly probes the dark underside of idealized emotions ... Her cool appraisals and meticulous plotting suggest insights that will only deepen."

— *The New Yorker*

"Excellent ... A formidable reminder that characters—girls and young women in particular—are still making their way to disturbing frontiers."

— *Time Out New York*

"A truly vibrant collection. The characters are bigger than the pages they inhabit, not because the stories themselves are small, but because the characters register a humor and terror that are so large."

— *Believer*

"Remember the first time you looked at your family and thought, How can I be related to these people? How about the first time you realized, 'Shit, I actually have a lot in common with them'? That's the horror you'll feel when you read Angela Pneuman's *Home Remedies* . . . Though these excellent stories are not gentle, recognizing the truths in them is somewhat comforting."

—Esquire.com

"Well-crafted, tough-minded stories of fractured lives."

—*Kirkus Reviews*

"Dark and spirited . . . Sharp, well told, and—most important— fearless in their capacity to explore the contradictions both between and within characters. The prose lights up."

—*Ploughshares*

"These amazing stories . . . possess intelligence and grace of every sort. Angela Pneuman must surely be one of the most gifted young writers around."

— LORRIE MOORE, author of *Birds of America* and *Bark*

"Smart, brave, and unflinchingly honest, Angela Pneuman is a writer of such flinty brilliance and such dead-on, deadpan humor it's often hard to believe you've arrived at the end of a story until stunned by the last gesture or word."

—ZZ PACKER, author of *Drinking Coffee Elsewhere*

"I love the way Angela Pneuman's characters soldier on in their curi- ous, comic, questioning lives. I believe in them, which is to say that their troubles seem real, and, like longtime friends, their foibles amuse and alarm me."

—ANTONYA NELSON, author of *Living to Tell*

"Time after time [Pneuman] illuminates the old harrowing corners of adolescence with her remarkable new light. This book is as fresh and astringent as a raw secret whispered just before church."

—RON CARLSON, author of *A Kind of Flying* and *Five Skies*

LAY IT ON MY HEART

Lay It on
My Heart

ANGELA PNEUMAN

A Mariner Original ✦ *Mariner Books* ✦ *Houghton Mifflin Harcourt*

BOSTON NEW YORK 2014

For information about permission to reproduce selections from this book,
write to Permissions, Houghton Mifflin Harcourt Publishing Company,
215 Park Avenue South, New York, New York 10003.

www.hmhco.com

Library of Congress Cataloging-in-Publication Data
Pneuman, Angela.
Lay it on my heart / Angela Pneuman.
pages cm
ISBN 978-0-15-101258-9 (pbk.)
1. Teenage girls — Fiction. 2. Mothers and daughters — Fiction.
3. Families — Fiction. 4. Mentally ill — Family relationships — Fiction.
I. Title.
PS3616.N48L39 2014
813'.54 — dc23   2013045636

Book design by Chrissy Kurpeski
Typeset in Dante MT Std

Printed in the United States of America
DOC 10 9 8 7 6 5 4 3 2 1

This is a work of fiction. Names, characters, places, organizations, and
events are the products of the author's imagination or are used fictitiously,
and any resemblance to actual persons, living or dead, events, or locales
is entirely coincidental. With the exception of Lexington, the author has
created fictitious county and town names for full artistic freedom.

For Shawn

"How strange it is that they can't tell us what they themselves seem to know," a tall, thin beast murmured.

One of Aunt Beast's tentacled arms went around Meg's waist again. "They are very young. And on their earth, as they call it, they never communicate with other planets. They revolve about all alone in space."

"Oh," the thin beast said. "Aren't they *lonely*?"

—Madeleine L'Engle, *A Wrinkle in Time*

LAY IT ON MY HEART

CHAPTER 1

M Y MOTHER AND I get along better with a room or two between us. The way she's humming now, to herself, is the kind of thing that would make me crazy up close: but there's something separate and free about the fact that she doesn't know I'm listening. Like she'd be doing this same thing if I didn't exist, or if I was someone else's daughter she knew only from church or the IGA. She breaks into a soft, nervous soprano. "My Favorite Things." The words lilt over the opening and closing of her dresser drawers, over the sound of Mayor James's lawnmower next door approaching and retreating like something that can't make up its mind.

It's August, hot, and I'm waiting in the foyer on the bottommost stair, trying to catch the breeze from the window.

"Charmaine?" my mother calls now from the bedroom, breaking off the song. She likes to exaggerate the French pronunciation of my name, for fun, in a way that pains me: *Shah-hah-mehnn.* "Come help me dress," she says. "I have something to share with you."

In the bedroom I find her pulling her beige half-slip over her head, letter from my father in one hand. The international mail was so slow that it didn't arrive until just this afternoon, as we're about to head out to collect him from the Bluegrass Airport.

"We're not French," I say.

"We're a little bit French," she says, speaking through the thin polyester fabric. "Maybe."

She shrugs the slip down past her shoulders and bra, settles the elastic at her waist, and flaps the letter at the bed, where our black cat, Titus, sniffs at the airmail envelope. "Your father's had a new revelation," she says.

I perch on the bed and study the Jerusalem postmark. God's own city. Where my father, a man after God's own heart, a prophet, has spent the past month. Prophecy is one of the rarest spiritual gifts. Usually it involves God telling my father what kinds of things to bring to people's attention, but sometimes it involves God telling him what to do. Like visit the Holy Land. Or before that, take a year's leave from The Good Word Press, where he writes up his prophecy, so that we can live, as we've been doing since last summer, on faith alone.

"What kind of revelation?" I say carefully.

My mother is frowning into the grainy mirror over the dresser, eyeing the tiny roll of loose skin that spills over the waistband of her slip.

"Phoebe," I say. "A revelation like to live on faith alone?"

"Let's hope not," she says. "*Charmaine.* I think we're done living on faith alone. It's exhausting. Look here. Never forget to draw in the muscles, see? See?" She waves her arms until I look, then sucks in her stomach, pointing at the way the loose skin disappears. "Then you'll never need a girdle. A project, he calls it, which sounds practical. If I had to guess, I'd say your father's starting a new series of articles. About our year, maybe, or his trip. Maybe he'll even write a book." She steps into the bottom half of a cornflower blue suit she sewed herself. *Bespoke* is what she calls it, if anyone asks.

Inside the airmail envelope is a postcard made out to me. It shows a tall, thin boulder rising from a faded landscape of rock, standing craggy and pale against blue, blue sky above an even deeper blue sea below. The Dead Sea. Which is really a lake, my father explains on the back, underneath which, quite possibly, lie the ruined, sinful cities of Sodom and Gomorrah. The boulder is supposed to be Lot's disobedient, unfortunate wife. That's all the note says. I flip the card back over and study the picture, wondering if this particular choice has anything to do with his revelation. Lot's wife. One way you can look at the boulder makes her seem stuck in mid-motion, like she's trying to move forward and turn back all at the same time. The other way makes her look like she's hunched into herself, maybe under a shawl, watching her home disappear under a merciless rain of fire.

Phoebe adjusts the skirt and squares her shoulders. She studies me with a serious, confiding tilt to her head, which usually means she's about to share something she'll want to stay just between us. Like her secret tailoring jobs that have kept us in peanut butter for the past year, which my father never thinks to question. Or how she has it on good authority that my grandmother, Daze, thinks my father married down. Since my father's been away, I'm beginning to wonder if all information can be sorted into what I wish I knew and what I wish I didn't.

"Listen," Phoebe begins, but I don't want to. I scoop up Titus and jiggle him in Phoebe's direction until he relaxes into my arms and starts to purr.

"I'm a fat black kitty," I say from behind his soft head.

Phoebe sighs and pinches the pads of Titus's foot. She loves him almost as much as I do. "Look at these little black beans," she says in her half-scornful, half-babyish cat-talking voice. By the time I let him down and stand up, she's already on to something else, giving me the once-over. "What's that you're wearing?"

It's a brown dress, one that Daze bought me.

"Where's the pretty white one I made for summer?" Phoebe says, pouting.

I shrug. I'm not about to tell her how tight it's gotten in the chest, how the roomier brown one does a better job hiding the bulky evidence of my first period, too — the awful belt, the safety pins, the cotton pad thick as my forearm. In 1989 you can't even buy pads for a belt anymore, but Phoebe found a year's supply at a closeout sale. Fifty cents a box. And if I reminded her of any of this now, I'd have to hear the words *your breasts* again, and *your flow*, whispered at me in her best private voice.

Outside, the sky is a low, humid ceiling. Everything under it is muddled with heat. We head north out of town, past the campus of the East Winder Seminary, past the retirement home named after my grandfather, the famous evangelist Custer Peake. Daze, his widow, lives there now. We pass the tree streets — Elm, Maple, Walnut — that dead-end at the seminary's neglected athletic field. On a hill in that field stands our huge water tower with the light-up electric cross on top. Underneath that tower, before I was born, Custer Peake led more than four hundred people to the Lord in one of the world's largest spontaneous revivals. It went on for two weeks. People stood or sat or camped, even, listening to my grandfather over the PA system someone rigged up on day three. They came from all over, even from other states, once the word got out. It made the papers. It made the television news in Lexington and Louisville, both. On day six, my father came home from college in Ohio to see what all the fuss was about, and on day ten, as the sun set, my grandfather sent him to meet a delivery truck from Clay's Corner carrying two hundred loaves of Wonder Bread for communion. That's when my father spotted her. A petite girl, standing at the edge of the crowd wearing a sun hat and cutoff dungaree shorts and the kind of halter top frowned upon in East Winder. She raised an eyebrow at him like she was waiting for something, like he'd already spoken to her and she hadn't quite caught it all. Right then and there, before he even knew her name, the Lord laid Phoebe on my father's heart as the woman he was supposed to marry.

There's a back road from East Winder to the Bluegrass Airport, two lanes that twist and turn their way out of Rowland County. Phoebe drives with one foot on the gas and the other on the brake, or sometimes the clutch, the knuckles of both hands turning white on the steering wheel. Shifting gears is a crisis, with a lurching that nearly sends me through the windshield. In the airport parking garage, she takes a moment to close her eyes, collect herself, and thank the Lord that we've arrived. She feels around for my hands, which I tuck securely into my armpits. I can't help it. But then I feel sorry, which is the kind of thing that happens when you're born again. First you have your original reactions and feelings from your fallen, sinful nature. Then the Holy Ghost kicks in and shows you what to feel bad about. After Phoebe says, "Amen" and opens her eyes, I give her a tiny smile and pray again, a short, invisible prayer of apology.

Unfortunately, where prayer is concerned, I do not have either my father's gift of hearing the voice of God, or my grandfather's gift of sensing God's presence. They say God was so close to Custer Peake that everyone standing in the room could feel the spirit when he prayed. When I pray, all I feel is my voice spilling into a dark, silent space, a space with its own force of gravity that could pull me right in after it. Like what happens at the edges of the black holes we studied in science. But even though they're called "holes," they're not empty. They are really full of very dense matter. And my father says that with God, there is no real emptiness, either. When we worry that we are forsaken, we should search our thoughts and behavior for anything that might be preventing us from closer contact. There is always something to find.

At the airport gate, Phoebe and I take a seat in a low row of chairs. People like to say we are the spitting image of each other. We are both five feet tall, though Phoebe has stopped growing, of course, and I am on my way up. We are both brunettes. Until a month ago we both had simple, short, bob haircuts that Phoebe kept up herself on Saturday nights in the kitchen after giving my father his trim. Now I'm trying to let mine grow so I can wear it in a ponytail, even though Phoebe warns that this will do nothing for my appearance. I have the

Peake face, is what my grandmother says. A set of squared-off bones and prominent features that can be a little severe in youth but that she has seen approach classic beauty by middle age. Phoebe's face is rounder, sweeter looking. She has her own grandmother's chin, which comes to a pretty, dimpled point and makes her look worried even when she's not. Which is not very often. Daze says this kind of face looks young for a long time, right up until the day it doesn't.

Now Phoebe stands up and nudges my calf with the toe of her blue-dyed satin pump.

"Stand up with me, Charmaine. Look alive." Then she remembers about my period. "How're you feeling?"

"Fine."

"No cramps?"

I look around to make sure no one is listening. "I don't think so."

"Nothing bothering you in your middle? In your *womanhood*?" She whispers the word *womanhood* and waggles her eyebrows. Phoebe has a hard time keeping her face still, is another thing Daze says. She doesn't just have her feelings on the inside like the rest of us; she stretches her face around them as if everyone needs a demonstration.

I concentrate on my stomach. Or right below it, a spot I haven't been aware of before recently. Now I can feel it, I guess, but nothing really hurts. Womb. Womanhood. "No," I say.

"Good," she says. Then she forgets she told me to stand up and sits down again herself. Then she thinks better of it and stands up again. "Are you nervous?" she asks.

"No."

"Good," she says. "Me neither. Excited?"

"Yes."

"Me too."

The flight's in already, just arrived from Chicago and getting ready to go on its way to Atlanta. The huge, parked plane stretches across all the airport windows, like a sea creature in the world's largest aquarium. I *am* excited. I have missed my father, and even though Phoebe says he's a difficult man, and she's been happy for the break, the truth is that when he's not keeping her occupied, she doesn't know what to do with herself. Or with me either. And I don't know what to do with her. Left to ourselves, we have not exactly brought out the best in each other.

When the people start trickling through the gate, they're blinking like they've been deep underwater instead of up in the air. One tanned, elderly couple passes through the doorway whispering and glancing behind them at a skinny man with a wild beard. He's dressed like an illustration from the Bible, in a brown robe and rope sandals, and for just a moment I think that's why he looks familiar. Then Phoebe's hand on my shoulder gets so heavy it hurts.

"Oh," she says, and suddenly, beneath the beard, I recognize my father. His lips are moving like he's talking quietly to himself, which means he's probably receiving prophecy. It can come upon him any time, like a spell.

"David," Phoebe says. She waves her arms until he sees and heads in our direction. His legs work slowly against the heavy robe, like he's wading through water. I'm used to thinking of him as a prophet, which some people consider unusual even in a town as full of churches as East Winder. But until now he's always kept his hair short and his face shaved, and he's always worn the regular clothes Phoebe picks out or sews for him.

Still, you never know what you're getting with my father on any given day. "The prophet," he has said in the past, "is different from the man."

Now he stands in front of Phoebe with his hands on her upper arms. His lips stop moving, and he smiles his warm, sad prophet smile and says her name. Then he turns to me and palms the top of my head the way he did when I was little, and that's when I smell him. Not exactly a bad smell. Kind of sweet and rotten at the same time, like fruit that's gone by. The people from the plane stare or look away, but they all give us a wide berth.

"Dad," I say, and he gives me the same smile he gave Phoebe, his I-love-the-world-and-you're-part-of-the-world smile, which means that right now he is more prophet than regular person. My stomach drops the way it does in the elevator at the retirement home. All of a sudden I do feel a pain there, a slow squeezing.

We turn and make our way back through the airport, me trailing them by two steps. On the escalator down to baggage claim, my father ducks his bearded head and tells Phoebe that he is not quite himself because he is full of the spirit of the Apostle Paul.

Phoebe waits, a rare blankness on her face.

"I have been given a vision much like his," says my father. "You may find that the Lord calls upon you to adjust your expectations."

"My ex-pec-ta-tions," Phoebe says, tasting each syllable like she's unfamiliar with the word.

"Isn't it interesting that the biblical Phoebe was a special helper to the Apostle Paul?"

"My expectations," Phoebe says again. "My expectations." It's like she's doing what I used to do when I was little, repeating a word but emphasizing a different syllable each time just to see what it sounds like. It's not a good sign, but my father doesn't notice.

"I stood where they all stood," he says. "I traced their steps. It was profound. It was real. It worked on my spirit until I was open in a new way, and you can't believe, you can't believe what's possible when we let go of the limits we place on God." He speaks in a hoarse voice that is also loud, and getting faster, and people gliding past us on the up escalator stare openly.

Phoebe nods once and bites her lips. She shoots me a worried glance, and part of me feels sorry for her. But a bigger part of me feels impatient, because she's the one always reminding me that mere humans can't imagine in advance what the Lord has in store, and she has gone ahead and tried to imagine it anyway, hoped for it, and it's her own fault if she is disappointed.

At baggage claim my father's lips start working again. I don't want to stare at him, and I don't want to see other people staring at him either, if they are, so I train my eyes on the suitcases snaking by on the rubber mat. One right after another, with a secret message for me: whatever's coming is going to come.

"Here it is," says my father, and reaches down for his deflated canvas duffle.

"What about the rest?" says Phoebe.

My father hoists the bag over one shoulder, which lifts the robe and exposes a constellation of small brown scabs on his ankle. "I divested myself of anything that wouldn't fit into a single bag," he says. "And anyway, I've been wearing this robe for two weeks now."

"I see," says Phoebe, and I know she's thinking of the trip organizer's list of suggestions we followed to the letter. The loose linen clothes that were supposed to withstand the heat of the Holy Land. The search in Lexington for the appropriate walking shoes, for the hat that would protect his face and neck from the Middle Eastern sun. The list had been specific. And expensive. And Phoebe said she felt humiliated to go around raising support for the trip from hardworking people while we ourselves were forgoing work in order to live on faith alone. Which my father said was her pride talking.

"I have shed many things," he says now, as if he's thinking of the list, too. "But I didn't come home empty-handed." He winks at me and pats part of the duffle that looks flat, like maybe it contains a shoebox.

Outside, the clouds have turned deep gray and it has begun to rain. Phoebe and I trot across the road to the parking garage, then wait for my father, who takes his time, palms and face lifted gratefully to the rain until he is soaked through. Phoebe watches him and says nothing, which makes me nervous. The rain steams up from the road, a metallic smell I usually love, but now it's just turning into a heavy, wet dread in my lungs.

"I haven't seen rain in a month," my father says when he reaches us. "You forget how nice it can be."

Phoebe slides a foot out of her satin pump and regards her toe, which has turned blue from the wet dye. She slides her foot back in without comment. She points her chin. She offers my father the keys to the Pinto, but he shakes his head and opens the passenger door, flipping up the seat for me to climb in back, which I do, holding my dress against my legs. Outside the parking garage the rain comes down steadily. Our windshield wipers keep time with the dull throbbing in what I can't stop thinking of, now, as my womanhood. Phoebe heaves the Pinto through its gears, and we grimly, silently make our way over the back road home.

Daze is chatting with Mayor James on the front porch when we pull up. At five feet nine she stands taller than the mayor, and straight as a pole, too, until her shoulders narrow and curve in on themselves like the tip of a canoe. She squints through the rain in the direction of the passenger window. When we get out, she smiles hard at my father and runs two manicured hands over her silver hair, which is pulled straight back from her forehead with a clip. Since she turned sixty-five a few years ago and splurged on permanent lip liner and eyeliner, she has been pulling all of her hair back from her face to tighten everything up.

"Well," Daze says to Mayor James. "I guess you can tell where he's been for the last month." She gives a single clap of what might be delight. A woman's real emotions, she likes to say, should hold some mystery.

"Surely," says Mayor James. He shakes my father's hand, looking him up and down with the deep, friendly brown eyes that make him a good mayor. "You keep me guessing, David. Can't wait to hear all about it."

"Can't wait to tell it, Mayor," says my father, "and a few other things too."

"No doubt," says Mayor James. He sticks his hand out from under the porch roof to check the rain, which is letting up. "And now I'm going to get after the weeding while the ground's still wet." And we all watch from the porch as the man hightails it back to his own yard, leaving family to deal with their own.

I've been trying to remember everything I know about the Apostle Paul. He never married, which might be what my father means when he says that Phoebe is going to have to adjust her expectations. Though the Apostle Paul did say it is better to wed than to burn, which means burn in hell for lustful activity outside of marriage. He didn't have children, either, that I know of, so I may have to adjust my expectations, too. I don't know what happens to Daze. The Apostle Paul had to have had a mother. But my father just does the same thing to Daze that he did with Phoebe. He doesn't call her "Mother" or "DeeDee," his pet name for her. He just pats at her thin upper arms and delivers the smile.

Over his shoulder, Daze makes big eyes at me; I make them back at her and shrug. Then she arches an eyebrow high into the middle of her forehead, which she knows I like, to let me know she's not worried.

In the kitchen, Phoebe takes two casserole pans from the freezer and peels back their tinfoil. I'm expecting her to launch into her encouraging speech, the one she makes whenever our lives change direction according to the Lord's will, but she just hands me the bowl of sourdough and says, "Biscuits, please." Then she switches on the oven and adds, "Feed the dough after."

"I know," I say.

"Flour and a little sugar water."

"I *know*."

When we're alone, Phoebe wants to talk to me like I'm an adult, but the second that Daze is in the room, Phoebe snaps back into treating me like a child, just to let Daze knows who's in charge. Daze would take over everyone's life, Phoebe says, if you let her. Which doesn't sound all that bad to me.

I spoon out eight biscuits onto the cookie sheet. The cramps come regularly now, like a slow, airless breathing deep inside me. As one fades I find myself waiting for the next, and when it comes, it's comforting, in a way. *There you are.*

Daze lowers herself into a seat at the table. She makes a teepee of her long forearms and props her chin on top. "Can I help?"

"No, thank you," says Phoebe.

"Got those biscuits okay, sugar?" Daze says to me, and I tell her yes. "I always say your sourdough's on the strong side, Phoebe, but then the biscuits turn out fine. I wonder what Mary James did that was different."

It's a sore spot that Phoebe didn't take her sourdough starter from Daze. Instead she took it from Mayor James's wife, Mary, who got her own starter twenty years back when she cleaned out a dead woman's refrigerator. There's no telling where the dead woman got hers, because sourdough can last for generations if you keep feeding it.

Phoebe snatches the cookie sheet from me and sets it on top of the oven.

"You never can tell, can you?" Daze says.

When Phoebe doesn't answer, Daze turns to me.

"No," I say.

"I guess this means he won't be going back to work right away," Daze says.

"We haven't discussed it," says Phoebe.

"I think—" Daze begins.

"We haven't discussed anything," Phoebe says. She smoothes

wrinkles from the two sheets of tinfoil like it takes all her concentration. I sit down and pull my knees up under my chin
to see if it makes a difference in the way my stomach feels.
It does, then it doesn't. I want to go find my father, who has
stopped off in the living room. Probably to pray. But I don't
want to miss what Phoebe and Daze might say about the situation, either.

"David is a man after God's own heart," Daze says, after a
time. "But it would be wonderful, maybe, if he finished with
this latest" — Daze waves her hand respectfully in front of her,
looking for the word — "it would be wonderful, maybe, if he
didn't go back to *The Good Word* until he was sure he could
fully focus on it." Daze is the one who set my father up with
the job in the first place. She doesn't mind reminding people
that the press was started by the late, great Custer Peake, with
Peake family money, the rest of which my grandfather ran
clean through before he died, but she leaves that part out.

"We haven't even had a chance to sit down," Phoebe says
through her teeth.

Daze's hands drop from her chin and hit the table in fists. "I
can get his job back, but I don't know if I can get it back over
and over."

"I don't need for anyone to get my job back," says my father
from the doorway. He raises his arms to the side, and the
sleeves of his robe spread out like wings. "The Lord has given
me new direction, and everything will be taken care of. Hasn't
he taken care of us so far?"

Phoebe turns to the sink, her back to him, and stares out
the window. Her shoulders rise and fall slowly with one deep
breath.

"Hasn't he?"

"I guess he gave me the means to cover your mortgage, praise Him," Daze says.

"And someday we will pay you back," says Phoebe, speaking toward the backyard. "And it won't be soon enough."

"We had plenty to eat, too," says my father. "And when it looked like we weren't going to, the Lord provided."

At the sink, Phoebe whips her head around so fast her bob whirls into a circle, the swingy ends of her hair crashing into her cheeks. I hold my breath, worried that she's mad enough to reveal her secret tailoring money. It seems possible my father would do something from the Bible if he found out, like rend his garments or smite himself on the breast, and I say a quick prayer that God will strike Phoebe dumb, if he has to, just for a moment, like he did John the Baptist's father for not having enough faith. You can ask God for things like that, but it's not really what prayer is for, and he often says no.

Phoebe keeps talking. "You want to know something? I lived on faith alone because it's what the Lord told you to do. And I prayed and I took charity from people with their own jobs, people who probably felt sorry for Charmaine."

"I don't know about charity," Daze says. "Charity is for the poor."

"We would all be so much happier if we came to him like children," my father says, laying a hand on my shoulder.

"And I did it, I took *charity*, because the Bible makes it clear that you are the head of this house." Phoebe is pointing at him, jabbing the air with her finger. "But I have to say, I have to say right now, that I have been a nervous wreck every single day."

My father nods as though he is considering her words. He looks at Phoebe's finger, then at my grandmother, then at me.

He's blinking a lot. "I walked the streets of Jerusalem," he says. "I offered prayers at the Temple Mount. The Lord's plan is vast and spans the ages, and as I understood that, I was filled with the spirit of Paul's special mission to the Gentiles." After he stops talking, his eyes keep moving over the three of us like he's tracing a shape with them in the air. "Even my body has been changed."

"Son," Daze says. "Do you need to sit down?" But he doesn't sit down or even seem to hear her.

"Are you smiling?" Phoebe says. Her pointing finger sinks to her waist. And he is smiling, right through his beard, and it would be better if he weren't, but when he gets like this, preoccupied with a vision, it's pretty much all he can see.

"If you could for once grasp how worry is just unnecessary," my father says.

I have been a nervous wreck, too, about living on faith alone, but I don't say this out loud. I want to show my father that unlike Phoebe, whose flesh sometimes gets the better of her, I have enough faith not to worry.

"Am I hearing that you do not plan to go back to work?" Phoebe says. "Is that what I'm hearing?"

"It's interesting the way everyone uses the word *work* to indicate what one does for money," my father says. "I have never stopped my true work. Not once. I am imperfect, and I have not always worked in pure accord with the spirit, but I have never stopped trying."

"David is a handpicked servant of the Lord," Daze says. "But, son, remember that you can do the Lord's work anywhere. Even at a job with a paycheck."

I am staring at the floor, now, feeling full-on sick to my stomach, either from the cramps or from the fact that we've all been waiting for my father to come home, and he's only been back an hour, and he and Phoebe are already going at it. Beside the doorway where he stands is a heating vent, and it looks like the hem of his robe is dancing with forced heat the way my nightgown does when I stand there in winter to get warm. But there isn't any forced heat, because it's not winter. And as I lift my head to where my father's fingers peek out from his sleeves, I see that they are all spreading out, then coming back together, very quickly, a motion like scissors that travels up his arms and causes his robe to sway.

I say, "Dad," and when he looks at me now he's blinking even faster, way too fast, like the fingers and eyes are all being run by the same engine that's overheating inside him. "Dad," I say, "are you okay?" And I don't know where this comes from since I've never asked him or any other adult if they're okay before. And he keeps blinking at me like he thinks he might know me but can't place how, can't remember my name. The clutching in my stomach moves up toward my heart.

"Charmaine, go upstairs," Phoebe says.

"I have a burden," my father says, talking right to me, as if I'm the only one who can understand. Sometimes I think I might be. "It has to do with the salvation of the people of Rowland County. Not this town, with all its churches, its phari-sees, but the dark, lost outskirts. I pray that I am up to the task," he says, "but I worry that I am not."

"But you're willing, right?" I say.

"Daze," says Phoebe, "Charmaine has some exciting news she might like to tell you upstairs."

"I am willing," my father says. "Yes, Charmaine. Char-maine, thank you for that." He closes his eyes briefly, seems to steady himself, then opens them. "What exciting news?"

"Nothing," I say, mortified at the thought of my period.

"It's not that I'm not concerned for the people of Rowland County," says Phoebe. "I'm just growing more concerned every day for the people of this family."

Daze stands up too fast and lurches to the right, which is the side that lags, still, from a stroke she had last year. "I'm fine, I'm fine," she says, though neither Phoebe nor my father has noticed. "I want to hear this news," she says to me. "And I want to see the clever new school clothes your mother's made."

"I'm a Christian, too," Phoebe is saying. "I'm willing, too. I lived on faith alone for the whole year, too. We all did, if you happened to notice."

"We were taken care of," my father says.

"And you said that the Lord said a year. One year. Which is over."

"I've had some further revelation," my father says.

"We're just heading upstairs now," says Daze. As she edges around my father in the doorway, she kisses him on his gaunt cheek, right above the beard, and says, "Son," but he keeps right on talking.

"The Lord was preparing us, Phoebe."

I'm standing up now, but I can't take my eyes off the opening of my father's sleeve, his scissoring fingers. "I saw lepers, Phoebe. In this day and age. Covered in sores. People who couldn't feel their own skin burning if they were on fire. And do you know there are children in this very county born with tails?"

"Charmaine," Phoebe says, pointing to the door.

I follow Daze into the foyer, and the kitchen door shuts behind me. Daze heads up the stairs, limping a little, and I'm careful to go slowly behind her so she doesn't feel rushed.

In my room she pulls me into a hug.

"I don't feel good," I say into her chest, which is bony above her low, flattened bosom.

"It's an unusual thing, the way God reveals himself to your father," Daze says. "But there's nothing for you to worry about."

"Have you seen any of those children with tails?"

"Not tails," says Daze. "Not really. Well, tails, but not like you're thinking. More like little growths along the spine. The county health system leaves something to be desired."

I reach around behind my back and finger the ridges of my backbone. My womanhood cramps up again. There seems no end to the treachery of the body. But when I share the news with Daze, who as a rule avoids discussion of bodily matters, she congratulates me and gives me Tylenol from a bottle in her handbag. She also fishes out the extra plastic egg of panty-hose she always has on hand for runs and places it on my bed-side table. "Now that you're a woman," she says. Then I lie down and she sits beside me.

Out my window, the rain is gone and the sky has turned clear. It's getting dark slowly, and the crickets sound like they're saying, "OKAY, okay, OKAY, okay," in a kind of resig-nation loud enough to drown out the voices of my parents downstairs. The cross on top of the water tower flickers on in the distance, as it does every evening at dusk. Some nights it's bright enough to wake me up, the white light playing off town rooftops in one direction and, in the other, spilling over the rolling county fields.

When my grandfather died, Daze came to live with us for a while. She used to tell me stories before I went to sleep, the same stories over and over, and even though I am thirteen, and less of a child than I have ever been, I ask her for one now, one that I know by heart. She tells me about the day I was born, how she and my grandfather got the call and sped to Saint Joseph Hospital in Lexington to meet my parents. It was January, bitterly cold, the road from East Winder treacherous with black ice. My grandfather prayed the whole way. At the hospital he took me out of Phoebe's arms and dedicated me then and there, with his booming evangelist's voice, to the service of the Lord. Two nurses stuck their heads in to see what the commotion was about and ended up laying hands on me right along with the rest of the family.

Daze tells me how sick Phoebe was afterward and how much help she needed and that she was sorry Phoebe didn't have her own mother at a time like this but glad she had a chance to step in. Taking care of me as a baby was the great blessing of her "second act," which is what she calls her middle age. Not that her second act is over yet, she says. Her second act is really just getting started, come to think of it. When she stops talking, things downstairs are quiet. "You hungry?" she asks. I shake my head. "You feeling any better?" she asks.

"A little," I say, and I am, but I make a face like I'm not, because I know Daze will sit there with me until I feel better or fall asleep, whichever comes first.

CHAPTER 2

I N THE MORNING, THERE'S a small, flat box at the foot
of my bed near where Titus is curled up sleeping. Inside
are four separate baggies. Two of them hold about a spoon-
ful each of dirt and rocks, and the third holds a large splinter.
The fourth looks empty. They're all fastened at the top with
rubber bands, and underneath them is an index card that says
what they are in uneven typewriter type: *Holy Soil from Bethlehem Hill; Stone from the top of the Mount of Olives; Sliver from the
Cross of Jesus; Water from the River Jordan.*

I shake the sliver of wood out onto my palm. Jesus' cross
was so large and heavy that he could hardly carry it up the
hill on his back to Golgotha—even if they hadn't been beating
him the whole time. Eventually, he gave out and someone else
had to carry it the rest of the way. But no matter how big the

cross was, it's hard to believe that two thousand years of slic-
ing it into souvenir splinters wouldn't have already used up the
wood. The rest, I don't know. Probably it depends on how high
the hill of Bethlehem is, or the Mount of Olives. I picture long
lines of nonstop pilgrims carrying away handfuls of pebbles
from a mountain for years and years, the mountain shrinking
just a tiny bit all the time, until it disappears.

My father knocks, then swings open the door. He's still
wearing the brown robe, and he still smells like he hasn't
bathed, and I'm wondering if Phoebe let him sleep in the bed
with her. Or if, inhabited by the spirit of the Apostle Paul, he
even wanted to.

"Are these real?" I ask him.

"Everything's real."

"I mean, are they what it says they are?"

"The River Jordan is a possibility," he says. "Also the Mount
of Olives. Their value may be more symbolic, however."

I hold up the empty bag where the water should be.

"Arid conditions," he says.

I pretend to examine the Mount of Olives bag, with its
rough gray and black gravel. My father seems calmer this
morning, but he's still blinking a lot.

"I bought these from a beggar," he says. "He was crouched
against the city wall with a stack of these boxes and a sign
that said HOLY RELICS. I gave him my shoes." While he's talking, my father's gaze shifts from the white sheer curtain at
my window to my bookcase. The walls of my room are pale
yellow with white woodwork, and the furniture, which was
Phoebe's furniture when she was little, is also white. All the
bright white things in the room show up in warped miniature
on my father's dark, glassy eyes. His cheekbones have become

so sharp you could fit an egg in the hollow underneath each of them.

"I missed you," I say, before I can stop myself.

My father gives me a stern look. "'Reject all falsity.' Ephesians four:twenty-five."

Then I have to think about what I really meant, because he hears something in my voice that indicates that what I said doesn't exactly match what I feel. That's the prophet in him. What I really feel is that I miss him right now, more than I did when he was gone, even though he's right here in front of me and we're joined together in the Lord, which is the most important way to be joined. More important than being family, even, because Jesus says in the book of Matthew, "Who is my mother and who are my brothers?"

My father picks up my children's Bible and opens it, careful not to let any of my bookmarks fall out. It's the full New King James Version text, just like in adult Bibles, only it's illustrated with pictures: Moses parting the Red Sea, Abraham raising the sword ready to sacrifice Isaac, Jesus as a shepherd surrounded by lambs.

"I started the Christian Education class at church," I tell him as he turns the thin pages. "At the end you get a new Bible. And you join the church. And if you haven't been baptized, then you get baptized too."

"Baptism is not something you do because you finish a class," my father says. "You will be ready for baptism when the Holy Ghost comes upon you, and not a moment sooner. Only you will know when the time is right."

"Okay," I say, wondering if you can still get the Bible, which comes in pink or brown leatherette, if you opt out of the baptism.

"Do you know what's so special about the word *apart*?" he says, closing the Bible on one finger to keep his place.

I want so badly to be able to guess this that my brain turns dusty. At my feet, Titus stretches and resettles himself with his head on the box of relics.

"Think, Charmaine. What does it mean? *Apart*."

"To be separate from something."

"Now break it up and tell me what it means. *A part*."

"To not be separate," I say.

My father flips the Bible open again and runs his finger down the page, and suddenly I'm staring at his fingernails, which I've only ever seen clean and clipped short. Now they are too long, and some of them look split, and there's a thin line of grime showing right where each nail meets the skin underneath. "You could say that *apart* is a perfect word, one that suggests opposite things at the same time. *Apart*," he says again, leaving the Bible open on his lap and raising his hands to either side of his head. "Now, *a part*," he says, clasping his hands together. "A part of something larger. We are a part of the church because we share faith. 'For where two or three are gathered in my name, I am there among them,' Matthew eighteen:twenty. But we must also hold ourselves *apart* from other believers at the same time because humans are fallen, therefore any human organization, like the church, is also fallen."

Now he runs a finger down a page in First Thessalonians, which is the Apostle Paul's first letter to the church at Thessalonica, a place in the Holy Land my father may have even visited. Titus pushes himself to his feet and does his black-cat pose, with the arched back. My father has liked this in the past, and I wait for him to notice, but he doesn't.

"Here's what I was looking for," my father says. "Read this."

He taps his dirty fingernail on 5:17. It's short, almost as short as "Jesus wept," the shortest verse in the Bible.

"Pray without ceasing," I say.

"In the nineteenth century, C. H. Spurgeon gave a sermon on this verse," he says, "and in it he makes some practical points about what is unnecessary to prayer. But even Spurgeon may not allow the words their literal meaning. Prayer without ceasing. This is what I have come to believe is possible, Charmaine. I am lining up with the old Russian monk, after all, and his Jesus Prayer."

"Spurgeon," I say. "The Russian monk." I try to nod like I have some idea of what he's talking about.

"Not that I use the same words," my father says, still tapping the page of my Bible. "The monk used 'Lord Jesus Christ, have mercy on me,' but I prefer a prayer of invitation. And the most important thing is the breathing. With a two-part prayer, you can think the first part as you breathe in and the second part as you breathe out." He closes his eyes and takes a natural breath in then lets it go. "See? Consider the rhythm."

I breathe in and then out. "You do it all the time?"

"Without ceasing."

"At the same time as you talk?"

"We are capable of much more than we ask of ourselves. Once you get into the habit of praying as you breathe, you can talk and even think about other things at the same time. It has been revealed to me that prayer without ceasing keeps one in a holy state of reception, which is the perfect undergirding for the full armor of God. This is important, Charmaine, as we reach out into the county. And you're no longer a child. You're at an age of transition."

I wonder, uneasily, if Phoebe has told him about my period.

"With a spirit of reception the Lord can fully inhabit you," my father says. "He can lay many things on your heart. You may receive your calling or find yourself manifesting one or more of the spiritual gifts."

The spiritual gifts are wisdom, healing, prophecy, miracles, discernment, tongues, mercy. Among others. I try to imagine being known for mercy or miracle working the way my father is known for prophecy. *There goes Charmaine, worker of miracles*, people might say. Then I wonder if that kind of thinking borders on prideful, and I try to imagine myself manifesting the gift of humility. *There goes Charmaine the humble*. But even that could be prideful, if you think about it.

"What words do *you* use when you pray without ceasing?" I ask him.

"That's between me and the Lord. And whatever you pick will be between you and the Lord. You don't have to keep it secret, but I think you'll find that exposing certain things to the air, even to other believers, can be frustrating. That's a good example of holding yourself 'apart.'"

I nod, but I wish he would just tell me what he prayed so that I could pray the same thing. Sometimes I think that I would rather share a secret with my father than with the Lord, but that's backward. A prophet helps people get closer to the Lord and the Lord's will, through revelation and interpretation, pure and simple. You're not supposed to try to get closer to the Lord just to get closer to a mere human, even if that human happens to be your father.

"I think I have it," I say after a moment. "My prayer." I know he won't ask what the words are, but I'm disappointed when he doesn't respond at all. His eyes are closed, and he seems to be listening to the summer sounds outside. The morning insects, the buzzing kind, instead of the chirping evening kind. And the slow, wavelike sound of each approaching car, now drowned out by the train rumbling across Main Street not a quarter mile away. I watch the way he listens, ready at all times for the voice of God, and I breathe in and think the invitation I've come up with, words that seem grave and receptive: "Inhabit me," on the breath in, then out: "O Lord God."

My father opens his eyes and follows the motion of the sheer at my window. It picks up the breeze, fluttering out toward my bed before being sucked back against the screen, a kind of breathing of its own.

At lunch my father drinks tomato juice but slides his grilled-cheese sandwich over to me, which means he's fasting. His hair is so greasy it looks wet. Between his beard and mustache, his lips are moving again. Possibly a prophecy, possibly his ceaseless prayer, which makes me remember to pray my own. *Inhabit me,* I think, breathing in deeply. I hold it for a second. *O Lord God,* I think, slowing down the words in my head so they fit the long breath out perfectly.

Phoebe tries to catch my eye, but I look down at my food. "How long is this going to last," she asks my father.

His mouth moves a moment more before the sound comes out. "I don't know," he says, finally. "As long as it takes. I'll be spending some time at the river."

"You just got back," she says tightly.

"Is the tomato juice still there?"

Phoebe closes her teeth and blows air through them. It sounds like she's deflating. Her face is white except for two high spots of color. "At the river? Yes. The cupboard is full of tomato juice. You can bet Charmaine and I didn't head down there to deplete your supply."

"Phoebe," I say, because she sounds so mean.

"She calls me 'Phoebe' now," she says to my father. He nods distantly, like he's hearing about the weather in another state. "I guess that's okay with you. 'Honor your father and mother'?"

"Your mother is angry," my father says to me.

"When was the last time you ate?" says Phoebe.

"I've been fasting for two weeks."

Phoebe presses her lips together. Today she has not bothered with lipstick. "I guess that explains a lot."

"Jesus fasted," I say.

"I realize that," says Phoebe.

"I'm fasting." I push away my grilled cheese. My cramps are gone, and I missed supper last night, and I'm hungry, but my father needs backup.

"The Lord does not ask growing children to fast. David?"

"That's true," my father says.

"I'm a woman," I remind her.

"Oh, that's right," Phoebe says. "I'd forgotten." She snatches my plate, then my father's plate, and crosses the kitchen to dump the sandwiches in the trashcan. It is not like Phoebe to waste food, ever. "Here's what we'll do. We'll take your father down to the river and then we'll come back here by ourselves, as if he hadn't even come back from the Holy Land at all. And I, for one, am going to spend some time on my own knees in prayer, because I am not feeling very godly."

"We will all be in prayer, then," my father says. "Which is as it should be."

I move my lips, praying as I breathe, in case he happens to notice.

After lunch we head south, Phoebe grinding through the low gears until Main Street becomes the river road. The open windows turn the Pinto's back seat into a wind tunnel, and I can't hear anything Phoebe and my father are saying. But they're not saying much. I'm figuring it will take a day or two for her to get over being mad and get on board with the plan. Then we'll all settle in to what my father's latest vision means to everyday life. Out the rear window, the cross on top of the water tower, unlit, is just a sharper white against the pale, muggy sky. In East Winder, you don't just pass churches on every corner, like in a lot of towns. Here, there are churches in the middle of each block and more churches in the tiny strip mall with the dollar store on one end and the dime store on the other. The New Beginnings Free Methodist Church meets in a corrugated building in the parking lot of the IGA. And there's still the old Free Methodist Church, which the New Beginnings Free Methodist splintered off from. There's United Methodist. There's Church of God, Church of Christ, Church of Jesus Christ. Church of the Savior, Church of Jesus Christ the Savior, Church of the Holy Savior. Presbyterian, Lutheran, Nazarene, Assembly of God, Christian Church, First Christian Church, First Community—where we've been going—Christ Evangelical, and Evangelical Free. There's the Salvation Army. There's a small Baptist church, even, though mostly county people go there, since you don't have to go to seminary to become a Baptist preacher and most people in town are tied up with the seminary. In fact, two out of three East Winder men are preachers, or they're at the seminary studying to be preachers, or they're retired preachers living out their dotage, Daze says, in the Custer Peake Memorial Retirement Center. The black community on the other side of the railroad tracks is divided between the African Methodist Episcopal and the African Methodist Episcopal Zion. The nearest Catholic church is over in Clay's Corner, and the only Jewish people I've ever seen are the Jews for Jesus who came through once and put on a musical show in the seminary auditorium. There are missionaries in town, too, home on furlough. Even though my father considers them a refreshing bunch, closer to the practical application of the Lord's will, he says, than seminarians battling it out over hermeneutics, their kids can be hard to take. They've been all over the world, and they like to rub it in. Like Seth Catterson, who went to school with me up to third grade, when his family left for Ghana. He's back now, and when I saw him in church last week, he said, *"Kawula,"* then pretended to look confused, hitting his head with the palm of his hand like he couldn't believe he was so African now that he'd forgotten how to say *hello* in English.

North of East Winder, what everyone calls the "city side" of the county because it's nearest Lexington, the land is wealthy—all tobacco fields and thoroughbred horse farms. But on the south side, what everyone calls the "river side," it's scrubby pasture as far as you can see, dotted with cows and hogs and a few swaybacked old mares. The black barns that held tobacco in better days are turning gray as the creosote wears off, and most of them list to one side like sinking ships. The river side is where Custer Peake's people all lived before the turn of the century. Before the Holiness Movement swept through the South and some great-great-great-uncle Peake was called to preach and ventured into town.

The old farms just south of East Winder are set back from the road, like they're holding you at arm's length. Closer to the river, though, houses begin to creep in toward the road, some with just a ribbon of gravel between the blacktop and the front door. We pass unpainted porches sagging under dishwashers, electric stoves, upholstered chairs, and one stacked high with bricks and clapboards pulled off from somewhere, nails still poking out into the air like they're surprised to see the light of day. Almost every rutted driveway has the shell of a truck propped up on cement blocks.

My father has always talked about the county as a place where instead of turning to the Lord, people turn to the worldly occupations of drinking, fornicating, gambling over cockfights, or listening to country and rock 'n' roll music that makes the blood boil for more of the same. We pass a yard where two red-haired girls about my age share a cigarette and glare at us. One of them raises her middle finger. "See?" my father says, gesturing to Phoebe as if they've been having a conversation about it. As if any of this is new. As if Daze, when she ventures down to the river, doesn't always comment on the particular type of red hair folks have in these parts. County red, she calls it, and she claims it comes with its own brand of hostility.

"We're going to get a flat tire," Phoebe says as we drive over a sprinkling of brown glass.

It takes ten minutes total to get from our house in town to the tiny piece of land on the river that's been passed down through the Peake family for six generations. The road is straight and flat until you hit Tate's Bridge, which spans the gorge high above the water. Three hundred feet high, to be exact, which everyone knows from the sign the state put up to mark it as a historic site. The bridge is rusted red and older than the Civil War, but the Norfolk Southern trains still make their heavy way across it every couple of hours. The whole thing is held up by two long piers that end in cement feet, each planted into the opposite riverbank far below. So far below that if you look down you start to get that pull that tells you that falling, jumping, even, is what you really want to do. Every so often someone fool enough to climb out onto the bridge slips. Or jumps. When they fish out the body, every single bone is broken.

After the bridge, the road drops into steep switchbacks that sink you deeper and deeper into the gorge until you hit the bottom. Then it straightens out again to run along the river. Folks live spread out on both sides of the blacktop, but everyone on our side, near the riverbank, built their houses on stilts for when the river overflows. Everyone except us, since our place is really just the old RV that my grandfather used to travel around the country in, evangelizing. After he died, and Daze said she didn't care if she ever saw the inside of the RV again, my father parked it on the river lot and raised it onto a stone foundation that's supposed to hold through all but the very worst flooding. "The wise man builds his house upon the rock," he'd said. Then he built up log walls around the door, windows, and all the sewer and electrical hookups. He did most of this with the nervous energy fasting brings on. Some of it he did during a dark night of the soul that lasted pretty much one whole summer. Now the RV looks like a real cabin, sort of. There's even a tin roof with just a little pitch to it, like on a lean-to, so the water runs off when it rains and collects in our cistern.

We pull into the short gravel drive, and Phoebe cuts the engine. She's out of the car first, standing and looking helplessly out to the river, which is brown and swift from the rains, then up to the bridge, which straddles the cliffs high above like an ancient, complicated skeleton, and finally to our cabin. My father's robe catches on the car door, and I wait while he struggles with it, then I push myself up and out of the back seat.

"Here we are." My father spreads his arms to take in the air, the green vegetation. In college, before the Lord made him choose between becoming a park ranger or a man of God, my father learned a lot about nature. He can name almost every tree around, from the blue ash and squat chinquapin oaks to the yellowwood with its smooth, gray bark. The river is high enough today that the old sycamores down the bank dip their lowest branches into the water. You can hear our tiny dock, just out of sight, straining its ropes, knocking against one of the trees. That's how strong the current is.

"This grass needs cutting," says Phoebe. "And the garden's a mess. I've come down for vegetables but I haven't done much weeding."

"Those are prayerful tasks that will serve me well during this time," says my father, but she's already heading off through the tall, wet grass down toward the small garden closer to the river. I follow my father to the shed on the side of the cabin and stand there, helpfully, because I have a feeling he might have forgotten the combination, which is 1-06-76, my birthday. But he hasn't, and the lock springs open against his hand.

"It's quiet down here," I say as he opens the door of the shed and begins wrestling with the mower. "Easier to hear the voice of God."

"Interior barriers to God's voice can be much more of a problem than exterior," says my father. He rolls the push mower to the side of the cabin and props it there, then crouches down over the reel and runs his finger over one of the blades, testing for sharpness.

"I bet you could write some interesting stories about your trip, down here," I say. "Or about the ministry of the Apostle Paul. Or how to pray without ceasing." These all seem like good ideas, ideas that fit both his vision and Phoebe's practical concerns without my having to bring them up.

My father, still crouching, rolls the mower back and forth, making it squeak. He rises and returns to the shed without looking at me. When he comes back with a small bottle of oil, his lips are moving.

"Dad," I say. "Did you hear me?"

He squirts oil onto the axle of the reel and rolls the mower back and forth again to work it in.

"Dad?"

"Internal barriers to God's voice include worry," my father says, speaking down into the blades.

"I'm not worried, though," I say, and my voice is chirping, chirping, as if it hasn't even entered my mind how we're going to keep on without any money coming in. "I just think you have a lot of interesting things to write about."

My father frowns at me over his shoulder. "You disappoint me, Charmaine. At least your mother acknowledges what she feels even as she allows it to come in between her and the Lord's work. At least she is not hiding her own thoughts from herself. At least she is not walking in total darkness." He shakes his head like I, myself, am a bad thought he's trying to clear himself of, and turns back to the mower.

I swallow hard. "I'm not walking in darkness."

"It is very difficult to retain a childlike faith as one grows older," says my father. He sounds more neutral now, less disgusted, like he's speaking to the mower because he's given up on me.

"I do have a childlike faith," I say, but the words come out high and thin. I hope Phoebe hasn't told him about my period.

My father rises with his back to me. The hem of his brown robe looks damp. He pushes the mower several feet, right up to the edge of the cabin and back, and the blades quickly become clotted with wet grass.

"I'm just at an age of transition," I say, moving up behind him. "My faith is still childlike. It is. Dad. Dad." All I want is for him to turn around and see me. Even if he's mad.

The prayer has come to his lips again, and I've already stopped mine. I say it twice quickly to myself, as he works the mower over the same patch of grass, forcing it through the tangled growth. Before I know what I'm doing, I reach out and grab a handful of his robe. That's when the reel locks up. The mower skids forward with all my father's weight behind it, so that my yank is hard, harder than I mean it to be. We rebound into each other, his back slamming into my front, where my chest already hurts most of the time.

When he whirls around, the back of his hand catches my chin. It takes me a second to understand that this is not an accident. I let go of his robe. My hand goes to my face, as if my fingers have their own curiosity about what happened there.

My father has never hit me before. He nods at me like he's confirming something, and I feel him see right through me, through my pretend-innocent suggestions. It's true that I don't have enough faith. That I am afraid. That I have been hiding my thoughts from my own self. I wish I could disappear, which is probably how Cain felt, running away after killing his brother, trying to hide from God.

I pick my way back through the wet grass to the Pinto, holding my throbbing jawbone. My eyes feel hot and dry. I didn't know that becoming a woman would do anything to my childlike faith. I didn't even realize there was anything special about it the whole time I had it. But I understand that when a lack of faith obstructs God's will, my father cannot let himself be bound by mere human attachment. "Who is my mother and who are my brothers?" also means "Who is my daughter?" If you love anyone, even people in your family, more than you love Christ, then you are unworthy of Him.

I wait in the passenger seat of the Pinto. Tiny, flat green grass bugs have collected around my ankles like confetti, and when I try to brush them away with my fingertips, they smear across my skin and die. "I'm sorry," I whisper, and try to shake off the rest. It occurs to me, slowly, that maybe my father would not be disappointed enough to strike me if he did not still consider me capable of faith. That if he did not think me capable he would treat me more like he treats Phoebe, like some things are simply too much to expect.

He has told me about the prayer without ceasing, after all, though of course I have already ceased again. "Inhabit me, O Lord God," I whisper now, breathing in and breathing out, keeping my eyes on the palisades that rise steeply across the river in front of me. Soon my eyes are burning a little less. The limestone walls, crowned by a ridgeline of deep green trees, seem like they're growing toward the sky with every exhale, lifting the old bridge above me even higher.

. . .

Phoebe climbs up the riverbank carrying tomatoes in her T-shirt. She pauses behind the cabin, says something to my father, then approaches the Pinto and lays the tomatoes carefully on the back seat. She missed the whole thing. We drive wordlessly up out of the gorge, jerking through the gears until we finally reach the top and the road levels off again. She checks her pocketbook, then asks me to scour the seats and floor of the car for change. Together we come up with a dollar thirty-eight, and she drives straight through East Winder and out the city side, then turns west toward Clay's Corner, where I'll be starting at the county junior high in a week. Clay's Corner put in a McDonald's last year, and when Phoebe is feeling really terrible, it's the only thing that can help.

"One hamburger each," she says on the way in. "No French fries. Water to drink. Unless tax has gone up, we'll be fine."

Phoebe waits in line, and I head down the short hall to the ladies' restroom. In the stall I am shocked to see that even though I feel none of the cramping from yesterday, I have continued to bleed since I changed my supplies this morning. Blood has stained my underpants and the inside of my shorts, though it has not yet leaked through to the outside. When I join Phoebe in line, I whisper that I need a quarter.

"What for?" she says, not whispering back. A man in front of us is getting ready to order.

"I need it," I whisper.

"We don't have it."

"Please?"

She points to the marquee sign above the counter, where all the prices are listed. "How much are hamburgers?"

"Sixty-two cents."

"How much is sixty-two times two?"

"One twenty-four."

"Plus tax," Phoebe says. "How much money do we have?"

"A dollar thirty-eight."

The man grabs his tray, and Phoebe, satisfied that she has explained herself to me, begins to order from the high school girl behind the register.

I creep back to the bathroom and sponge up what I can with toilet paper. I roll more toilet paper around my hand, and when it feels as thick as a pad, I add it to the top of the other one, then I wind toilet paper around the whole thing, including the crotch of my underpants. I try to pull it all as tightly against myself as I can, and I manage to button my shorts and waddle out of the restroom and down the hall to the dining room, where Phoebe has taken a table for two by the plate-glass window and already unwrapped her hamburger.

"Let's pray," she says, and bows her head. "Oh, Lord, for what we are about to eat, make us truly grateful. Amen." Then she pops open her eyes. "What did you need the quarter for?"

"I don't want to talk about it."

Phoebe bites into her hamburger and chews it reverently. Her pointy chin moves up and down. "There's nothing in the world that tastes like this," she says, placing her fingers over her lips since she is talking with her mouth full.

I unwrap my hamburger, too.

"Tell me what you needed the quarter for," she says.

"My period," I say as quietly as I can.

Phoebe swallows and frowns at me. "Part of being a woman, Charmaine, is thinking about that kind of thing before you leave the house."

"I know."

"With a new body comes new responsibilities. You can't be caught out just anywhere without supplies. Where's your purse?"

I shrug. Phoebe sewed me a purse from a pair of brown corduroys that I outgrew. The rear pockets of the pants decorate the front of the purse, which is cute as an idea, but in real life the material still bags out in the shape of my bottom.

"You're talking about the machines in the bathroom?" Phoebe says. "That's what you needed the quarter for? Those are tampon dispensers, Charmaine. Do you know what tampons are?"

"It's not just tampons in there," I hiss, glancing at two women at the next table, willing Phoebe to lower her voice.

"You're too young for tampons, anyway," Phoebe says. She takes another big bite of her burger, which is going fast, and nods toward the remaining half on my wrapper. "Does yours taste funny?"

"No. Does yours?"

"No. But if yours did, and you took the rest of it up to the counter, they'd probably give you another one."

"Why don't you do it?"

"Because mine tastes fine, too," she says in a small voice. "It tastes great." She finishes the burger off and wipes her mouth with a napkin. "Listen, Charmaine, I'm not like some folks in East Winder who think tampons compromise your virginity."

The women at the next table stop talking to each other and turn toward us.

"Phoebe," I say. "Please."

"Oh, relax. As if this particular matter is the biggest thing we have to worry about in the grand scheme of things. However, it should be said that someday you will want to get married to

a good Christian man, and you will want to give him the precious gift of your virginity, and the issue is not do we believe
tampons compromise that, but whether or not the man you
marry will have been raised to believe that. It's a good idea to
honor that possibility."

Now the women at the next table are staring deep into each
other's eyes, holding their breath, daring themselves not to
laugh.

"What happened to your face?" Phoebe points to where my
father caught me on the chin. "You're a little flushed there.
Does something hurt?"

"No."

"Listen. You need to consider what I said about tampons."

"If you say *tampons* one more time, I'm going to die," I say
under my breath. "I hate my period."

"One day you'll have the joy of your own children," Phoebe
says. "In the meantime, don't be melodramatic."

I stuff the rest of my burger into my mouth and chew miserably over the thought of these imaginary future children. I
would sacrifice them in a heartbeat if it meant I could get rid
of my period.

"We simply don't have quarters to go squandering on tampons. Not when we have perfectly good supplies at home.
Especially now that your father has thrown us a curve ball."
Phoebe crumples the wrapper of her hamburger. "We don't
have money for this, either," she says. "That was our last hamburger for a long, long time. Sixty-two cents is sixty-two cents.
Times two. Plus tax. Not to mention what it took in gas."

"God's will isn't a curve ball," I say.

Phoebe sighs and turns to the plate-glass window. Outside is
a plastic playground, with a high fence so kids can't run out into

the street. A woman sits on a bench, sipping her drink through a straw and watching four blond children tumble around on the slide. You can hear their shrieks, muffled through the glass. Phoebe's chin has begun to quiver, as though she is about to cry, right here in McDonald's. She closes her eyes for a quick prayer, and then I realize that I've left off the praying without ceasing again, and I start in.

"Did you say something?" Phoebe says, opening her eyes.

"No."

"Under your breath?"

I don't know why I don't want to tell her about the prayer, but I don't. "No."

She shakes her head slowly. "I hope the teenage years aren't going to be full of resentment and attitude. But it's not looking good."

"I'm not resentful," I say, clenching my jaw in pure resentment.

"It's not every woman who could be a helpmeet to your father. Hear me? It's no walk in the park. But the Lord brought us together. So I don't need a teenage girl telling me about God's will. I have my own front-row seat, and I'm barely hanging on."

I drop my head and keep it low, but I can feel the women behind Phoebe, listening.

"When someone speaks to you," Phoebe says, "please respond."

"Okay," I say.

"I am at the end of my rope. You get that, right?"

"Right."

"This is hard," she says.

"I know."

"What do you know?"

"That this is hard."

Phoebe sighs again. "Your tone is unkind."

"I don't know what you want me to say," I say.

"I don't want a puppet," Phoebe says, "but I don't think a little compassion is too much to ask for."

I am trying to think the prayer while I talk, but it stops and starts around the words I say out loud. Still, I like having something private in my head, especially when Phoebe starts in on compassion. I heard her telling Daze, while my father was away, that she worries about my "diminishing capacity" for. it. This includes my capacity to understand that the world does not revolve around me, as well as my capacity to imagine what it might feel like to be another person and to imagine what that other person might like to hear in order to feel better. But Phoebe has it wrong, because even though I say I don't know how she feels or what she wants to hear, it's not true. I do know. She wants me to tell her how sorry I am that this latest thing with my father is hard on her. She wants me to say that I will start helping her out in little ways around the house. Doing my chores without being asked and taking over some of her chores, too. I know she'd like to hear this because this is the kind of thing I used to be able to say to her when she was overwhelmed or worried, like during the summer of my father's dark night of the soul. And when I said these things, she would hug me and cry a little harder and tell me I was sweet. I remember what it felt like to want to say these things, too, but whatever made me want to has flipped over inside me into the most intense not-wanting-to that I have ever felt about anything.

The women who have been listening to us gather their trays

and move to the trashcan. One of them sneaks a look back and shakes her head, just barely, in disapproval or disbelief or disgust. First this embarrasses me, but then it makes me mad, more mad than I am at Phoebe, even, and I stare right back at the woman. I keep myself from blinking until she stops shaking her stupid head and turns away. By the time Phoebe turns around to see what I'm looking at, the women are gone, the glass door of McDonald's already closed behind them.

CHAPTER 3

*E*VERY SUNDAY, BEFORE THE main service in the sanctuary, my Christian Education class sits in a circle of folding chairs in a cinder-block room of the church basement. Besides me, the teacher, and two adult women, there are these two girls I know, Mary-Kate and Karen, best friends joined at the hip, and now Seth Catterson, the missionary boy back from Ghana. This morning, one of the women, a thin, blond seminary wife, starts us off by saying that in her old church whenever anyone was baptized, they spoke in tongues. "Baptized not just with water," she says, "but with the Holy Ghost." The teacher, Connie Bowls, nods so hard that her soft, powdery skin quivers. It's like she's agreeing, but she's not. No one will expect the blond woman to speak in tongues at First Community Church, Connie Bowls explains. In fact, First Community considers tongues to be a private prayer language. To be used in private. The seminary wife writes this down on her notepad.

"But if there's a translator, then it doesn't have to be private," says the other adult woman. She's also blond, but heavier set. With her Bible, she holds an old issue of *The Good Word,* the one with my father's revelation on fasting.

"In Ghana lots of people speak in tongues," Seth adds.

"It's more a matter of church unity," says Connie Bowls. "Of time and place."

"Once I even translated myself," says the second blond woman. "Translation is one of the gifts of the spirit." She looks pointedly at me. "Like prophecy."

"Prophecy is an Old Testament gift," Seth says, beating his pencil against the rubber sole of his shoe. "Speaking in tongues is a gift of Pentecost. Acts. New Testament."

"I thought speaking in tongues was from the Tower of Babel," says Mary-Kate. She and Karen wear their hair in identical French braids, while I have managed only to pull my bangs straight back into a barrette. I wonder if either of them has started her period, but I'm glad you can't tell from looking.

"The Tower of Babel is where different languages come from," says the seminary wife. "Like French and Spanish."

"Something like that," says Connie Bowls, nodding.

"My father says the Lord has always spoken to him in plain English," I say. "And there are plenty of prophets in the New Testament."

"What do the prophets have to foretell in the New Testament after Christ already came?" Seth asks.

"What about interpretation?" I say. "What about revelation? What about John the Baptist and the Apostle Paul? What about Agabus? What about Philip's daughters?"

"Debatable," says Seth, though I doubt he even knows about Agabus and Philip's daughters, since most people just skim over their mention.

Connie Bowls smiles brightly. "This lofty discussion falls right in with today's scripture from First Corinthians, where Paul says the church has one body but many parts. A role for every member. Let's get quiet, for a moment, and contemplate some of the ways the disciples supported the early church. Then we'll write down what this says to us about our responsibilities today."

I don't even have to crack open my Bible to write *prayer* and *outreach,* and to come up with examples, the most obvious being prayer in the Garden of Gethsemane and the writing and preaching of the apostles throughout the New Testament. *Today,* I write, *this means supporting the church in prayer and witnessing to others. And,* I add for Seth's benefit, *being open to new revelation from the Lord.* When I look up, everyone else is scowling down at their Bibles, turning pages, except Seth, who has also finished. He pulls a thick square of paper out of his back pocket and unfolds what looks like a script, with a broad white margin on the left.

I love plays. Seth and I were in one together, a church play, back in the third grade. It was directed by Dr. Osborne, a man in town who is famous for never marrying, for having never known a woman, biblically. In addition to directing plays, he teaches sermon delivery at the seminary. In the play, Seth and I were supposed to be husband and wife. When he came home from work, he was supposed to kiss me, which we both refused to practice, and the night of the performance he came toward me like an attack and banged into my cheek with his teeth.

"Is there a new church play?" I ask him after class.

"By 'church,' do you mean a play *about* church or a play *for* church?"

"Either one."

"In that case, the answer is yes." He refolds the paper and pushes it into his pocket.

Connie Bowls places one hand on my shoulder and the other on Seth's, as if this will help us get along. "It's nice to have you and your family back from the mission field, Seth," she says. "And Charmaine, I know you're glad to have your father home from the Holy Land."

"Yes," I say, even though he's been home all of a day and a half and he spent last night down at the river, not at home.

"Ghana's farther away than the Holy Land," says Seth.

"Maybe one day I'll be lucky enough to see both Ghana and the Holy Land," Connie Bowls says as she steers us toward the door. She is so nice to everyone that I don't know how I'm going to explain about not getting baptized if the end of class comes upon me before the Holy Ghost does.

My father doesn't show up for the main service like I thought he would. I've assumed that the heat of his revelation has been cooling into a new workable vision, and that he will ease back into being not just *apart* but also *a part* of the community. As much as he ever is. Usually when he's fasting down at the river and needs to get home for church or any other reason, he walks to the tiny gas station in Tate's Bend and calls Phoebe from the pay phone. Today, though, Daze, Phoebe, and I sit by ourselves in our regular pew. The two of them take turns telling people that yes, David got home okay, but he's still exhausted from traveling.

The sanctuary of First Community is big and barn shaped, with a red-carpeted floor that slopes down to a stage in front and two small alcoves in either corner. The choir sits on the right, and on the left is the worship band, a group of seminarians with two electric guitars, two acoustic guitars, a drum set, and a keyboard. Their warm-up sounds like a bag of cats. The windows that look out over the bank parking lot are wide open, but the ceiling fans just churn up stale, hot air. The only other windows, near the ceiling on the opposite wall, open not to the outdoors but onto the Upper Room, domain of the Youth Group leader, Pastor Chick. This is the year I'm finally old enough for the Sunday-night meetings, which will start up again when school does.

As the band launches into the first song, Daze hands me a funeral-home fan and raises her eyebrow. The song is called "Spirit of the Living God, Fall Afresh on Me," which my grandmother lumps under "contemporary music," a category she cannot abide. *Melt me. Mold me. Fill me. Use me.* The side of her lip curls up like the words taste bad. Sometimes I try to stand, unsinging, beside her until we get to a respectable hymn like "What a Friend We Have in Jesus," or a gospel song like "I'll Fly Away." But if Phoebe catches me not singing, she switches places with Daze and pokes me until I open my mouth.

Soon a woman to my left slips out from the pew and heads down the center aisle. Then another woman on the right a few pews up. Then two more women, then three, all while Daze's face becomes more and more grim. The women are headed to the spirit-flag box mounted on the wall of the choir loft. The flags are decorated with felt crosses and doves and flames. One red flag has a pair of hands that are supposed to look uplifted in prayer. But they're both left hands, and the cutting job on the felt makes them look creepy, with craggy, too-long fingers and wrists that just end like they've been hacked off. The hand flag is almost always the last one picked, but today, the thin, blond woman from my Christian Education class timidly lifts it from the box. Probably she's too new to know which one she's choosing. The other women, including Seth's mother, spread out in front of the stage and wave their flags in time to the music. The idea is that the flags help lift people's hearts in prayer, and that flag waving is an opportunity to get more people involved in worship, which is one reason we stopped going to the United Methodist Church, with its one-way delivery of the gospel. That's not to say, however, that First Community supports dancing any more than it supports speaking in tongues. And even though most Sundays it would be hard to call what's happening up front dancing, today the thin, blond woman is wiggling her hips just a little, as she jerks the hand flag back and forth. Every few seconds she changes it up, swaying the flag to one side and kicking her foot to the other, like the chorus girls from Daze's old movies. Several people in the congregation bring their hands to their mouths, and Daze and Phoebe steal a quick look at each other. The question to ask yourself, if you feel moved to keep time with music in church, is whether you intend to call worshipful attention to the Holy Ghost or whether you're inviting lustful attention to your own body. Watching the open-mouthed smile on the thin, blond woman's face, it's hard for me to believe that she means to be inviting lustful attention. I am imagining the church she comes from, where people freely speak in tongues when they are baptized. Maybe they dance in the aisles, too. I want to run down front and warn her, but I just stand there while everyone gasps as she raises the flag over her head with both hands and begins twirling in joyous, oblivious circles. She is so caught up that she doesn't even notice the other flag wavers, who one by one lower their arms to watch. In a unanimous, unspoken decision, they file past her in a slow line, and by the time she opens her eyes and stops twirling, the rest of the women are already replacing their flags, dropping them into the box with a hollow *thock* we can all hear just below the music, turning away from the thin, blond seminary wife as she stops twirling and scurries to catch up.

Later I will find out that during this church service my father, down at the river, is tramping around in the scrubby woods at the base of the limestone palisades. I have seen the way he does this when he thinks no one is watching. Tears on his face, eyes lifted toward heaven, allowing the Holy Ghost to descend upon him. Maybe this time he has his eyes closed, imagining the Apostle Paul from when he was still Saul, struck blind on the road to Damascus. Maybe he's just wrapped up in his prayer without ceasing. What he is not doing is watching where he is going, or he would never have stumbled into poison ivy, which is the first plant he taught me to identify. By the time he realizes it, his robe is already tangled in the underbrush, but he struggles on through the scrub, not wanting to interrupt his communion with the Lord. The itching won't come until later on, anyway. Even then, it will seem like nothing more than a nuisance, a distraction like hunger or worry. He will ignore it all day Sunday, first while Phoebe and I are having dinner with Daze in the cafeteria of the Custer Peake Memorial Retirement Center, then while Phoebe sits at our kitchen table

scouring the *Lexington Herald-Leader* for employment ads, telling me that even though doing this counts as working on the
Sabbath, it's okay because our ox is in the ditch. He will ignore
it while Phoebe and I head back to church for the evening service to listen to Seth's father give his presentation about their
school in Ghana.

Sunday-night dinner for us is always a can of tuna mixed
in with a can of cream-of-mushroom soup, heated up and
spooned over saltine crackers, a meal Phoebe calls "tuna wiggle" because of how it turns gelatinous as it cools on your plate.
The trick is to eat it fast. About the time we are sitting across
from each other at the kitchen table, in the half dark because
the electric lights just seem too hot when it's this muggy, the
itching begins to get the better of my father. Under a bright
half-moon he drags Daze's old tin washtub from the shed, the
big one that I used to splash around in. There's a gallon of
bleach in the shed, too, and he empties it into the washtub and
adds water from the hose until it's half-full. And then, because
it doesn't look like the neighbors are home, he drops his filthy
brown robe in the grass, steps into the tub, and squats, wedg-
ing himself in until the bleach water rises to his waist. He sits
there a good long time, praying without ceasing and killing the
poison ivy, the itch that Satan has brought upon him to test his
devotion to the Lord's vision.

I'm sitting on the floor of my room with the contents of
an old box I keep under my bed spread out beside me on the
braided rug. It's a wooden Swinburne's gelatine box Daze
picked up somewhere, built to last, with a hinged top and
mitered corners. Titus has jumped in and filled the box with his
whole body, corner to corner, squeezed in tight as my father in

the washtub. You can tell by the way Titus purrs that he thinks it's a good, solid feeling. Some of what I keep in the box is special, like Daze's bone pen from Niagara Falls, which she bought on her honeymoon. A tiny lens at the top of the pen is a viewfinder that shows you the different parts of Niagara Falls, like Goat Island, Horseshoe Falls, and Whirlpool Rapids—all places I would like to see someday. But most of what's in the box is junk. There's a matchbox I saved because it reminds me of a drawer. There's an empty Tic Tac container that still smells good. There's a queen-of-clubs playing card I found on the street in Lexington and pocketed. You can't even have a deck of playing cards within East Winder city limits because they're the tools of gambling. I also keep a small notebook in the box, with a list of things I might like to become, including actress, veterinarian, and prophet. And even though I am not in danger of forgetting the words to my prayer, I jot them down now on the notebook's back page. I know that every time I come across them I will remember to start praying again, if I have stopped. I whisper the words now. "Inhabit me, O Lord God." I bend down close to Titus's head and whisper them again into one of his velvety black ears, which flattens in annoyance. I tip up the box and he spills out onto the rug. Then I reload it with all my things, arranging them to make space for the Holy Land relics. I also slip in the postcard of Lot's unfortunate wife.

I don't know at what point the bleach starts to burn my father worse than the itching. When he manages to throw the wash-tub on its side and crawl out on all fours, he has red rings from the pressure of the tub halfway up his back. He must under-stand that his robe has poison ivy oil all over it, but he wants to cover his nakedness, suddenly. To warm the chill that's coming over him. To soak up some of what's oozing from his skin below the waist and down his legs. He clutches the robe to his private parts, then wraps himself in it and sets out for the gas station a mile and a half away. But the pain, the pain forces him to stop at a trailer lit from within like a tin lantern on the side of the road.

When Ruthie Pope opens the door, my burned, blistered father can hardly speak. The robe has stuck to his legs and his privates, which are unspeakably raw. When she peels it away, the lower parts of his back and stomach look skinned. Ruthie Pope is a practical woman, and the first thing she does is cover a patch of her wall-to-wall carpet with a sheet so he doesn't soil it. The second thing she does is grab her cylinder of Crisco and oil my father's naked body from the waist down while four of her seven children watch, open-mouthed and silent. My father, she will say later, pushes air through his lips with pain. He seems to be talking to himself, and Ruthie reckons he's delirious. There's something familiar about him, but she can't put a name to the gaunt, glassy-eyed, bearded face. And he doesn't give her his name, or she would find the number for Daze or for Phoebe. The Peakes and the Popes, old Rowland County families both, know of each other, though it is possible they haven't crossed paths in years. She keeps asking, though. "What's your name, child? What's your name?" and when he finally manages a name, she believes she hears him say he is the Apostle Paul. Then he says it again, and she figures the best she can do for this man, and for any and all concerned, is call the police.

I am closing the lid on the Swinburne's gelatine box, sliding it back under my bed, when the phone rings downstairs.

Phoebe has been sitting at the kitchen table, listening to the Sunday-night Christian soap-opera broadcast by the Salvation Army, the stories about streetwalkers and drug users who hit rock bottom in Chicago or Cincinnati and stumble into churches on their last legs, where they meet kind people ladling out hot soup right alongside the gospel.

The radio goes off, and I hear her friendly, public voice fall flat. She's still on the phone with Police Chief Burton, Ezra Burton, when the doorbell rings, and there's Mayor James, having got the first call from the chief who thought Phoebe Peake should have someone with her, should have someone drive her to the hospital. Phoebe either thinks I'm already asleep or is too shocked to think of me at all. For the first time ever, she leaves the house without telling me where she's going and when she'll be back.

At my window I follow the mayor's taillights until his car disappears up Main Street. I stay at the window awhile longer, whispering my prayer, listening to a long, slow train come through and watching the moon, which has risen to sit opposite the cross on the water tower, the two lights hanging on either side of town like the very eyes of God.

CHAPTER 4

THEY KEEP MY FATHER in the first hospital for four days. His legs are covered in gauze, but the doctors leave the more serious burns, in the more serious places, exposed to the air. When Daze and I get there Monday morning, everything but his head and shoulders is shielded by a curtain, for modesty, while he sleeps away next to his IV bag. Someone has shaved his beard and clipped his hair close to his head, which makes him look younger. And smaller. And it's awful the way his jaw has dropped open to one side, his mouth a stretched-out hole. I want to pull the curtain the rest of the way closed so no one can see him sleep this way without him knowing it.

"The bleach did a number on him," Phoebe says when she finds us in the hallway. "Not to mention the fasting. They want to run a few more tests."

"Tests?" says Daze.

"They want to rule out a head injury. He said some things when they brought him in."

"He's exhausted," says Daze. "My poor boy." She gives me a hankie, in case I'm about to cry, but I'm not. I'm whispering my prayer so fast my mouth turns dry.

"What's all the muttering about?" says Phoebe.

And Daze says, "Oh, leave her be. It's too much for any of us to take in."

For the summer, I have an off-and-on part-time job helping Mrs. James clean out her attic, and, with Phoebe and Daze tied up at the hospital, she enlists me again to take my mind off the situation. Mrs. James has her own part-time job in the county clerk's office every morning. Sometimes, like this week, she says she's too pooped by the time afternoon rolls around to go through boxes dredging up the past. So she makes iced tea, and we sit on the couch in the air-conditioning and watch back-to-back reruns of *I Love Lucy* and *Batman*. My father says that television hijacks the mind, filling it with something other than God. We've never even had a set. But as long as the TV's running at the James's house, I don't feel bad about anything. Right up until Lucy does the dance with Ricky and all the eggs break in her shirt, and I start laughing so hard I can't stop, and then there's a bad moment, and a bad sound, a croak, and it's coming from me. It's the sound of laughing switching to crying so fast that my face and neck are wet with tears before Mrs. James realizes what's happening.

She sits with me and pats my back. She calls me "sweet patootie." She tells me when they made my father they threw away the mold, which is just how some folks are, and that he's going to be fine. She tells me chemical burns are better than fire burns because your insides don't heat up. She gets out her notary-public stamp and lets me notarize a bunch of junk mail envelopes, squeezing hard until the paper takes the impression. It actually does make me feel a tiny bit better for some reason.

Each night, Phoebe brings home brief reports before falling into bed. Tuesday she says he's alert but disoriented. They're making sure nothing gets infected while his skin's scabbing over. Wednesday he's out of the woods enough, infection-wise, to tolerate a brain scan and to meet with a different kind of doctor, a psychiatrist.

Thursday afternoon, Mrs. James feels a migraine coming on and needs absolute quiet. So I sit at my own kitchen table at home, Titus sprawled out beside me, trying to read a book the bookmobile lady thought I might like. It's about a girl whose father is mysteriously away from home. Townspeople are speculating that he ran off with another woman, but her mother is trying to keep a stiff upper lip.

"I hope you've done your Bible reading first," Phoebe says when she comes back from the hospital. I'm supposed to read the Bible every day before anything else. Right now I'm making my slow way through Jeremiah, for the second time, and I tell her so. She pulls out the chair opposite me and nudges Titus off the table. She's still smiling as politely as she has probably done all day, which makes her look strained, like something she's wearing underneath her clothes—the same outfit she wore to the airport not even a week ago—is too tight.

I wait for the rest of what she has to say, but then I see that she is waiting for me. When Phoebe is very upset, she switches from confiding in me, which forces me to listen, to keeping information to herself in a way that forces me to ask questions. Only she gives me the shortest answers possible, so I learn only as much as everything I can think of to ask.

"Well?" She dips her chin in my direction.

I open my mouth to speak, but I am afraid suddenly of sounding afraid out loud. I am afraid I will start crying again.

"Your father won't be home for a while," Phoebe says, and waits again. "Why not?" she asks finally, for me. "What's going to happen, Mother? Well, Charmaine, right now it's anybody's guess. He's been moved to a smaller hospital, a facility, really, where your grandmother's second cousin has found him a room. For long-term recovery. In the meantime, things are going to be a little different for you and me."

I know I should be asking why he can't recover at home, which is what I don't understand. But Phoebe is watching me from across the table, eyebrows raised, mouth tight with expectation. She sighs and places both hands flat on the place-mat. She lifts an index finger and we both watch the tendon move around under her skin, rippling the delicate veins.

"How?" I say.

You can see how the question from me makes her feel better, the relieved look that comes over her face just after she is asked and before she answers, even if the answer she's about to give is going to be incomplete or upsetting. "For starters, we're out of money," she says. "Let me rephrase that. We were out of money and now we are not only out of money, we owe money. Lots of money."

"To who?"

"To whom. Whom do you think? To the hospital. The first

one, not the one he's in now, praise the Lord, which is more of a rest home than a hospital. Daze worked that out, but let me tell you, money's not the only kind of debt."

She waits for another question, and I cast around for it but my head feels hollow.

"How are we going to get by, you wonder?" says Phoebe. "Well, your mother has put in her name as a substitute teacher. Which will be a drop in the bucket. What else, you'd like to know? Well, your mother has secured a renter for this house. For the next few months. You and I will be staying down at the river."

"The next few months?" I say. "He'll be gone that long?"

"It's hard to tell what's going to happen," she says, "but one thing's for sure. We either rent out the house or lose it. And the Cattersons have three months furlough and they can't shift around according to your father's condition."

My throat is starting to get tight. I bite down hard, and I keep my eyes on the cover of my book. It's blue, with three tiny white silhouettes of the main characters, each in their own series of circles, like you're peering at them through a Slinky or the fat end of a tornado, a vortex, like a black hole, which is maybe what you're supposed to think, since the book is about traveling through space and time. Space and time act differently near a black hole, stretching out, slowing down the closer you come, right up until you get sucked in and pulverized. This is what feels like is happening to the information Phoebe's giving me. My ears suck it in, but my brain pulverizes it. I imagine peering all the way through a vortex, with my father on the other end, tiny, and then I realize that I haven't prayed without ceasing since I saw him in the hospital bed.

"What's wrong with him?" I say finally, keeping my eyes on the book cover. *Inhabit me, O Lord God.*

Phoebe is moving her finger again, watching the back of her hand. "They're talking about something gone wrong in his brain. A chemical imbalance."

I have only ever thought of chemicals as household products like bug spray or ammonia or windshield-wiper fluid or paint. Or like the bleach that burned my father's skin. Substances with sharp odors and warnings and childproof caps. I never knew the brain had chemicals with hazards all their own that could poison you, maybe, from the inside out. A crazy-feeling giggle bubbles up in my throat.

"In the meantime," Phoebe says, "I told the Cattersons they can move in right away. There's no reason to draw out this whole ordeal." She stands, then squats before the cupboard under the sink and hands me two brown grocery bags. "Pack your things."

Upstairs, in the middle of the braided rug, I unfold the two bags that have to hold everything I'm taking, everything I will need for school. For one stunned moment I don't remember where I keep any of my clothes, even though I'm staring right at my dresser. Even though junior high starts on Monday. Then I am on my feet and packing in a frenzy, stuffing the first bag with my two pairs of jeans, the hand-me-down Jordache ones from the charity box and the new ones Phoebe sewed to look like Levi's, with the fake orange felt tag that makes them impossible in a way she will never understand. After the jeans go my cut-off shorts, my T-shirts and button-up shirts, then my brown church dress from Daze. Into the other bag go my shoes and socks, my underwear, and a nightie. I find the belt and safety pins for the sanitary pads and stuff those into the bottom of the second bag so I'll know where to find them next month.

I am praying again under my breath, and it gets faster, like my racing heart. The prayer keeps out the image of my burned, sleeping father. It keeps out the worry over what will happen if the Cattersons are still living here when he's ready to come home. It keeps out the idea of Seth, sleeping in my bed, looking out my window, touching all my books. But it's as if all this is just waiting at the corner of my mind, so that when I forget the prayer again it can come rushing back in.

Titus slinks into the room and pads his way over to me. We will be taking him with us because Seth is allergic to cats. And dust. And carpet. And even air, probably. The Cattersons, Phoebe says, will be rolling up my rug and storing it in the basement. At the river, Titus will get to try being an outdoor cat, which Phoebe says will be a treat for him, but which is another worry for me, and now I'm praying so fast that I'm spitting a little bit as my lips form the words: *Inhabitmeolordgod, inhabitmeolordgod, inhabitmeolordgod.* I sink to the rug again and pull Titus onto my lap. I bury my head in the back of his neck, which he lets me do for a long time, purring, nosing his face into the crook of my elbow as I pray. We stay this way until Phoebe calls from downstairs that it's time to go.

Halfway to the river, I remember my box under the bed. "I need to go back," I say, caught between wanting the box and not wanting to see the Cattersons as they arrive.

But Phoebe is squinting into the setting sun. If she hears me at all, she is concentrating too hard on driving the river road to answer.

• • •

That it is not the best idea for me to see my father for a while is a rare point of agreement between Phoebe and Daze. Phoebe says that the medicine he's taking makes him very subdued. Not great for visitors. But the next day, our first full day of living down at the cabin, she returns from the hospital with a short letter from him.

"I didn't read it," she says, holding it out to me.

I take the folded sheet of paper. I have been tracking Titus around the perimeter of the cabin, warning him when he seems about to explore farther. Cats roam, my father has told me. Cats establish a territory and know, always, where they are in it and how to get back home.

"He'll just want out again," Phoebe says when I scoop him up and return him to the cabin. But I am already letting the flimsy screen door, original to the RV, slap shut behind me, heading down to the dock to read the letter in private.

A few things I did not expect, it begins without greeting. As if maybe he wrote it first and then decided it might as well be a letter. *They asked if I fell. The first time in the tube, the screen was off. This time, pictures and words, which I remember they told me about, only I'd forgotten. The words said "a rubber hand will touch you in five seconds." Then the noise from the camera, mapping the ocean floor. But the noise can be the prayer.*

A letter of groggy half thoughts. My father has always printed in capital letters—sharp marks that slant forward and dent the paper. His handwriting here is looser, large and nearly cursive but not quite. I lie on my back, on our dock, and use the letter to block the sun, which is about to dip behind the western palisades.

Everything inside me is outside the machine. I was in the tube.

Then I swallowed the pill, and the tube I was in was in me. That's the whole letter.

It's a warm day. The big leaves of the sycamores look limp and tired after the long summer. A red-tailed hawk shuttles between the steep rock walls. I try to imagine myself inside myself, with my own breathing and heartbeat like weather around me. The river lifts and settles, pressing the warped planks of the dock against my shoulder blades. The water smells oily. My father has told me that at one time Kentucky was under a large inland sea. That's why it's full of limestone, which is made up of millions of tiny skeletons of tiny fish. Now all that's left of the sea is the river, which flows eventually into the Mississippi. For centuries the river has pushed its way over and through and along the rock, carving the gorge.

I hear Phoebe before I see her, grunting softly as she makes her way down the grass bank, dusty yellow summer squash in each hand. "I forgot all about these," she says. "We can eat off the fruits of our labor."

"Technically, it's not *our* labor," I say, since my father is the one who kept up with the garden before leaving for the Holy Land.

"Technically, I found them and picked them. That's pretty laborious." She steps out onto the dock, holding the squash out to her sides to keep her balance.

"You're wearing my jeans," I say.

"Not your new pair. Not the ones I made you." She is wearing the charity box Jordache pair, which fit her better than they fit me. Under stress, Phoebe gets smaller and smaller. She has new finger-sized shadows between her ribs. My ribs don't even show anymore, and above them my breasts just get bigger and more painful. Sometimes I think they're going to keep on swelling forever, the way my father's tomatoes do on the vine, splitting wide open if you don't pick them in time.

"Did he say anything about me?" Phoebe says, lowering herself to a crouch. Then she loses her balance and sits down hard. A corner of the dock dips into the river, picking up a film of water.

I hold out the letter. "Read it yourself," I say. Which is rude. Phoebe's mouth turns down and her chin points. She will hold the face until she gets an apology.

"He misses being home," I say quickly.

"Really?"

"He says he loves you."

"Maybe I should take a look at that after all." Phoebe sets down the squash and holds out her hand.

As she reads, I watch the surface of the water. Sometimes it's a black-green sheet of glass, but today you can see the current, flexing and unflexing like a long muscle. Soon Phoebe's mouth is doing the pre-crying thing, like she's sucking on a piece of hard candy. I know I should feel bad about lying, but what I feel instead is angry.

"I want you to close your eyes with me, Charmaine," Phoebe says, tucking in her chin. "Lord, first of all we thank you for teaching us not to take our mental health for granted."

I try to pray what she prays, but I can't. Then I try to start up my own prayer, but I am fully in the grip of my fallen nature, and the only words that surface are ugly: *Lord, make my mother shut up.*

"We also give you the glory for this fine day," she goes on.

Shut up, shut up, shut up, I pray. I can't help it.

"Help Charmaine and I to support each other with honesty

and respect. Amen." Phoebe raises her head. "I just thought he might have said 'Look after your mother,' or something. You don't have to make things up."

A breeze stirs the leaves around us and they flip over, changing entire trees to a paler, grayer shade of green, then back to normal. "What happened with the rubber hand?" I finally say, cross because she's the only person I have to ask.

"He's a little confused," she says. "It's what they've got him on. He's had an MRI, so I guess that's the tube part." As she speaks, Phoebe contemplates the squash, then the river. Tiny puddles of loose skin form at either side of her mouth, which makes her look young and old at the same time. It draws the anger right out of me. Now I wish the words I made up had been in my father's letter. I pray, in my head, *Forgive me.* I pray, *Help my father* and *Help my mother. Inhabit me, O Lord God.* Out loud I say, "I'm sorry."

"It's a tough time," Phoebe says. She leans over the side of the dock and wiggles the squash around just under the surface of the water. Then she brings them out and wipes the dust off, in long dirty streaks, down the legs of the jeans I'll be wearing to school.

On Sunday, for the first time ever, we miss morning church. It's been exactly a week since the bleach incident, and Phoebe says she feels tired of explaining things to people. "And besides," she says, "I feel worshipful right here, with the river. It's another adventure, really, like living on faith alone."

"You hated living on faith alone," I remind her.

"The point," she says, "is that we lived to tell."

Late summer in Kentucky is usually dry, but today it's drizzling again, which makes the built-in tweed sofa I'm sprawled on—also my bed—smell like an old coat. We keep the windows open to catch the slightest wet breeze. At the miniature sink, Phoebe scrubs potatoes. She tries to use as little water as possible, because even though there's been plenty of rain, our cistern only holds so much at a time, one tank barely enough for two showers. The cabin feels suffocating. If I reached out my arm, I could touch the back of Phoebe's leg—that's how cramped we are.

"It's hot," I say, then wish I hadn't. Saying so only makes it hotter.

"It's like a sauna," says Phoebe. "People pay money for sauna treatments. And I'm telling you, Charmaine, plenty of people would love a front-row seat to the changing of the seasons down here. Just wait. Someday after I'm gone, you'll tell your children, 'One time my mother and I lived all by ourselves in a real log cabin down on the Kentucky River.' Then you'll show them the spot and get all choked up."

I send my skepticism, telepathically, toward Titus, who's watching us from the passenger seat. He hates rain. I can't imagine a time after Phoebe's gone. Then all at once I can, and an unwelcome bolt of grief runs clean through me.

"You won't have to give them all the details," Phoebe says, misinterpreting my face. She wipes the sweat off her forehead with the back of her arm, then stabs each potato with the paring knife. "We can look at this situation in terms of the challenges or the opportunities. If you never have to persevere, Charmaine, you'll never know you can. And I, for one, am feeling positively buoyant after winnowing down my earthly store."

"You sound like Daddy," I say. "Divesting yourself of things."

"This is different. Less prophet, more pioneer."

The two paper bags that hold my own winnowed store are wedged between the RV's passenger seat and driver's seat. I picture Seth sitting at my desk, opening the box under the bed and discovering the Holy Land relics, the secret glimpse of Niagara Falls, the notebook with my prayer written inside, which I have forgotten all about. Again. I breathe and run through it twice.

Phoebe hands me the potatoes and two pieces of tinfoil. "All I'm talking about, here, is to get a little less attached to the things we have. Not to see if we can do without things we actually need."

"But we'll move back home anyway," I say, crimping the foil around the potatoes. "All three of us. Even if we get less attached to our things."

Phoebe perches next to me. She starts to grab my hands, but she ends up laying her hands on top of the potatoes instead, as if we could bake them between us. "You're more important to me than anything else in the world," she says.

I try giving the potatoes a little lift. The cabin feels too stuffy, too damp to be hearing any of this. Phoebe presses the potatoes back down, pushing the backs of my hands into my lap.

"Thank you," I say.

"Are you really listening?" Phoebe asks. "I said you're more important to me than anything else in the world. That should mean something to you."

"What about Daddy?" I say. It doesn't seem right to be more important to her than he is. Or for any of us to be ranked in importance at all. Or for her to say it.

"That's different."

"What about Jesus?"

"That's different, too," Phoebe says. "You'll understand when you have a child of your own. There's no bond like it." She moves a hand to my forehead, pushing back my bangs, which hang into my eyes because I have forgotten my barrette. It makes me even more hot, and I lean away. On the stove, a small pot of water begins to boil. "So?" Phoebe says, standing up.

"What?"

"Am I important to you? Because it's getting harder and harder to tell, these days."

"You're important," I say, and even though I mean for the words to come out in a careless way that would let her know this conversation couldn't be less important, they come out thin and strained. "Please," I tack on, but even that word, sarcastic as it feels in my mouth, sounds more like pleading by the time it hits the air. Like it could mean *Please believe me,* not *Please don't make me say these things.*

For the first time since my father came back from the Holy Land, Phoebe smiles. She sips from a can of tomato juice and drops two big handfuls of spinach from the garden into the pot. We eat some manner of boiled greens every night, which Phoebe enjoys. She even enjoys the worst part, which is afterward when she splits the leftover water they were boiled in between us, a kind of vegetable tea, to make sure none of the nutrients go down the drain.

The rain patters on and on against the cabin's tin roof. I think about what Phoebe's said, that there is no bond like the one between her and me. And whether or not I believe it, or want it, I feel it, as real and deep inside me as if we shared a single vital organ that neither of us can survive without. A liver. A heart.

The air coming through the cabin's small trailer windows feels thick and smells dark and wet, like the tangle of grass and weeds outside. It's not hard to imagine this tangle on the move, creeping up to and then over the thick logs of the cabin, so slow we don't notice, until one day the only thing to be seen from the outside is a gentle hill, like an Indian burial mound, with Phoebe and me trapped forever inside.

CHAPTER 5

Y OU CAN HEAR THE school bus before it comes into
sight, whining down into the hairpin turns of the river
road. Soon it rounds the stone foot of Tate's Bridge, then
it's pulling closer to where I'm standing in the gravel, then it
looks like it's going to run right into me before it stops, and I
step back into the wet grass. The doors fold open, and a long-
boned black woman in the driver's seat says, "Hey there, baby,
hop on."

"Ravenna," someone yells from the back of the bus.

"I'm talking right now," says Ravenna. She looks me up and
down, checks her clipboard. All the woman's hair has been
wound into a tight knob on the top of her head, like the handle
on a pot lid, and what looks like a tiny piece of straw has been
stuck through a hole in her earlobe, where an earring should
be. "You Charmaine Peake?"

I nod.

She half stands, twisting up out of her seat.

"Ravenna." The voice comes from a pudgy, redheaded girl near the back. "You deaf?"

"Tracy Payne, sit down," says Ravenna.

"Just so you know, I'm saving this seat," says the girl.

"That's right. You saving it for Charmaine." Ravenna sweeps her arm out toward the aisle. "Go on, sit with her," she says to me. "That'll be your assigned seat."

There are only four other kids on the bus and plenty of empty seats, but I follow the rubber mat toward the red-haired girl, Tracy, who has scooted to the outside edge of the seat bench and crossed her arms. She makes her body so stiff that I have to high-step over her, nearly sitting on her lap. I arrange myself by the window and hold my breath until I can't anymore, and the *whoosh* of my breath out reminds me to pray. "O Lord God" comes out in a louder whisper than I mean it to, and Tracy, still shooting hate toward Ravenna, narrows her eyes.

School's just starting, and already the bus window is layered in tiny scallops of grime, from the rain. Out of the corner of my eye, I watch Tracy stretch a leg into the aisle and withdraw a rusty screw from her jeans pocket. She elbows me hard in the shoulder, then holds the screw up to my face. "Give me lip," she says, "and I'll give you something you won't forget."

Except for yellow shadows under her eyes, and the large tan patches where freckles merge together, Tracy's face is very pale. Even her blue eyes are pale—cold and ghostly, as if more blue used to be there but found the conditions too hostile. She talks like they do down at the river. *Lip* is *lee-yup*.

"This is *rust*," she says. "You want to get lockjaw?"

"I have lockjaw already." I wiggle my jaw to make it pop. "TMJ."

"TMJ?" the girl looks insulted. "Well, I have ESP. You know what that stands for?"

"Yes."

"What, then?" *Wuht, they-un.*

Tracy's words are like little darts, or insects hitting a windshield. They don't hurt, but it's hard to have your own thoughts when they're coming at you. I know what ESP is from a *Good Word* article on the occult. I just can't remember what the letters stand for.

"If you don't know," she says, "I'm not going to tell you."

Then it comes to me. "Extrasensory perception."

"Whatever," says Tracy. "I can predict the future. I predict you'll be sorry if you give me lip."

I have no idea what to say to this. A kind answer is supposed to turn away wrath, but there's no question on the table, and she's not exactly wrathful. *Ornery* is the word that comes to me. One of Daze's words. The special kind of red hair.

"Close your mouth," Tracy says. "You wanna catch flies?"

I close my mouth. ESP is kind of like being a prophet in the way you know things other people don't, only it doesn't come from God, and whatever doesn't come from God is of the world, which is Satan's domain. I would say some of this to Tracy, maybe, but she has propped her foot onto the opposite knee and is digging into the rubber sole of her tennis shoe with the screw like she's forgotten I'm there.

From inside the bus, the river road seems narrow as a wire. Every curve feels dangerous, like we might tip over and crash back down the scrubby hill. I breathe in and out. I remember the prayer again. I pray.

We stop every quarter mile or so to collect kids. Some of them look like they slept in a pile of dirt; some are so clean and red-cheeked they could have been boiled in a pot. Ravenna makes seat assignments right and left, but the bus stays pretty quiet—just the hiss of the brakes and the high drone of the engine as it works harder. Tracy's eyes have closed, and she sways, trancelike, every time we make a turn. She smells like cigarettes. I feel the sway of the bus, too, but I sit carefully, not wanting to touch the girl's arm or leg in case it wakes her up.

Then her eyes pop open so fast it's hard for me to believe she's been asleep at all. "You know who's kin to me?" she says.

"Who's kin to you?" I repeat, stupidly.

"That's what I'm asking."

"How would I know, though? I don't even know you."

"If you knew, you'd know it," Tracy says, and closes her eyes again. Her thin lips twitch into a smirk.

When the bus stops next, Ravenna gets up and pulls a sheet of plywood from behind the driver's seat. She bangs it down on the steps and latches a latch. There's a heavy first step on the plank, then it's step and shuffle, step and shuffle.

"Here he comes," Tracy says. "You better not stare at him like you're staring at me."

"Hey there, Cecil Goode," says Ravenna, peering down the ramp. "You got it, baby?"

If there's an answer, I don't hear it. There's a couple of thumps and some more shuffling and then the boy's standing at the head of the aisle. "Child of God" is what I heard him called at church once. His head and abdomen are normal-sized, but his legs look like they've been cut off below the knees, and instead of a right hand, a metal claw pokes out of the cuff of his plaid shirt. The other sleeve, the empty one, is tied into a knot right above where the elbow should be. He ignores the handicapped bench behind Ravenna and moves down the aisle toward the back of the bus, yanking his shoulders with a powerful effort that slaps the claw into the back of each seat he passes.

Is it worse to look or to look like you're trying not to look? He has the face of an adult, with a heavy ledge of a brow and a mustache trimmed close to his lip. Everything about his head is golden, from his burnished skin to his blond, wavy hair. He even breathes heavily through his nose the way a golden lion might, if you got close enough to hear.

"Cecil," Tracy says hopefully beside me. "Hey there, Cecil."

He nods at her. Then he lifts his chin and looks down his nose at me, and I feel my mouth stretching into a wild, encouraging smile, as if a smile can convey that I don't really notice anything different about him, or that, like Jesus, I see only what's inside.

That's when he stops himself by our seat. As he leans over Tracy, a golden curl falls into his eyes. Then his face is in mine, and he smells of pine needles and sweat, and his light amber eyes are hard. What he says is: "I can smell your pussy."

I swallow, my face stuck in the smile. "What?"

He says it again, separating the words with his smooth voice, a higher voice than I would have expected. It sounds golden, too. Musical. "I. Can. Smell. Your. Pussy." Then he rears back and makes his way on past. Tracy shrinks down in her seat with a proud little yelp, and I turn my burning face to the dirty window and cross my legs as tightly as I can, in case what he said could possibly be true.

• • •

I have worn the homemade Levi's to school, to please Phoebe. Once inside, however, I duck into the first bathroom I find and dig the dirty Jordache pair from the bottom of the butt purse. I give them a thorough smell in the crotch before I put them on, just in case, but all that comes through is a trace of damp earth.

The only person from East Winder in any of my classes the first half of the day is Mary-Kate, in homeroom and second period, but her assigned seats are far across the room. The rest of the kids, from the county or from Clay's Corner, have all gone to school with each other for years, and after we hear about supplies and write our names in the covers of our text-books, they talk around me while I flip through the pages and try not to look conspicuously alone. I don't know anyone in fourth-period English either, but in that class, all extra time gets absorbed by freewriting. Today's topic on the board is "summer pastimes," but we may also choose our own top-ics. Freewriting can be anything, says the teacher, a woman in bright red slacks tight enough to show the outline of her bikini panties. As she walks up and down the rows, a couple of boys snicker. Even a letter, the teacher says. Which we can even mail after she checks it for completion. I have my father's let-ter with me in the butt purse, and now I begin a letter back to him. *I'm in English class,* I write. *This fall, our first assignment will be preparing and giving a "how-to" speech.* When I realize that I have written what the teacher has just said word for word, I erase it. *Praying without ceasing is hard,* I write instead. But then I wonder if that sounds like I'm complaining about a direct instruction from the Lord, so I erase that too.

"No erasing," says the teacher from over my shoulder. "The only criteria for freewriting are that we do not erase and that we keep moving forward."

I've read your letter a few times, I begin again. *Right now we're doing freewriting, which this page is part of. After I turn it in for a grade, I will be able to send it to you. I have to come up with something to demonstrate. It has to be something I already know how to do, and the title of it has to be "How to 'something.'"* I stop writing. *Quotidian* was the word of the day this morning in homeroom. It can mean "routine," or "drab," and that's exactly what my letter is.

Our classroom, like every room in the building, is a flat hexagon with green fluorescent lights that make us all look like we're coming down with something. The windows are floor-to-ceiling slivers the width of my hand, set so deeply into the cement blocks that the outdoors seems like a distant, separate world. The high school is a mirror image on the other side of a shared lunchroom, which is the biggest hexagon of all. We are bees in a honeycomb. Drones. Already I feel like I've been here forever.

Beside me, a girl with a long brown ponytail writes steadily. "No stopping," says the teacher, behind me again. "Even if you have to write, 'I don't know what to write' over and over, I want you to keep your pencil to paper. Get used to it, men and women, because this is how we'll start every class period." On the chalkboard, she has written *Miss Shipps,* then crossed through it triumphantly to write *Mrs. Teaderman* underneath, because one of her summer pastimes, this year, was getting married.

I don't know what to write, I write. *Everyone around me is writing, except for one boy over near the window who might be mainstreamed. Did you get to see the pictures of your brain? Do you still feel the spirit of the Apostle Paul? I'm reading Jeremiah in the Old Testament, and Romans in the New Testament. The part about cir-*

cumcision. Then I'm embarrassed to have written *circumcision,* and I cross it out and still try to look like I'm writing. *The boy they call the "Child of God" rides my bus,* I write, the page now cloudy with smudges. Then I am wondering about the boy and how he holds a pencil, eats his food at lunch, shaves his face around the mustache — all with the claw. I wonder how he goes to the bathroom too, which makes me think of the time I walked in on my father. I had seen a diagram, but I had not expected any of the parts to look like they did in real life. Pinker than skin and with the deflated pouch underneath. Like something that really belonged inside his body, an intestine maybe, that had escaped. It made me sad for him, and for all men. And now my father has burned himself there, which is impossible to picture.

After fourth period there's "activity," for which our English class follows Mrs. Teaderman to the gym and up into the bleachers to an assigned section near the top. I find a seat against the wall as the entire seventh grade files in, a sea of people, with teachers waving their arms and trying to make themselves heard. If you plug your ears and don't think of them as teachers and just watch their faces, you get a good idea of what they might look like when they are in pain or about to cry. I'm trying to spot Mary-Kate, Karen, or even the red-haired girl from the bus when the bell rings right over my head, loud enough to loosen my brain in my skull. The brown-haired girl with the ponytail is beside me, and she jumps and claps her hands over her ears, too. Down below, the doors on either side of the gym clang shut. On stage, the PE teacher, Coach Doran, steps to the podium.

"Quiet," he says into a microphone, which buzzes then squeals. Coach Doran waits for the sound to peter out, then explains that on some days, activity will involve a dance contest or spelling bee. Other days we can talk or balance our homework on our knees. When one of the sports teams has a game, activity will become a pep rally, and today the cheerleaders are on hand to show us the meaning of school spirit. Coach Doran motions to someone offstage, and in two seconds rock music blares from the speaker above me.

By now, most of the boys in the bleachers have parked thick slugs of chewing tobacco under their bottom lips. They try to hide it, but if you turn too quickly, you'll catch them spitting into empty pop cans.

"Disgusting," says the girl with the ponytail as a boy wipes his lips with the back of his hand.

I pull out the letter from my father and smooth it against the cover of my social studies book. I read it once through and start in again, as though it will begin to make more sense.

"Who'd you get the letter from," says the girl.

"My dad."

The song ends and then they restart it louder. "Eye of the Tiger." Beside me, the girl dances with the upper half of her body.

"I'm going out for cheerleading," she says. She stops dancing and starts making the rigid motions of a cheer with her arms. "My sister used to cheer at my old school. My used-to-be stepsister. My parents are divorced, too. My dad lives in Omaha."

"My parents aren't divorced."

"Then how come your dad's writing you letters?"

I look down at the letter in my lap, which is starting to fold itself back into thirds. "He's just away for a while."

"In prison?"

"No," I say. I hadn't considered prison or expected anyone else to. The girl has straight dark eyebrows, and when she speaks, her lips move carefully over a delicate set of braces. After she stops speaking, it is hard to believe her face ever moved, much less that she was talking about prison.

"Theresa's dad is in prison," she says. "It sucks that there's no one popular in English. No offense."

I dimly perceive the insult and shrug it off. "Who's Theresa?"

The girl lifts a thin, graceful arm and points to where the cheerleaders have sprung out onto the floor in their blue-and-white uniforms, doing an "Eye of the Tiger" cheer routine. At the song's chorus, a blond girl in ribboned pigtails, legs tight with muscles, takes a running start and turns handsprings down the entire length of the gym floor. The rest of the girls in the squad wait their turn under the basketball hoop. "I can only do a round-off back handspring," says the girl beside me. "I can't do a standing back tuck, and that's what you have to do to make cheerleader. I have a week to learn, though." On the gym floor, Theresa, having landed and thrust her arms ceiling-ward in a jubilant V, snaps them back in, crouches, then lofts herself in a back flip and lands on her feet again, rising into another V. "That's a good one," says the girl beside me. "Theresa's dad wrote bad checks. He wrote a check to cheerleading camp that bounced, but they let her stay because she has such good spirit. She even won the spirit stick. Are you from East Winder?"

"Originally," I say, which I already know is obvious. Everyone from East Winder looks wrong here. Our jeans are too thickly cuffed. Our shoes are mostly plain canvas sneakers from the dollar store. Mine have a crackling white layer of shoe polish to make them look more new. The Clay's Corner kids wear name-brand sneakers or brown leather lace-up shoes I don't even have a name for.

"That's where all the churches are," says the girl. "Have you ever thought about growing your hair out?"

I touch my hair. Today I have pulled my bangs straight back into a barrette again, but some have escaped and curl on either side of my forehead in the natural wave Phoebe says I should be grateful for.

"The thing to do is wear it in a ponytail every day." The girl moves her face from side to side to make her ponytail swing. It's as straight and smooth as water poured from a pitcher. "Then one day you just wake up and your hair is long, which makes you prettier. Unless you're like them." She points again, five rows below us, to twins from East Winder whose parents are missionaries, like Seth's, only to Honduras instead of Ghana. Ida and Martha Hughes. Their flat, dishwater-blond hair dangles below their waists in a line of brittle points. "They look like they haven't cut their hair since they were born."

"They haven't," I say. "The Bible says a woman's hair is her crown in glory, and some people think that if you cut your hair in this life, you won't have a crown in glory. *Glory* means heaven."

"Not even a trim?"

"That's just how their family takes it," I say. "It doesn't really say not to cut your hair, except for Samson in the Old Testament, and there it was just that if he cut his hair then he would lose his strength. But when he let it grow out again he got his strength back and brought the temple down."

The girl blinks at me a few slow times, looking confused at the mention of Samson, then entirely bored. "Do you have a boyfriend?"

In my head I break down the word into *boy* and *friend,* and say, "I guess so."

"What's his name?"

"Seth," I say, experimentally. "He doesn't go to this school."

"Have you kissed him?"

"Kind of."

"You know what's better than having a boyfriend? When someone else's boyfriend likes you. Even if the boy is a little bit scummy, like from down by the river."

"Scummy," I repeat, swallowing hard. It's an awful word.

"Because when you have your own boyfriend, they could always be about to like someone else. You have a lot to lose. Another thing: it's good to have a brother or sister who's popular."

"I'm an only child."

"When your parents get divorced, maybe one of them will marry someone who's also divorced and has kids, and maybe those kids will be popular at the school where you end up. That's what happened with my stepsister. Then my mom divorced her dad."

"My parents aren't getting divorced, though. I already said. My dad's just away for a while."

"That's code for getting a divorce. That's Divorce One-oh-one. My mother's been divorced twice."

"Stop saying 'divorce,'" I say. In my head I hear Phoebe telling me she loves me more than anything else in the world. "God told my father to marry my mother."

The girl blinks at me again, like I'm speaking in another language and she's not curious enough for a translation. Then she keeps talking like I haven't said anything at all. "This is my fourth school, though I did go to Clay's Corner Elementary for third and fourth grade. When my name was Melinda. Now it's Kelly-Lynn. But my old junior high started in sixth grade, not seventh, so this isn't exactly my first rodeo." Kelly-Lynn takes a tube of lip gloss from her small leather purse, uncaps it, and taps it onto her mouth. Her face gives nothing away. It's possible to imagine that she has already thought of every single thing anyone could say, ever, and every single thing that could ever happen anywhere in the world, and all of it has already bored her.

This is exactly the opposite of Phoebe, and I am Phoebe's daughter, and right now I know that I have a face full of divorce. In the book with the missing father, the girl has to pass through an evil, dark specter that's spreading itself over the earth and even throughout the universe. That's the way the idea of divorce feels, like a specter creeping over my heart. Beside me, the girl watches cheerleading, her ponytail switching gracefully against her back. In each of her earlobes nests a tiny pearl. Not like a planet coated in evil, but like a clean little moon, still and serene unto itself.

In the ten-minute break before final period, I join a group of about forty East Winder kids outside the lunchroom for a prayer meeting. I'm standing at the back, next to a long, skinny window, and when I peer through it, there he is. Right outside, the Child of God. Cecil. He grinds a cigarette into the dirt with his awkward, booted foot. Three boys tower over him, dressed in jeans and concert T-shirts that you can tell used to be black. Quiet Riot and Iron Maiden. One of the boys flicks a lighter and holds the flame to the edge of a textbook. He looks toward the window, and I turn my head away as fast as I can.

In front of the group now, one of the long-haired missionary twins stands on an upturned milk carton. "Separation of church and state does not mean we don't have the right to free assemble," she pronounces.

"Yeah," holler some of the kids. They raise their fists like they're protesting something, but it's not as if anyone's trying to stop us from assembling. In fact, none of the kids trickling in and out of the lunchroom for study hall seem to be paying that much attention.

"Charmaine, hey," someone whispers behind me. It's Mary-Kate with Karen, from church, both clutching their clarinets. "Where were you Sunday?" asks Mary-Kate.

"Out of town."

Up front, the missionary twin says, "They can take the Ten Commandments off the wall of the classroom, but they can't take them out of our hearts."

"Did you bring a lock for your locker?" Karen says. "I forgot."

I shake my head. The twin up front is detailing how the prayer requests will work. You submit your request on a folded-up piece of paper, and each day the person leading prayer will unfold as many as there's time to pray for. Around me, kids start tearing paper out of their notebooks and scribbling requests.

"We were going to see if we could put our clarinets in your locker," says Karen, "but now I'm going to write a prayer request that they don't get stolen." I hold both clarinets while Mary-Kate and Karen write their requests and pass them to the front, where the other missionary twin collects them in her bag. Then she reaches in, selects several, and hands them to her sister.

Behind me, the outside doors open with a heavy *clank*. The high school boy who tried to burn the textbook sneers at our group, lips pulling back from sharp yellow teeth that look too small for his mouth. He holds the door until Cecil's made it through, then he and all his friends line up at the back of our group.

"This is a good one," says the twin up front. "It says, 'Remember to pray for David Peake, who's still in the hospital.'" All the East Winder kids turn this way and that until they spot me at the back. Heat creeps into the roots of my hair. I don't know how many people knew about my father before the request, and I don't know who wrote it, but I can't even hear the next two requests because of the blood pounding in my ears. When everyone lowers his or her head in prayer, I get ready to slip away from the first and last school prayer assembly I will ever be *a part* of. That's when one of the high school boys behind us yells, "Jesus fucking FREAKS!"

Not a single East Winder kids moves. We've been trained for persecution, and we know how to keep our heads down.

"Those boys?" whispers Mary-Kate. "They don't even steal stuff out of lockers. They pee through the slots in the locker doors."

It has the horrible ring of truth, and I turn around and look. I can't help it.

"What's your problem?" says the textbook-burning kid.

Cecil looks at me hard. "Girl from the bus," he says. He lifts his nose in the air like he's trying to smell me again, and I shut my eyes against what comes next. "Girl from the bus on the God Squad." Then he does a little hop with his foot, pivots awkwardly, and shuffles away down the hall with his friends.

CHAPTER 6

*E*VERY MORNING BEFORE SCHOOL, Phoebe drives to the pay phone at the gas station in Tate's Bend to find out where she's substitute-teaching. If it's far out and she will be late, then she will leave a message for me at school to take the afternoon bus that stops in East Winder. On these days I am to stay with Daze, if she's available, or at my old house, where I have been handpicked by Mrs. Catterson for the unlucky task of socializing Seth, who is homeschooled. If Phoebe won't be late, then I'll ride the river bus back to the cabin. I'll sit in the RV's passenger seat and do my homework on the dash. Daze says this makes me a latchkey kid, like she saw on *60 Minutes*, but Phoebe says it most certainly does not.

On the second day of school, a Tuesday, I get the message to ride the bus to the Cattersons, and Seth's mother meets me at the door of my own house. She is tall and blond, with a strong-looking nose and a wide red smile. Inside the front door she stoops to give me a little hug as I stand there looking around for our shoe tray.

"How's your father, dear?" she says. "We missed you in church."

"I don't know, I know," I say, like an idiot.

Even though the cabin is a very cramped space, the inside of my house seems smaller than I remember. It has the invisible feel of other people, a strange, clear layer that distorts all the familiar things in a way I can't pin down. For the first time ever, I keep my shoes on while I cross the pale gray carpet, the carpet Phoebe says is for sock feet only. Already there's a faintly soiled footpath between the front door and the kitchen, right through the foyer. There's a small television set too, on the shelf opposite the couch.

"You can set up your books on the table," says Mrs. Catterson as she pours two glasses of milk. "You and Seth can do homework, and then we'll see about the rest of the afternoon, if there's time left over. Maybe even watch television."

What I would like to do is go up to my room and get my box. Only not in front of Seth.

"Make yourself at home," Mrs. Catterson says. "I mean, I know this is your home already, but you know what I mean." Then she pulls on yellow rubber gloves and heads off to clean the bathroom. I've just opened my history book, which is the only real homework I have so far, when Seth thumps a red clothbound Bible down on the table across from me, at my father's place. He doesn't say hello and he doesn't drink his milk. He just flips to a page in the middle of the Bible and begins reading. I am already on the history chapter about Puritans, how they believed in the "Elect," and how some women would throw their babies into wells so that they knew they would go to hell and wouldn't have to worry over it anymore.

Seth jiggles his knee, shaking the table. When I look up, he's staring right at me. "Guess how many times I've read the Bible," he says.

I shrug. I've never read the Bible from start to finish. I always end up skipping Leviticus and Numbers. Right now, I'm still on the book of Jeremiah, the part where God tells him he's going to lay waste to Judah and make Jerusalem a haunt of jackals.

"Three times all the way through." Seth pushes the red book toward me. "This Bible has four versions all on one page, see? Tell me a verse you know, and I can probably figure out which translation you have. Then we can look it up and see what the differences are."

"Jesus wept."

"You know what I mean."

I could give him "Pray without ceasing," but I don't want to, because then I'll probably have to hear, in my own house, all about how Seth spent a whole year mastering ceaseless prayer in Africa. When I have let my own prayer slip away again. I think the words now to myself. *Inhabit me, O Lord God.*

Seth pushes up his wire-rimmed glasses, waiting. He seems taller every time I see him, and his eyes are clear brown, like iced tea. Under the table his knee continues to jiggle, and the surface of my milk rocks up against the inside of my glass. "Come on," he says. "A verse."

"'The harvest is past, the summer is ended, and we are not saved.'"

"That's not even biblical."

"It's Jeremiah."

"Doubtful," he says. "Give me another one."

And because I can't remember exactly where in Jeremiah, I reach for the red-cloth Bible. Seth pulls it back.

"I have school," I say. "I can't just sit around memorizing the Bible all day."

"You could read the Bible on the bus, if it was important to you." Seth's mouth, wide like his mother's, twitches with the challenge. It's like he's trying not to smile, only teasing, maybe, but when I start to smile back, he presses his lips together, serious. "You think reading the Bible is a laughing matter?"

"I read the Bible every day," I say.

"In some parts of Africa, people can't even read the Bible, because it hasn't been translated into their own language yet. It's something Americans take for granted. Like having enough to eat."

I go back to my history book with a show of concentration. In the Puritan chapel, an usher carries a stick with an iron ball on one end and a feather on the other.

Seth stands up and walks around behind me, just like a teacher. I have to reread the caption three times. It says that when children misbehaved in church, they got knocked on the head with the ball, and that when adults fell asleep, they got tickled under the chin with the feather.

"I did Puritans last year," Seth says. "When you're home-schooled you can move at your own pace. What are you, in seventh grade? I'm already in ninth and I'm only thirteen."

I keep ignoring him, and he returns to his seat and bends his head over the Bible, holding his hair off his forehead with one hand, thumping a pencil on the table with another.

"Seth has an exceptionally high IQ," says Mrs. Catterson from the doorway. She peels off the rubber gloves, and her smile breaks open over the whole lower half of her face. "He was reading at a very early age, but he was memorizing even before that. He could recite whole children's books before he turned four."

"Mom."

On her way across the kitchen, Mrs. Catterson pauses at the table to squeeze Seth's shoulder.

"I really can memorize anything," Seth says when his mother disappears into the pantry. "It comes in handy for Doctor Osborne's play."

I flip another page in my book, like I couldn't care less.

"You could be in it," he says. "Except it's kind of a limited cast. Of two—Doctor Osborne and me."

"Is it a missionary story?" I ask in spite of myself.

"I'm not at liberty to say."

"So you can brag about being in it but you can't say what you're in?"

"Hey." Seth smiles crookedly. "I may be able to memorize, and I may be in a play, and I may have a high IQ, but I'm not saying I think I'm better than you because of it. That would be bragging."

"I don't even have an IQ," I say. "I don't need one. I have ESP."

"ESP is of Satan," Seth says.

I grit my teeth and force myself not to say anything more. In my history book, I'm getting to the part about the first Thanksgiving, and I try to practice reading and thinking my prayer at the same time, glad for something spiritual to do that Seth can't see. I am hoping to be receptive enough that by the time my father comes home, I can help with his new vision. I may have a spiritual gift to offer by then, or maybe even a calling that will show me how to use it. The problem is, when I think the prayer words, then the words on the page about Pilgrims become shapes, and when I read the words on the page, the words of the prayer in my head just stop.

"Do you know what lust is?" Seth says after a time. His voice is low, and when I look up, he's staring at my chest.

I look down at where my breasts push painfully against my T-shirt, then I bend over my book so that the whole heavy front of me is hidden beneath the tabletop. This brings me so close to the page that I can smell the clean paper, like split wood, and the tangy hint of ink, too.

"It's when a man looks upon a woman and thinks about having sexual relations. 'Therefore God gave them over in the sinful desires of their hearts to sexual impurity for the degrading of their bodies with one another,'" Seth reads from the red Bible. "Lust."

"I know that."

"Men are weak when it comes to lust," Seth says. "Doctor Osborne says that sisters in Christ are called to help men practice looking without lusting. Like right now. I'm looking at you and not lusting."

Receptive or no, I refuse to believe this is my calling. "Stop it," I say.

Seth grins. "Stop *not* lusting? You want me to stop *not* lusting?"

"I can see why you need socialization," I say. The grin dies on his face, and I make it through the whole section on Thanksgiving before he speaks again.

"Guess who we prayed for last night? Someone who thinks he's a prophet."

I snap up to full height in my chair, breasts and all. "You

shut up," I say, dropping my voice to a hiss as Mrs. Catterson enters the kitchen. She opens the refrigerator door, then closes it, turns, and says, "No whispering." Frowning, she approaches Seth from behind and palms both sides of his face. "I don't know what you and your family practice, Charmaine, but in our home we have a policy of full disclosure." Seth's face, under his mother's, wears a complicated expression of satisfaction and sorrow. His mother's hands smush his cheeks toward his nose, and his lips pucker up like a fish. "And we never, ever tell other people to 'shut up.'"

Phoebe believes that elegance is a state of mind, not a station in life. Candlelight is elegant. A set table is also elegant. So even when the meal at the RV-cabin is just canned tuna and sliced tomatoes, washed down with powdered milk, I put a cloth napkin in my lap, and I lay my unused knife across the top of my plate, blade in. Polite conversation is elegant, too, and so she tells me about the second-grade class where she subbed that day, and she asks me about being at the house with the Cattersons, which I tell her was fine. She won't mention my father until after dinner.

While I do the dishes, she takes herself outside to the old lawn chair with a back issue of *The Good Word*, and when I come out to dump the dishpan, she tells me that he slept through her visit again.

"He's exhausted still, the doctor says. But his burns are healing." On her lap, the cover of *The Good Word* shows a green pasture dotted with pale, woolly sheep. "I was reading what he wrote about that one summer. That month he worked down here nonstop, then the next one, remember? When he couldn't get himself out of bed? I should have seen something in that."

"It was a dark night of the soul," I say. "Everything went back to normal."

"Normal," Phoebe says. "Very often your father sleeps only two nights a week. When he gets worked up." She fingers the edges of *The Good Word* and watches the river, which tonight is still. Just a quiet splash here and there from a fish or bird. After a time, she opens the magazine to his column, which includes a photo of him peering seriously into the camera.

"When can I visit?" I say.

"Soon," she says. "Once he's rested, they'll start figuring out if the medication is working, which I guess can take a while. It's different now. Not like the times he got worked up. Then it was like talking to, I don't know. A radio broadcast that couldn't hear me. Now he just seems confused. When he manages to wake up."

As she's speaking, the crickets fall quiet, but after a few moments of silence they gear back up, hesitantly at first, then throbbing with song. A long way down the river road, someone starts a car.

"I never told you about the first time I met your father," Phoebe says.

"You told me a million times."

"My friend and I had been to a wedding in Ohio. This was right after Mother died. We were just passing through East Winder, and we stopped when we saw all the people. It was the funniest thing."

"Daddy saw you, and God told him you were the one. You told me."

"This boy," Phoebe says, like I haven't spoken. She watches the river like she's calling the memory up out of it. "This boy who was getting married in Ohio, this brother of my friend?

His bride had been abducted a few years before when she wasn't much older than you. Sixteen, I think. Some man. Her parents were frantic."

"For ransom?" I say. This part I haven't heard.

"Not exactly. I guess the man did things to her. At the wedding she testified how the Lord restored her virginity. But my friend said the rumor was that when the girl showed up back at her own house she just shut herself in her room for a week and wouldn't talk to anyone. By the time she finally told her parents that she'd escaped a man's apartment and they called the police, the man was gone, and so was all trace of the things he'd done to her."

Behind me, Titus squeezes himself out of the window over the sink and drops onto the pile of cement blocks underneath, left over from when my father built the foundation. The sun falls fast behind the palisades, but it takes a while for the gorge to grow fully dark. You can look way up to the top of the cliffs and see sunlight filtering through the leaves and shining on the limestone ridge.

"My friend and I talked about it the whole trip back," Phoebe says. "If the girl was telling the truth, and whether or not your virginity could be truly restored if you lied about the circumstances, and what kind of life her brother might be in for. I'm ashamed to say it, but I remember wondering what it might be like to be abducted. Or to run off with someone. Whatever it was. And that's what was on my mind when God pointed me out to your father, even though I let him think differently. I let him think I was there because I'd heard about the revival. 'The heart is deceitful above all things,'" she says, quoting Jeremiah. "Isn't that how it goes?"

"'And desperately wicked,'" I say. "'Who can know it?'"

"Right," says Phoebe. "Who indeed."

Before bed I wash my face and wonder if maybe the man left the girl behind and that's why she shut herself in her room. My father said that during his dark night of the soul he had trouble hearing the voice of God, and he wondered if he'd been abandoned. But in *The Good Word* article, he explains that God was teaching him that he is always there, even when it doesn't feel that way. Unlike people, who are with you when they're with you and not when they're not, no wondering about it.

When I fold back the accordion door to the bathroom, Phoebe is sitting on the narrow tweed sofa waiting for her turn. "I've been thinking," she says, nodding thoughtfully, like she already agrees with what she's about to say. "It would be nice if we could remember to tell each other 'I love you' every day. Otherwise whole weeks might go by without either of us hearing those three important words. We can make that the first of our house rules, now that it's just the two of us."

"I don't need to hear 'I love you' every day."

"Yes, you do," says Phoebe. "You just don't realize it. Come over here."

I sit beside her on the sofa and she leans over me, inspecting my face. Then she unclips the gooseneck lamp from the kitchen counter and clips it to the tiny windowsill over the sofa. We have two of these lamps in the cabin, with cords long enough for us to fasten them where they're most needed.

"Maybe we'll even write them up," she says, "—the new rules. And tape them to the wall."

"We didn't make new rules when he was in the Holy Land."

"This is different. This time, we don't know what to expect. I might just discover that I like being an independent woman."

I keep myself very still. Phoebe has a way of trying ideas out, even ideas that she doesn't really mean. But if you challenge her or react in any way, she can start to argue for what she's only been trying out and start to convince herself. The word *divorce* comes back to me from the girl in activity, and I taste tuna in my throat. I have never considered Phoebe and my father anything but a pair, even when they're an unhappy pair.

Phoebe positions the lamp so it's shining right into my eyes. She leans in and plants her thumb on my nose, pushing the tip to one side. I squirm away from her and stand up.

"Come back here," she says. And because I am afraid that if I don't she will launch back into the subject of her independence, I sit down again. She traps my head between her hands, pins it to the sofa. "Your nose is a nest of blackheads," she says, then starts going after them with her two thumbnails. On my cheek, her breath advances, retreats, advances again like a small, soft army.

"You said not to pick," I say, my voice nasally.

"I'm not picking," she says. "I'm extracting. Hold still. And all I'm saying, Charmaine, about the rules, is that with me at this new job, I'm going to need some serious support from you. That should be rule number two. Support each other. I always wanted to be a teacher, and now I'll see if I've got the stuff."

"You're just a substitute, though. Ow. All you have to do is follow the teacher's notes and tell people if they can go to the bathroom or not."

"I don't need your back talk." Phoebe's thumbnails skid toward each other on the side of my nose, and I feel a layer of skin peel away. I wrench my head up from the sofa and clap a hand over my nose. "What I do need, is to hear an 'I love you' every day."

I press my fingertip to my nose then hold it up to her, bright and bloody in the glare of the bulb.

"So you're bleeding a little," she says. "Don't be dramatic."

While Phoebe gets ready for bed, I slip outside to check for Titus. I like to shut him in at night when I can, but if not, then I'll leave the window open and he'll steal in to sleep in the passenger seat or at my feet and wake me up in the morning to be fed. Tonight the moon is thin as a nail paring. Almost not there at all. There is such a thing called a black-hole moon, which I used to think was how the moon got thinner and thinner each month. Like it was disappearing, little by little, into the overwhelming gravity of the black hole at the center of our own galaxy. What it really means is that once a year the moon sits right in front of the black hole, almost like it's trying to warn us about where it is.

I make my way down to the dock, calling for Titus, hoping he'll come. Then I'm praying he'll come, and I catch myself. In *The Good Word*, my father explains that it's not that you can't ask things of God, it's just that you have to be okay with whatever answer you get back or with his silence. What I want to ask is for Titus to stay inside, where no larger animal can get him and where no teenager, drunken or cruel or both, can catch him and throw him from Tate's Bridge, which is something that you hear about happening down here. I want to ask for my father to be okay, for things just to go back to the way they were. Or maybe even a little better than the way they were, for him to be just a little more like other people, who sleep every night, and for him to pay just a little more attention to Phoebe so that she will love him as much as she loves me and forget about being independent. But even if, like my father says, God's silence is an opportunity to appreciate the power of faith, it's a wretched feeling to ask for something you want so badly and to hear nothing. It's the kind of silence that turns familiar things, comforting things like the presence of the moon or the way the river smells after dark, strange and a little scary.

You can't go wrong, though, with the prayer without ceasing. I don't know how my father manages it even as he's talking or eating. That's the part of him that isn't like other people. The prophet part. I start up now, whispering to the sliver of moon, but later as I'm going to sleep I realize I've stopped again already.

From her loft bed over the dash, Phoebe hears me sigh. "You still awake?"

I don't want to answer, but I do, because our first night here, when she believed me to be asleep, she started to cry, quietly to begin with and then so loudly that the sound carried across the lawn and down the riverbank, where I imagined it spreading out across the water, echoing against the cliffs.

"Isn't there anything you'd like to say to me?" she says.

"I don't think so."

"Think harder."

"I'm sorry for back-talking?"

"Something else," she says. "Remember?"

Then I remember, and even though I would be hard-pressed to say I do not love my mother, the words she wants to hear drop from my mouth like reluctant stones.

"I love you too," she says. "Good night."

CHAPTER 7

"I KNOW WHO YOUR DADDY is," Tracy says in the morning, poking me hard in the stomach as soon as I sit down. "The preacher? I watched him make that trailer of yours into a cabin."

"He's not a preacher," I say, leaning my head against the dirty window.

"You think you're the only one who's been to church? I'm baptized and everything. Right there in the river."

"My grandfather was baptized in the river," I say. "I didn't know they did that anymore."

"Well, they do," she says. Under her breath she says, "Dumbass." Then: "Where do they do it at your church?"

"At the altar," I say. "You just get a little sprinkle on your head. Some altars have bathtubs behind them. Baptismal fonts."

"Whatever that means," Tracy says. "We had my sister's baby baptized, too, but now my mother says if the Lord wants anything else he can come down and tell her himself with a tongue of fire. She says she'll kill me if I get pregnant before I'm through school. What?" she says at the look on my face. "You want a baby?"

"No."

Tracy cocks her head. "You got something against babies?"

I blink hard, caught in the net of a question with no good answer. "No. Do you want a baby?"

"Hell, no."

"Then what're you asking me for?" I say. I take a deep breath and add: "Dumbass." I've never called anyone a name before, and I like the tiny, stunned gap of silence in its wake.

Half of Tracy's mouth twists into a smirk. "You got a scab on your nose," she says.

Outside it's getting light, the slow, gray way it does down at the bottom of the gorge. I never knew all the different ways dawn could look. The rim of the cliffs above glows brighter and brighter as we climb, and my eyes well up against it. We're nearing the set of trailers where the Child of God lives. The bus hisses and stops. I close my eyes with dread. This is the point of the morning where I start pretending to be asleep.

"Here he comes," Tracy says in a low voice. Then, as if she wants to see if I am really drifting off, she tells me, "Sometimes he picks a girl to sit on his lap. He can't finger nobody, but they can sit there and feel his you-know-what."

My eyes pop open. I look doubtfully toward Ravenna.

"She don't drive every night," Tracy says. "She's got her class."

"I know you're not about to smoke that on my bus,"

Ravenna says as Cecil Goode makes his way up the ramp. His head appears over the first seat, an unlit cigarette in his mouth.

"You're early," he says around the cigarette.

"Same time I get here every day."

"If you say so," says Cecil when he reaches the top of the ramp.

"I say that and a whole lot more," says Ravenna.

"A *whole* lot more," Cecil agrees. He shoulders his way down the aisle. "You got more words in one morning than most people got all day."

"Pearls of wisdom," Ravenna says, "cast before swine."

Ravenna doesn't move the bus, though, until Cecil's settled himself in. When the rest of us first get on, we have to get to our seats fast before she lays on the gas and whatever we're carrying goes flying. But Cecil she waits for, sassing him the whole time, letting him sass her back, even though he's a kid and white, and even though people down here say "nigger" this and "nigger" that like it's just information. And he always lets her have the last word, even though she's black and a woman.

When Cecil reaches our seat, he leans over Tracy. "Hold on to this for me," he says, "and don't smoke it, neither." Tracy pinches the cigarette from his mouth and opens her purse. "Girl?" Cecil says, and I almost answer "She won't" for her, out of distress, but then he's looking right at me with his light amber eyes. "What?" he says. "You want your own cigarette?" I open my mouth and try to look somewhere else, which ends up being at his empty sleeve. My neck burns. "Look at me," he says. "You were all fired up to look a second ago." He knocks Tracy's shoulder with his gleaming chrome claw. "What's her name?"

"Charmaine," Tracy says, dropping the cigarette into her purse.

"No," I manage to say.

"Her name's Charmaine," Tracy says, screwing up her face at me like I've gone crazy.

"No, I don't want my own cigarette," I say.

"Listen up, ladies' man," says Ravenna. Her eyes appear in the sliver of one of the complicated rearview mirrors. "I got a route, here."

Cecil Goode just nods like he's amused. He moves on by, and I let out my breath.

"Cousin," Cecil says from two seats back. "You tell your friend there that if she likes to look, there's a lot more to see."

"I'm a telephone operator now?" Tracy calls back to him. "You hear?" she says to me.

"Yeah."

"You scared?" Tracy says.

I shrug and try to move my eyebrows bravely, carelessly.

"You are," she says. She digs her pen into the seat in front of us, opening up a space between stitches. "You really are a dumbass. He's only mean because he likes you, and he only likes you because you're prissy."

I don't know what's hardest to believe, that Cecil Goode likes me, that I am prissy, or that prissy could be why he likes me.

"You know what *prissy* means?" Tracy asks.

"Yeah," I say. "Do you?"

"You think I'm stupid?"

"No one ever called me 'prissy' before."

"You're all carry-your-books-to-school-every-day. You talk like people on TV."

"Which ones?"

Tracy throws up her hands. "All of them. Or like a teacher. You talk like a teacher, through your nose, like you think you're better than everyone." She pinches her nose with her thumb and forefinger. "At my church you just get a little sprinkle," she says in a high nasal, wiggling her shoulders back and forth. "Baptismal font. I don't want my own cigarette."

"I don't sound like that."

"I don't sound like that," says Tracy, sounding more like me than I care for.

"Girl," Cecil Goode calls from his seat.

"She don't want to talk to you," Tracy says. "She don't want to talk to nobody on this bus."

I open *A Wrinkle in Time.* I am halfway through it the second time, and if I could, I would tesser myself right off the bus. I stare at the page like I'm reading, but it's impossible to read with Tracy glowering at the side of my face.

"She just wants to read her prissy book," says Tracy, ducking her head to look at the cover. "Wrinkle Dinkle."

The road curves upward, the bus chugging into gear like something settling into place far beneath me, like a reminder. Not praying. Not praying. I am as bad as the vestal virgins, whose only job was to stay awake and wait for the bridegroom, and they couldn't even do that much. *Inhabit me, O Lord God,* I whisper to myself.

"You're not supposed to do that," Tracy says. "Read with your lips moving. I thought you were smart."

• • •

Mrs. Teaderman says we are transcribing, through freewriting, a record of our movement from the *prison* of the unconscious to a *prism* of the unconscious. She writes both *prison* and *prism* on the board, with a big arrow to indicate the right direction.

After freewriting, if you are called upon to share what you wrote, you may say "Pass" and it won't hurt your grade. You may also write DO NOT READ at the top of your entry if you have written something you don't want even Mrs. Teaderman to read when she collects them. She says that the movement from *prison* to *prism* can sometimes be very private, which makes the boys snicker.

Phoebe is fine, I write to my father, though I know he has seen her briefly in and around his sleeping. *We are fine down at the river. I think I am going to see you very soon. Once everything is okay with the medication. How is the medication going?*

As we write, Mrs. Teaderman patrols the rows on her long legs. Today she wears the red slacks with a billowy pink top, and she looks like a flamingo, the way she steps and stops, steps and stops. "The truth can set you free," she says from somewhere behind me. "But it can also bind your hands. Inventiveness can be a ray of light in the prison of the unconscious."

I think about Seth and the play he's doing with Dr. Osborne, and then I am writing, inventively, that I'm the one who will be in a new play. I pick Ruth, for its strong female lead. *I have to sit at the feet of Naomi and receive her wise counsel,* I write. *Boaz and Naomi haven't been cast yet.* I can see the whole thing—myself in Old Testament dress, acting out the motions of collecting leftover wheat on the threshing-room floor.

In activity, Kelly-Lynn measures my tiny ponytail with her fingers. "Better," she says. "Maybe next you should think about cutting out junk food and pop. Your clothes are tight."

"I never drink pop," I say. Before I can stop myself, I say what Phoebe says about pop: "We can't afford it." I wish I hadn't said it, but it doesn't matter, anyway. Everything you say to Kelly-Lynn passes over her and disappears, like a flock of migrating birds.

"What's the matter with your nose?" she says.

"Nothing," I say, touching the scab. Down on the gym floor a dodge-ball game is going on, more than fifty kids on each half of the basketball court. I spy Tracy's red hair just as she hurls the rubber ball hard into a girl's knee.

"We used to be poor, too," says Kelly-Lynn. "We lived in an apartment before my mom met my stepdad. Then again in between my stepdad and Rob. And my dad was poor, he said, because he had to send us money for the apartment. I had to wear my mom's pre-diet fat clothes. Everything hung off me."

"My mother knows how to take things in," I say. "She sews a lot. Or she used to." Below, Tracy slams the ball into the feet of another girl. Then she takes out a boy who doesn't see it coming. Then someone else beans the ball right back at Tracy, catching her on the shoulder, and she slinks back toward the bleachers and disappears into the crowd.

"The trick is to stay away from anything salty or sweet," Kelly-Lynn says. "Salty and sweet food just makes you want to eat more. I'm only eating cucumbers and carrot sticks until cheerleading tryouts. You have to think, what do you want more, to not be fat or to eat? Or, for me, to be a cheerleader or to eat?"

This is what I ask myself after school, when Daze offers me a Ding Dong in her apartment at the Custer Peake Memorial Retirement Center.

"No thanks," I say.

"How about some RC Cola and peanuts?"

"Do you have any Tab?"

Daze gives me a hard look. "What happened to your nose?" When I shrug, she sighs. "You're not getting fat, sweet pea. You're just developing a figure. The less you fight your shape, the better. Your bosom still hurt?"

"A little," I say.

"It's growing, then. You're turning into an hourglass." Daze hands me one of her slinky robes, and I change out of my clothes in her bathroom. Her whole apartment smells like the Pine-Sol and Windex she uses to chase away the "vapors of death," which is what she calls the odor of old people trying to cover up their smells with potpourri. In the living room I hand over my clothes. Daze has her own stackable washer and dryer, and she loves to use them. Back in the day, she says, she had to wash everything on a washboard and wring it on a wringer and then hang it up to dry and take it back down and iron it. Now everything in her apartment, every towel and every piece of clothing, has just been washed and dried.

"I wish I was skinny like you," I say.

"I'm skinny all right. And spent my whole life pining for an hourglass figure." She pours detergent into the washer, then turns and makes wavy motions like she's moving her hands over breasts and hips. "Your mother, she's always been an unfortunate pear. Only she's so thin now, you can't hardly tell."

"What's Daddy?"

"Your father is a man after God's own heart," says Daze, "any way you look at it. But I take your meaning. Men are short or skinny or tall. Your father's on the tall side, like his father, but not too tall."

"Is he still a man after God's own heart?"

"Of course he is. Who said he wasn't — your mother? Once a man after God's own heart, always a man after God's own heart." Then Daze draws each of us a footbath, with bath beads, and turns on her small black-and-white television set. Daze loves soap operas, which she calls "the stories," and I'm not supposed to tell anyone, because they are all secular. Except for *Ryan's Hope,* which has a priest character, which is better than nothing, she says.

In the prime spot over Daze's television hangs a framed black-and-white picture of my grandfather. It's a famous shot. *The Good Word* still runs it during camp-meeting season, and my father keeps a yellowed clipping of it from the *Lexington Herald-Leader* in his Bible. It was taken during the "Great Revival," and shows my grandfather standing under the water tower. He wears a thin tie and wire-rimmed glasses. One hand points to the audience, and the other grasps the pulpit so tightly that his knuckles bulge big as golf balls. His specialty was father-and-son sermons, which start out with stories about modern-day fathers who have to choose between saving their sons and saving lots of people they don't know. The situations are complicated — bridges that hold only so much weight, viruses so strong and spreading so fast that doctors' own sons must be experimented on, burning buildings where hundreds of crippled senior citizens make their homes. There is always a moment when the father and son look at each other above the syringe or across the flames, and each understands the decision and feels the love and pain. I never heard my grandfather preach, but I've read the reprints in *The Good Word.* Even though I already know the outcome of every sermon, it is still hard not to hope that one of these fathers, just one of them, one time, will choose not to sacrifice his son, even in order to save the rest of the world. But the world is always in luck.

When the buzzer on the dryer sounds, I change back into my jeans and T-shirt—even tighter now—and we head down to the lobby. Phoebe is already there, using the front-desk phone to call Ron's Towing. She wears her black bespoke pants and blue blouse, and she looks pretty. I sometimes forget she can look that way until I see her in public. None other than Dr. Osborne himself stands tall behind her. He is the only grown man I know with hair long enough for a braid that rests between his shoulders. He wears a necklace, too—a large cross made of two entwined iron nails, like those that pierced the palms of Jesus, strung on a leather cord. I feel like I've conjured him by making up the play about Naomi and Ruth in freewriting.

"Let me give you a lift," he says to Phoebe after she hangs up.

Over the front desk looms a large color print of the same revival picture of my grandfather in a gold frame. Phoebe glances at it uneasily.

"You're down at the river these days," says Dr. Osborne. "Am I right?"

"Doctor Osborne likes to keep up," Daze says crisply. "He's a regular around here, visiting shut-ins."

"Daze," says Phoebe.

"I'm not so old and infirm that I can't take my own daughter-in-law home," says Daze. "I still have the Buick."

Phoebe puts her fingers to her temples. "That Pinto," she says. "It made it to the hospital, then here, then it just sputtered out. I don't know what to do with that car."

"You'll get it fixed, the way the rest of us do," says Daze. "Let me get my jacket."

"Ms. Peake?" Dr. Osborne dips his body from the waist in Daze's direction. "I don't want you to miss dining hall."

"Very often I prepare my own meals," Daze says, even as Phoebe is saying to Dr. Osborne, "If it's really no trouble."

Whatever Daze is thinking, she will not make a family scene under the watchful eyes of the receptionist, or even in front of Dr. Osborne. "If it's no trouble, then," she echoes Phoebe, then squeezes me extra long, as if I'm supposed to take meaning from it.

In the parking lot, I open the back door to Dr. Osborne's Toyota to see the seat and floor covered with books.

"Let me move some of those," he says behind me, but when I step aside to let him, Phoebe says, "She can squinch in there just fine, Doctor Osborne."

"Morris," says Dr. Osborne.

He holds Phoebe's door while she climbs in, leaving me to push one sliding stack of books across the back seat and into a big pile. Under my feet are more books, and I nudge at them until I can feel the car mat beneath my shoes.

"My, what a lot of books," Phoebe says as Dr. Osborne slides behind the wheel.

Dr. Osborne shakes his head and peers with her into the back seat. "I always check out more than I have time for," he says, "and soon as I know it, they're overdue and I haven't even finished reading them."

Through the window I watch the tow truck pull our Pinto backward out of the lot. We follow it to the garage, and when Phoebe gets out to speak to Ron Deeds, Dr. Osborne gets out, too, and stands beside her like it's as much his business as it is hers. Ours. When they come back he opens and closes the car door for her with extra care, like he's acting out the word *gentleness*.

The pile of books on the seat beside me shifts.

"Don't bother Doctor Osborne's books," Phoebe hisses.

"I'm not," I say, and when Dr. Osborne gets behind the wheel again, I ask him, as if I couldn't look for myself, if any of the books are plays.

"No," says Dr. Osborne. "I'm working strictly from biblical inspiration these days. 'A Series of Spiritual Scenes' I'm calling it."

"Fascinating," says Phoebe.

"Naomi and Ruth are inspiring to me," I say, because why not?

"The mother figure," says Dr. Osborne, "if not the actual mother." He smiles at Phoebe. "I can see how that would be inspiring."

Then he does something different with his voice, not whispering, but dropping into a kind of private tone, which excludes me, to ask Phoebe about my father. *David*.

Phoebe starts nodding before she speaks. I prepare for her standard, public response, which is "Better, fine, just overtired and under stress, getting some much-needed rest." But after she opens her mouth she just closes it and nods some more.

"It must be hard," Dr. Osborne says. "I've known David since we were kids."

"Of course," Phoebe says. "Doctor Osborne—"

"Morris."

"Morris. It's hard." Which is not something she should say, because it is discussing family outside family. Then he starts nodding with her, and a tear slips down the side of Phoebe's face.

I poke my head in between the driver's and passenger seats. "He's been under a strain," I say. "He's getting some much-needed rest. He's exhausted from his work. And his traveling."

Neither of them respond to me. They just keep nodding together, like they know each other much better than they really do. After a time, like I'm not even there, Phoebe says, "It's hard on Charmaine."

"It's not hard on me," I say.

"You're a tough cookie," Dr. Osborne says, keeping his eyes on the road. It could be a compliment.

"She's a tough cookie, all right," says Phoebe, making it sound less complimentary. They both laugh. Then they are talking about the car again, Dr. Osborne asking about future rides needed, Phoebe explaining that she can catch the children's school bus to East Winder Elementary, where she will be subbing for the rest of the week.

I pick up a book called *The Cost of Discipleship* and flip through it, snapping the pages loudly. In the index I search for Ruth or Naomi, but neither is there. *Prayer* is there, but not *pray without ceasing*, which of course I have stopped. I force myself to think the prayer in my head now, even though I'm angry. *Lust* is in the index, and I look up the passage, which I find underlined lightly in pencil:

Both eye and hand are less than Christ, and when they are used as the instruments of lust and hinder the whole body from the purity of discipleship, they must be sacrificed for the sake of him.

Sacrifice of eye or hand. This is what Seth will have to do if he slips up and looks at me with lust, even while practicing not to. And if Dr. Osborne looks at Phoebe with lust, he will have to do the same, though perhaps as the man who has never known a woman, he has conquered the desires of his eye and hand.

Up front, Phoebe is laughing, and when we pull up to the cabin, she tells me to go inside first and she'll be right along.

I close the door to Dr. Osborne's car harder than I have to.

"What a nice man," Phoebe says when she comes in a few minutes later. "What a thoughtful person."

I push past her and settle myself in the passenger seat.

"We had the nicest conversation." When I don't ask what they talked about, Phoebe sighs. Then she starts humming "My Favorite Things."

"Homework," I say, and the humming stops. We are late getting home, and it's already dusk. High above, a slow, heavy train slides over Tate's Bridge with a rumbling that ricochets deeply through the gorge. I watch it through what used to be the RV's dashboard, now a picture window of sorts. The trains run all night, and the sound used to wake me, but it's getting more familiar. Most nights I sleep right through.

Down by the trees, I spot Titus making his way up from the riverbank. Phoebe lets him in, and he jumps into my lap, on top of the social studies book, right under the warm goose-neck lamp. "I love you," I whisper into his velvety ear, and he purrs and pushes his head into the crook of my elbow. Behind me, the humming starts again as Phoebe runs the faucet to begin boiling something for dinner. She keeps it quiet, but the sound runs beneath everything else the way I wish my prayer would—like something that comes so naturally to her she can't help it.

CHAPTER 8

*P*ASTOR CHICK IS NOT your run-of-the-mill youth minister. He's a leading expert on the subject who teaches at the seminary with Dr. Osborne. He recruits his team from among his students. Like Conley, a tall Texan guitar player. To kick off the first meeting of fall, Conley bounds through where we've all gathered in the Upper Room, plants himself in front of the marker board, and starts strumming hard to an up-tempo song we all know called "The Horse and Rider." It's from the Old Testament, the part where Moses and the Israelites sing their thanks to God for parting the Red Sea and drowning the horse and rider, AKA the Egyptians, behind them. Conley's voice rises high on the song, then skims just over the surface of the other voices, like a hunting bird on the river. Someone in back starts clapping, and soon the music rolls through the room until everyone is keeping time, and when we get to the end of the chorus, Conley changes up the chords and launches us right into "I'll Fly Away." Mary-Kate and Karen have allowed me to perch on their best-friends beanbag, and we sit at the edge of the room, just underneath the row of windows that looks down on the sanctuary. We try to do the harmony part, all three of us together. Even Seth, sitting a few feet away, is singing, and it's easy to feel like everyone's on the same side, the Lord's side. I'm concentrating so hard that I don't even see Pastor Chick and his bald head in the doorway. Then he starts making his way to the front, weaving around kids sitting Indian-style. A few of the high schoolers stick their legs out as if to trip him, and he laughs and pretends to fall, waving his arms and staggering to recover.

Pastor Chick is stocky as a bulldog. He wears his old plaid shirt tucked into faded jeans like a lot of the county kids do, but his shoes are rich brown leather with heavy rubber soles. Expensive shoes. Daze says the Collinses, Pastor Chick's family in Tennessee, are "old money." Daze's own family used to be old money, generations back. Custer Peake came from old money, too, before the honorable Peake ancestor took a stand against growing tobacco. Daze says money's not important, though. She says you couldn't pay her enough to drive around in a Cadillac like a dime-store millionaire. Pastor Chick drives a beat-up Ford pickup truck like it's all he can afford, which is just the way old money behaves, Daze says.

Now Pastor Chick stands humbly to the side of Conley, singing. "When I die, Hallelujah, by and by . . ." Near him, one of the missionary twins lifts her hands in worship. Conley quietly shifts into the "Hallelujah" song, where you sing that word over and over until you work yourself into a prayerful state. Even though I can't think the words of my own prayer and sing at the same time, I feel prayerful all the same.

"You are a mighty God," Pastor Chick begins as the last Hallelujah fades. "You know everything we've ever done, all the ways we've hurt you by disobeying your word." Pastor Chick pauses, and when I sneak a peek at him, he's frowning down at his shoes, palms spread flat to the space in front of him, like he's blind and expecting to run into a wall. I crane my head to peer into the darkened sanctuary below. Today is the second Sunday in a row that Phoebe and I have skipped services. This morning she slept until noon, which she never does, and I had to remind her about a ride to Youth Group.

"We hurt you when we hurt the people in our lives," Pastor Chick is saying. "How many opportunities have we missed to share Christ's love? How many times this week have we said things that are unkind?" He gives us a moment to think, and what I think of is how unconvincing I sound saying "I love you" to Phoebe every night, wishing I didn't have to. I close my eyes again.

"How often have we laughed when someone takes their sexuality, that precious gift for marriage, and turns it into a dirty joke?" When he pauses this time, the silence in the room slithers into my ears and inflates there like two tiny balloons. "How many times have we been too cool to pick up our lunch tray and sit beside that lonely girl in the cafeteria? The one with the wrong kind of clothes. The one who looks like she hadn't washed her hair. Maybe we wondered what others would think if they saw us sitting with her." He lets this sink in. "Maybe we were that cowardly."

"We ask forgiveness for forgetting that you walk among us

in the people we meet, that everything we do unto the least of these, we do also unto you. Amen."

We all open our eyes and blink, dazed to find the room still there. The beanbag makes its quiet husking sounds as Mary-Kate, Karen, and I settle in more comfortably.

"Folks," says Pastor Chick, "we've got a big night." Conley does a drumroll on the guitar with his knuckles. "Many of you know that years back our town was home to one of the world's most exciting revivals. Any of you heard your parents talking about the Spirit of 'Seventy-three, when a Wednesday-night evening Bible study led by brother Custer Peake turned into a two-week celebration with hundreds coming to the Lord?"

Pride lodges somewhere between my ribs, with the special power only pride has to crack a person wide open. "When the word got out about the joy, people, the joy unspeakable and full of glory, well, folks just had to see it for themselves." Pastor Chick sucks his lips against his teeth and nods, thoughtfully. "What if I told you . . . ," he begins again, then waits so long we're all dying to hear what comes next. "What if I told you that right here, in this very room, could be the beginning of an underground revival in our school, our town, the whole great Commonwealth of Kentucky?"

He turns to the marker board and gropes around for an eraser that isn't there. Someone hands him a roll of paper towels from the windowsill, but before he begins wiping down the board, he steps back and checks out two idiotic messages: "Billy was here," and then below it, "Seth was here." Pastor Chick shakes his head, smiling as he wipes the board. "Seth and Billy," he says, with his back to the room. Then he turns around and sweeps out a hand to where a chubby, red-faced boy with shaggy hair sits against the wall opposite me. Then he nods at Seth, and I wonder if he already knows who I am, too. As if he reads my mind, Pastor Chick says, "People, let's back up. Before we go any further, let's take a moment to meet our newbies. Seventh graders, stand up."

Beside me, Mary-Kate and Karen spring to their feet, which sinks me deeper into the beanbag. By the time I'm standing, Pastor Chick has greeted the first few newcomers, studying each one in turn like he's memorizing their faces.

"Mary-Kate," says Mary-Kate when he gets to her.

"Mary-Kate," repeats Pastor Chick, savoring her name in a way that makes Mary-Kate's pale hair and even her slumping posture and new case of acne seem special.

"Karen," says Karen, and my knees lock into place. I am next.

"Karen," repeats Pastor Chick. "Sister of Brian, legendary eater of pancakes." Whatever this means, it makes Karen smile so hard her lips catch on her braces.

Then Pastor Chick is looking at me, and I understand that he knows. Not only who I am and who my grandfather was and who my father is, but also where my father is, and everything that has led up to it. I open my mouth, and when my name won't come out right away, Pastor Chick scans the ceiling, pretending to have to recall it. "Gotta be Charmaine," he says finally. "Scion of the holy Peakes." Now Pastor Chick smiles, and it might be the kindest-looking smile I have ever seen. I have not cried even one time since the crazy laughing tears at Mrs. James's house, and as long as I don't blink, I won't be crying now. But when I try to smile back at Pastor Chick, I can see him seeing me, seeing right into how I feel, only what he sees stays private, like he's momentarily switched channels to a frequency only the two of us can pick up. Then he does the perfect, merciful thing by moving on to the next new-comer, and I drop back down into the beanbag away from the roomful of eyes.

"An illustrious start," says Pastor Chick when he gets through everyone. He sounds like he's teasing and like he means it all at the same time. He pushes his hands deep into the front pockets of his jeans and rocks forward, then back-ward on his expensive leather shoes. "Operation Outreach," he begins, then takes another one of his long pauses. He nods seriously into each corner of the room. "How many are we in this room tonight? Fifty? Seventy?"

"Seventy-two," calls out Seth after a moment.

"Seventy-three," says Mary-Kate.

"Seventy-two, seventy-three," says Pastor Chick. "I like the enthusiasm of our new seventh graders. Now in a moment, I'm going to ask you all to close your eyes again. I'm going to ask you to think of the people in your life. People at school or on your Pony League team. Members of your family, even. Ask yourself if the people in your life have the information they need to connect that something special about you to Jesus. To the light of our Lord shining through. I hope you get questioned about that light on a regular basis, people," he says. "I do."

Pastor Chick claps and does a little jump like he's waking himself up. "We'll call that the first thing." He spins to the marker board and starts squeaking out letters. "Pray for the light of God. People ask your secret. That's one kind of oppor-tunity." He spins back to face the room. "Two. In a moment, when I ask you to be very, very still, we're each going to ask God to lay three people on our heart." On the board he writes, *three people on your heart.* "You may find yourself thinking, sud-

denly, of a person you don't really like that much. Pay attention to that. We'll take them one at a time." He raises his
hands, says, "Dear Lord," and I close my eyes and wait in the
emptiness where Pastor Chick's voice used to be. The room is
beginning to heat up.

I breathe in and then out. I pray my own prayer one time,
two times, with my breathing, and then there is a face. Kelly-
Lynn from English and activity, with her pearl earrings and
ponytail. Behind my eyelids, I consider her with dread, because
I know that when I witness to her she will lump me in disdain-
fully with the missionary twins. My father would be deeply
ashamed of me for this thought. It is not the job of the prophet
or any other servant of the Lord to care what others think of
you.

"Now ask God for someone else," says Pastor Chick, and
Tracy Payne's face appears to me so fast it's like she's been
lying in wait.

"Thank the Lord for the first two people," says Pastor Chick.
Thank you, I pray. *Inhabit me, O Lord God.*

"Seventy-five of us in this room, and already we've thought
of a hundred and fifty more individuals. Think of it, people.
Soon we'll be so many in number that we'll grow out of the
Upper Room and spill over to the sanctuary down there. I love
it. Now," Pastor Chick pauses, and Conley starts up with some
low guitar strumming. "Pray for the last one."

I pray even though I already know who it is. I give God
some extra time in case he wants to change his mind, but this
person has been hovering at the edge of my thoughts ever
since he first spoke to me. Hovering in my unconscious, Mrs.
Teaderman would say. Cecil Goode. The golden-headed Child
of God.

After the prayer, Pastor Chick records more instructions on the board. *First: Pray for your people. Second: Pray for an opening. Third: Witness to them or invite them to the Main Event,* which Pastor Chick explains will be a thrilling, town-wide scavenger hunt the Friday after next. After scavenging East Winder, we'll congregate at dusk, at the base of the water tower, in honor of my grandfather's revival. We'll have communion and an altar call—without the altar, of course—and then we'll all spend the night in the seminary rec center, a lock-in. Unless the revival spirit moves again. Then who knows how long we'll keep on worshiping.

We sing one more song and pray one more prayer before Pastor Chick sends us to the basement for refreshments.

"Who'd you get?" Mary-Kate asks me in the stairwell.

"I don't think you're supposed to say," I say.

"I got my uncle and my two cousins. Only I can't invite them to the scavenger hunt because they live in Ohio."

"I got the missionary twins," says Karen. "And Hannah Boykin."

"The twins are already in Youth Group, though," I say. "They're thinking of their own three people to bring. They're already missionaries."

"I didn't pick them," says Karen. "God did."

"What about someone from your bus?" I suggest. "Or activity?"

Mary-Kate shrugs. "We ride the bus with church kids, too. And we practice clarinet in the band room during activity."

In the basement hallway, I tip back my head and regard the low ceiling, just to be looking somewhere else. Its speckled rectangular panels feel like they might be closing in. "What if the people you got don't like you?" I say to the ceiling. "What if they're not people other people make fun of, but they're the people who make fun of you?"

"Turn the other cheek," says Karen easily. "Maybe tell them how fun the Main Event is going to be."

"Or maybe don't invite them personally," says Mary-Kate. "You could write them a note on the back of one of the flyers."

I imagine writing Tracy a note and handing it to her on the bus, how confused we would both be. I think of how stupid my voice would sound when I tried to explain to Kelly-Lynn why going around town asking people for things is supposed to be fun.

In line at the refreshments counter, Seth pokes me in the back, which I ignore. The thin, blond seminary wife from the Christian Education class, the spirit-flag dancer, has laid out napkins in a perfect grid and is depositing one dark brownie on the center of each.

Seth's finger hits my backbone.

"What," I say loudly, without turning around. The blond woman snaps her head up. "Sorry," I say to her.

"I've missed you in class," she says, offering me a brownie and pretending to pout.

"Guess who I got," says Seth, close to my ear.

"I've been reading back issues of *The Good Word*," says the blond woman. "I want you to know your father's columns really speak to me. I love what he had to say in that one piece about fasting."

"Thank you," I say as Seth pokes me again. While he grabs his brownie, I scoot away across the rec hall and lean up against a pillar, half-hidden.

Seth finds me anyway. "What are you doing back here?" he says. Even when he's just standing, his arms and legs spaz out in different directions, like each part of his body has its own idea about what to do next. I try to hold my brownie and cross my arms over my breasts at the same time, in case he wants to practice not lusting again. Then I remember that if he lusts, he has to pluck out his offending eye, and I uncross my arms. "You still don't know who God gave me," he says.

I look around the room. There are Mary-Kate and Karen in a corner, looking shy. There are the missionary twins giggling with Conley, one of them reaching for the guitar he still wears on a strap around his neck. "Anyone I would guess would be someone you and I both know," I say. "And anyone you and I both know is going to be saved already. Which doesn't count. You got someone who's already saved?"

"There's saved and there's saved," says Seth. "My dad says your dad's misguided. And you quit Christian Education. You can't even join the church now."

I stuff the rest of the brownie in my mouth and feel it give way comfortingly around my molars. The chewing fills up my ears too, which is good. If he has anything else to say, I don't want to hear it. But I hear it anyway.

"That's why God laid you and your family on my heart."

"What's going on over here with you two newbies?" says Pastor Chick, approaching in his expensive shoes. He grins first at me, then at Seth, then rocks back in the shoes and grins at both of us at the same time.

"How can you tell if someone's a prophet or not?" Seth asks. "Nowadays."

I look at my sneakers. The white shoe polish is peeling off now, making them look even older than they did before.

"Prophets, huh," says Pastor Chick. "Parts of the Bible that are most helpful to me were written by prophets."

"Like Jeremiah," I say.

"But there are false prophets," Seth says. He looks slyly at me. "Jeremiah himself says so: 'They speak visions of their own minds, not from the mouth of the Lord.' Chapter twenty-three: verse sixteen."

"To be sure," says Pastor Chick, scratching his chin. "To be sure. But to answer your question, I don't know how you tell them apart. I haven't reached that level of clearance with the Heavenly Commander in Chief. He tells me I have enough to worry about in my own heart. Whether ole Chick Collins is being false or true. Know what I'm talking about, soldier?" Pastor Chick punches Seth in the elbow. "But I do have the low-down on the brownie situation, and Missus Whitson is serving up seconds." He gives Seth a push and says, "Go get 'em, brother."

Then Pastor Chick turns to me, and I'm struck by something astonishing. His own Operation Outreach, with the three county people God laid on my heart, fits right in with my father's vision, with the spirit of the Apostle Paul and his ministry to Gentiles. I wonder if Pastor Chick would be interested in hearing this. I wonder too if he would be interested in trying out the ceaseless prayer. But Pastor Chick never stays in one place for too long. He is already winking at me and turning in his shoes and across the room slapping Conley on the back before I can say anything, even thank you.

CHAPTER 9

I KEEP THE FLYERS FOR the Main Event in the butt purse, in the bookmobile copy of *A Wrinkle in Time,* so I can pull one out quickly as the opportunity arises. I have another letter from my father in there, too, which I have waited until school to read, away from Phoebe's curiosity. This one's written on the back of a printout from his brain scan. The sheet has ten brains, in two rows, perched on ten skeleton necks. *Everything you feel shows up on the brain,* he writes. *Happy, sad. Afraid.*

The brains are identical except for the white blotches in different places, brain to brain, like a traveling storm. Or like those storms on the surface of the sun, where after a minute of staring at them you can't tell what's actually there and what's coming from your own eye.

I am having trouble hearing the voice of God, he writes. *That's happened before, but it's different now. And my thoughts are different, too. I used to think many thoughts at one time. Now each one comes slowly. I see it coming, like a car on the road, then I think it, then I wait for it to fade. It all takes so long. To write too. They tell me this is the medication. It's possible that God's words are also coming that slowly, and I'm not receptive enough in my current state to put them together.*

His handwriting is still loose, but at least his sentences are making better sense.

We're doing Operation Outreach at church, I write back during freewriting. *And guess what? The three people God laid on my heart are county people, and they can already see the light within me.* I glance over at Kelly-Lynn, who raises one bored eyebrow and keeps writing. *This letter could be like an epistle, like Paul wrote to the people of Galatia and Thessalonica. I hope reading hasn't gotten as slow as your thoughts.* I print DO NOT READ across the top of the page for Mrs. Teaderman, words I will erase before giving the letter to Phoebe to deliver. I don't want to make him more confused.

I'm making friends with the people, I write, shaking my head to get rid of the memory of Tracy calling me prissy, of Cecil's hard stare. *And after I bring them to the Lord, I can help you with the rest of the county. And I am praying without ceasing a lot*—which will not be a lie, exactly, if I redouble my efforts starting right now. Part of an epistle's purpose is to shore up the spirits of those in captivity. With my pen, I make a small hatch mark on the ball of my thumb, and promise myself to make another one every time I catch myself not in prayer.

"Does your dad have a brain tumor?" Kelly-Lynn says during activity, pointing to the printout.

"I don't think so," I say, though the possibility almost appeals to me. A tumor could be removed, maybe, once and for all.

Under the letter on my lap, I'm holding *A Wrinkle in Time,* with the Main Event flyers poking out. All I have to do for Operation Outreach is hand one to her. My hand tingles, poised on the edge of doing this, but then cowardice floods my stomach and I hold back.

Kelly-Lynn eyes the book. "My mom's boyfriend has lots of books," she says. "Last night he flushed her cigarettes down the toilet and she called him a fag." She stops talking and peers into my face, and I'm wondering if she's observing the light of the Lord within. I am peering closely at her, too, at the gentle way her eyes lead into a small, straight nose. Even as I show her my teeth in what I hope is a beatific smile, it is sinking into me that I don't look anything like Kelly-Lynn and that I wish I did.

"Your scab's getting smaller," she says. "How's your boy-friend?"

"Okay," I say, alarmed by the way untruths return. "I saw him last night." I imagine this lie to be one of the things that comes between me and the Lord, making it harder for me to keep up my prayer. Which I have stopped, again, and so I dig out my pen and make another hatch mark on my thumb. *Inhabit me, O Lord God.* Out of nowhere, I hear myself sharing an actual truth with Kelly-Lynn. "He wants to look at my, you know." I dip my chin toward my chest and feel my neck grow hot.

"Tell me about it," she says. "It feels funny once you figure out what they want, but then you get used to it."

"Lust," I say with some authority, wondering if lust shows up on your brain in its own white storm.

The flyers for the Main Event are right there on my lap. I say the prayer a few more times. I separate one of the flyers with my fingertips and take a deep breath, preparing to smile so invitingly at this pretty, indifferent girl that it will seem as though a great idea has just occurred to me. But when the bell rings, Kelly-Lynn turns her head the other way and I end up slipping the flyer into her bookbag instead. Which, depending on how the Lord wants to look at it, could be seen as cowardly or as taking advantage of an opening he may or may not have provided himself.

"You tell your mother to watch herself around Morris Osborne," Daze warns me after school as she loads the washing machine.

"She says it's nice of him to help out," I say.

"There's helping out, then there's helping out. Some people just can't stop helping out. You can bait those types like fish with the lonely and the sick."

"He says he's been friends with Daddy since they were kids."

Daze frowns.

"Or has known him," I say.

"It's hard for people not to know people in this town," says Daze, "whether they want to or not. But it's true, Morris Osborne came around when they were boys. Right up until his mother showed up at our back door and said, 'Morris, there's nothing wrong with your own house.' She was proud that way, and your grandfather believed in preaching from the pulpit, not meddling one-to-one. Which is exactly the kind of man Morris Osborne turned into, a meddler. In everybody's business, and when everybody means a married woman, living on her own for now—a moderately attractive married woman like your mother—and the oh-so-helpful person in question is a bachelor, well then . . ."

I think of how Phoebe called Dr. Osborne "Morris." How she admitted the hard times.

"There's some married folk who should have thought better of it, for sure," Daze says. "But there's plenty never-marrieds who would have been well served. So don't talk to me about helping out."

"Okay," I say, hands up. Daze is almost never cross with me.

"Sorry, doll," she says, softening. "Your mother's still young."

"She's almost forty."

"She has a pert figure," Daze says. A shadow of worry crosses her face. "Let's pray your father gets home soon."

The next day, while our English class makes lists of possible how-to speech topics, I watch for some sign that Kelly-Lynn has found the Main Event flyer, but it doesn't come.

"How to cheer," Kelly-Lynn says, when called upon to share the best of her brainstorming options. "How to babysit."

Mrs. Teaderman prompts her to be more specific, to show how one writes one's own cheer, or how to care for infants.

"How to sew," I say when it's my turn, and then, "How to sew a skirt."

"Those might be complicated props," Mrs. Teaderman cautions.

For freewriting, I tell my father that two of my three people are already on board with the Main Event. This is on the inventive side, but it will motivate me to invite Tracy right away, before he gets my letter or I lose my nerve. *I feel in my heart that*

if I get them to the Main Event, the Lord will guide me from there.
I'm not sure I feel this in my heart, exactly, but I am trying to
have faith. Then I am erasing the "I feel in my heart" part and
writing "I have faith."

"No erasing," Mrs. Teaderman says.

Maybe by the time I see you, maybe this week? I will have reached
the last person. Maybe I can invite them all to more things, maybe
to see me playing Ruth. I stop writing but keep my pencil tip to
the page. I would like to show him how much I remember
about biblical lineage. Ruth, a Moabite, descendent of Lot's
unfortunate wife, is an ancestor of David, who is an ancestor
of Christ. But my father knows all this and knows that I know
he knows, and trying to impress him never works. In a town of
seminarians, he considers biblical knowledge a duty, not something to be congratulated for.

"How come you only ride the bus home sometimes?" Tracy
asks me after school. She's already in our seat, waiting. "I seen
you getting on that other bus. That town bus."

"I go to some people's houses," I say. "Where's Ravenna?"

"Cigarette break," Tracy says. "And it's not Ravenna, it's
that damn fool sub."

This morning, Tracy's hair was a scraggly mop and her face
was blanched white, bare of makeup. Now all her hair has
been slicked back into a tight ponytail that bushes out behind
her in a giant ball of frizz. She has lined her eyes in bright blue
and applied so much mascara that her eyelashes look thick and
spiky as thorns.

After the junior high lets out, there are ten minutes before
the high school bell. That's the time they give Cecil Goode

to make his way to the bus, and now he emerges from the building with the skinny textbook-burning kid. When Cecil moves slowly enough, he walks with less of a hitch. Almost with a swagger. And the skinny guy's talking the whole time, or singing, using his hands to play an invisible guitar. When they reach the bus, the skinny guy hooks the bag he's been carrying crosswise over Cecil's chest, taps him on the back, then hunches away down the row of buses.

The sub has started in on his second cigarette behind the bus while Cecil waits at the bottom of the steps. He's still waiting when the high school bell rings. Then the school doors open and kids start to swarm out onto the lawn.

"That bus driver should fix the ramp," I say.

"He will," says Tracy.

"Before the other kids get here, though."

"All right," Tracy says. "Don't have a conniption."

But as the first of the high school kids reach the bus and clamber aboard, Cecil is still waiting. Then there's a hollow banging as he starts swinging his claw into the side of the bus next to the door.

Finally, the sub, a gray-haired man in jeans, emerges from around back, climbs the steps, and struggles with the plywood while the rest of the kids keep collecting on the blacktop.

"Any day now," Cecil says. When the ramp's finally in place, he lurches up it more violently than usual. He falls into his seat behind us with a grunt, and I can hear him trying to catch his breath. I'm thinking it's got to get to him, having to wait for other people's help. Two seconds later, though, he's pitching his voice in my direction. "Looky who it is. Cousin, you tell that girl she's next."

Tracy arches one of her nearly invisible eyebrows me.

"I'm not going to sit on his lap," I tell her. "No one can make me."

"It's just for a second," Tracy says. "Just until you can feel his thing. If you don't do it, you have to take what's coming. You get a choice, like truth or dare."

"What do you mean, 'what's coming'?"

"Hard to say," Tracy says.

I hunker down and push my forehead against the dirty window. The rest of the river kids jostle each other down the aisle with a lot more noise than they make when Ravenna's behind the wheel. The bus feels heavy as it fills up, sinking a little on its tires. It smells different than it does in the morning. Even more strongly of cigarettes, and then I see that one of the girls coming down the aisle is still smoking.

"You wish," says the girl to a boy behind her.

"What," says the boy, pushing at her back. "What?"

Through it all, the sub just stares out the windshield at the emptying lawn.

"It doesn't hurt none," Tracy says.

"Did you do it?"

"No," she says, squinting at me until her crusty eyelashes stick together. "We're kin. It's not for real, anyway. I mean it's for real but not really."

"That doesn't make any sense."

"That doesn't make any sense," she says, mimicking me again. "Don't give me your dictionary talk." She throws herself back against the seat. "You just can't help yourself," she says in disgusted wonder.

"Tell her," comes Cecil's voice. I raise myself up and turn toward him, and he looks down at the front of his pants, then back up at me and licks his lips. I duck behind the seat again. In my lap, my thumb is covered in hatch marks, and I dig out my pen and cross a group of four for a bundle. *Inhabit me, O Lord God.*

"You counting something?" Tracy says.

"No," I say. I pray the prayer over and over again, and I keep praying as the sub pulls the lever and the bus doors swing closed, as he backs the bus out slowly and we creep down the school drive in the long line. It's like we're part of a segmented tapeworm, like we saw diagrams of when Mr. Catterson gave his missionary presentation. One of their friends, he said, had a worm like that in his stomach. The friend, a prisoner, got so hungry that he could feel the tapeworm coming up through his throat, poking around at the back of his mouth for food. The tapeworm was starving, too.

Behind us, Cecil says, "Rosemary Cooney, you know what you want."

"Rosemary," a few kids start in. "Rosemary."

Inhabit me, O Lord God, I pray.

"That's right," Cecil says. There's a shuffling behind us.

"Rosemary, Rosemary." Most of the back of the bus is chanting now. Everyone keeps it low, but we're crawling slowly down the highway and the sub doesn't even check the rearview.

I peek over my shoulder. The girl who was smoking when she got on the bus, a girl with enormous breasts and stiff, brassy hair, shifts over her seatmate in the back and does a crouched walk up the aisle to Cecil's seat, while Cecil's seatmate makes his way back to hers.

Still nothing from the sub. "He just lets this happen?" I say to Tracy.

"What did I tell you? He probably wishes Rosemary would come sit on *his* lap. You see those titties?"

It's true. The girl's chest, in her deeply scooped T-shirt, is so ample that it makes me think of Daze's word, *bosom*. My own breasts haven't stopped hurting, but I'm getting used to the way it feels, a fact that makes me gloomy. Even my bra has turned a dingy gray, as if depressed by its big job.

"What size are you now?" Tracy asks, catching me looking down. "C?"

"I don't know," I say. When I check behind me again, Rosemary is sitting on Cecil's lap, her knees to the aisle. He fits the top of his head underneath her chin and ducks his face into the deep crevice of her bosom.

"I see you in activity," says Tracy. "With that girl everyone hates. The one who used to be Melinda when she lived here before. I hear she gave Mister Cooper a pair of her panties. I hear she's a lesbian. A girl who likes girls."

"Then why would she give her panties to Mister Cooper?"

"I hear she gave them to Missus Teaderman, then. You-all both have Missus Teaderman. I have her first period. You have to do speeches?"

"How-to speeches," I say. I try to imagine Kelly-Lynn giving her panties to Mrs. Teaderman, and all I can think is that Mrs. Teaderman would wash them, maybe, and give them back, like Daze does with mine.

We're approaching the turnoff to East Winder, where the shoulder gets shaved down to only about a foot. The tire catches the edge of the asphalt, and for a second it feels like we're about to tip over. I look down again at my marked-up hand. *Inhabit me, O Lord God.*

"I feel it," Rosemary is saying, behind us. She's squirming

on Cecil's lap, his face still buried deeply in the front of her shirt.

We roll through town and out the other side by the time Rosemary untangles herself and makes her way back to her seat. Everyone in the back of the bus cheers.

"Cousin," Cecil sings softly when the cheer dies down. "I got time for one more."

I hold my breath. We pass the historic sign for Tate's Bridge, then we near the gas station where Tracy gets off, high above the river on the ridgeline.

"Tell your friend," Cecil says, but Tracy ignores him. She stands up into the aisle, and light from the window panels travels across her pale face and neck, turning her skin yellow. The sub brings the bus to a stop.

"Girl," Cecil says to me, and just like that, I stand up, too. "Next time," he promises as I follow Tracy off the bus with a small group of kids. We wait there in the dirt while the bus rolls away and the rest of the kids disappear into the tiny gas-station store. I'm almost a whole head taller than Tracy, and I never realized it before.

"You following me?" she says.

"No."

"What, you need something from the store?"

I nod. I don't know what else to do.

"Well, come on, then," she says, and I head inside after her. A bell over the door tinkles. The light overhead is dim and the air smells old. The other kids from the bus are all bent over a cooler of pop, lifting cans out of the ice.

"What do you want, chips?" Tracy says.

"I forgot money," I say. I make a show of going through my purse as if there might be money in it.

Tracy plucks two bags of potato chips from clips on a rotating stand. "Momma," she calls to the woman behind the counter. The woman has orange hair like Tracy's, only it's fading to gray and tied back in a red bandanna. Behind her, floor to ceiling, are cigarette packs stacked neat as cells between narrow plastic barriers.

The woman behind the counter lifts her hand, but she's keeping her eye on the kids at the cooler.

"I don't have any money," I say, wondering if Tracy missed it the first time.

"Two bags." Tracy holds up two fingers toward her mother. "You get that?"

The woman raises her hand again and nods. She's scooting change across the counter with the fingertips of her other hand. Several of the kids grab their sodas and leave, and when Tracy and I start to follow them, the woman calls out, "What's your name, girl?"

"Me?" I say.

"I know Tracy's name."

"Charmaine Peake."

Tracy's mother tucks a red curl into her bandanna. Her eyes are small, bright blue chips of glass set deep into a squint. "Daddy knew some Peakes."

I wait for her to say something more, but she goes back to counting change. Tracy pushes open the door.

"Thank you for the chips," I say.

"Tracileen, wipe off that handprint you just made," says her mother, and Tracy swipes at the glass with her sleeve.

Outside, she heads across the dirt yard of the gas station to a cinder-block house in back of it that I never noticed before. "You coming or what?" she says to me without looking back, and I follow her. It seems like the right thing to do after the chips.

You can hear a dog barking inside, throwing himself against the door as Tracy tries to shoulder it open. "Sometimes this sticks," she says. She takes a step back and rams it hard, bursting into a dark, damp room lit watery blue from the television set. A brown-and-white-speckled dog growls at my knees. "Careful," she says. "He only likes Momma."

The place is a mess. Dishes on the table, beer cans on the floor, ashtrays on either side of the velour sofa, and another two on the coffee table in front of it, all of them spiky with cigarette butts. The dog is still growling at me. I reach my hand down to let him sniff, and he snaps at my fingers.

"Corky, stop."

"I have to get home before my mom does," I say.

"What's stopping you?" Tracy says. "Corky, shut up." She holds the dog away from me with her foot. He's really snarling now, baring long yellow teeth.

"Thanks," I say, holding up the bag of chips. I back away from Corky onto the stoop and am relieved when the screen door closes.

I don't know exactly how long it will take me to get home, walking from up here on the ridge. The days are getting a little shorter. Already the sun's falling behind the palisades, turning the gorge gray under a bright swath of sky. Then I remember the flyer, and I'm crossing back over the yard, knocking on the frame of the screen door. Tracy appears with a cigarette in her mouth. "This is for you," I say through the screen, and when she cracks the door, I thrust a flyer into her hand, then turn and walk away fast, before Corky breaks free.

• • •

That night, over the dinette, Phoebe informs me of what I already know: the shirt I'm wearing, like every other shirt I own, is too tight to keep wearing much longer. She pulls it away from my chest, trying to stretch the fabric, and I wince when she lets go and it stretches back against my nipples.

"Does that hurt?"

"Not really."

"I don't know what 'not really' means," she says. "How many days since your period?"

"Since it started or ended?"

"Started."

I think back. "Twenty," I say. "Twenty-one."

"You have to keep track, Charmaine. But it might not make much difference. I've never been regular." Phoebe brings her hands to either side of her face and draws her cheeks down with her fingertips, dragging her lower eyelids open to reveal the red rims underneath. I look away.

"Go sit on the toilet and take your shirt off." She drops her hands, and the skin on her face reshapes itself slowly.

"What? Why?"

"You heard me. I'll be in in a second." Phoebe stands and starts running water in a pan. I fold the dinette against the wall, stalling. She puts the pan on the burner and turns it on.

"What's that for?"

"Go take your shirt off," she says. "Bra too."

"Nothing hurts," I say. "I don't need you to do anything."

"Charmaine, I don't have the energy for a fight."

I step into the bathroom and pull the accordion door shut behind me.

"Leave that," Phoebe says, but I keep it shut. I sit down on the lid of the tiny toilet and peel my shirt off. It's the nipples, sore against everything, but it's also the rest of my breasts: they're heavy, and there's a tightness, like whatever's inside is growing too fast for my skin. When I release my bra, it's only a small relief.

I listen to the water starting to boil. After a time, Phoebe switches off the burner. Then she is there, collapsing the accordion door with her foot, a dishtowel in one hand and the pot of hot water in the other.

I cover my breasts with my hands.

"Don't be melodramatic," Phoebe says. She settles the pot into the sink and dips the dishcloth in it. "Take away your hands."

I won't. She stirs the dishtowel into the hot water, then picks it out gingerly. She wrings it out over the pot, sucking in little gasps of air, it's so hot on her fingers. Steam rises.

"Take away your hands," she says again, crouching in front of me. "This will help."

"But nothing hurts," I say, keeping my hands where they are. "I don't feel anything."

"At your stage of development, calcium builds up in your breasts if you don't use compresses."

"Calcium?"

"Calcium, caffeine," she says. "All kinds of things." She pulls my left hand away and then she is touching me, probing the underside of my breast with her fingers. "Hard as a rock. We need to break up some of that mass."

"Stop," I say. "Please. The mass is okay." I don't even know what she's talking about—a mass.

She covers my left breast with the dishtowel. It's so hot that tears come to my eyes.

"I can do it," I say, blowing out air through my teeth. "Let me do it myself." But then she begins to knead my breast with her fingers, through the towel, and I want her to stop. I want her to stop. I long again for tessering, like in the book, disappearing into another time and space. Titus has been approaching the bathroom with curiosity, and now he sits carefully outside the narrow doorway, watching.

While she does this, Phoebe stares into the mirrored medicine cabinet over the sink. "I'm getting old, Charmaine." She takes away the cloth and again probes my naked left breast, which has turned a deep pink from the heat. I press my teeth together. I don't want to look at her this close up while she's doing such a thing. "If you didn't know how old I was," she says, "what would you guess? Thirty?"

"I can do the other one," I say, clapping my left hand over my left breast, wishing I had an extra hand to reach for my shirt. "Thank you. Thank you for showing me."

"Stop it," she says. She pries my right hand away from my right breast. The bathroom is just big enough for our bodies. She is breathing in my exhales, and I am breathing in hers. Even the words of my prayer don't have room to surface in here, though I close my eyes and rummage around for them, desperately, in my head.

She holds the hot, wet towel to my right breast and pushes my hand away from the left one. Now she is squeezing both at the same time, harder and harder. "I think I could pass for thirty, still," she says. And then something weird happens, because I can still feel her hands and I can still hear her, but it's as though there's a bunch of parts of me, like there are parts of the body of Christ, and all the parts of me are climbing up my neck and into my head, like water's rising and we have to move to higher ground. We're all crowded up there together, watching what's happening right underneath our chin. Now I can pray again, but I am careful not to move my lips.

"When you see your father tomorrow, I don't want you to be alarmed," she says, and it's as if the words come at me from far, far below.

I make a small sound in the back of my throat.

"It's been an interesting couple of weeks. He looks a little different from the last time you saw him. He's a little puffy from the new medication. In funny places, like his neck. And he doesn't have quite the same . . ." She takes her right hand off my breast and flaps it around her mouth as if encouraging the right word to come forth. "I don't know, Charmaine. He's just not quite the same. They've got him on something very strong. I just want you to be prepared."

"I'm prepared," I say, though I may or may not be. Phoebe makes a big deal about some things that turn out to be okay, and the things she thinks are no big deal, like her hands on my breasts, are awful in ways she can't even imagine.

"They've got him on 'mood stabilizers.' So his mood is very stable, I guess, and that's what everyone wants. But he looks bad. Tired. And he doesn't communicate well. He's working on a pair of moccasins for you, though. Sewing them himself. The doctor says it's good for his motor skills."

Then both of her hands are gone. "There." says Phoebe. All the parts of my body that have gathered up into my head drop back to their regular places. I grab my shirt and hold it in front of me. She stands up, blocking the light, and sighs. "Go ahead and act like I'm killing you, Charmaine, but you can't tell me that doesn't feel better."

CHAPTER 10

*I*T'S DR. OSBORNE'S TOYOTA that pulls up to school Wednesday. I'm standing out front, and I keep on standing there until Phoebe rolls down the passenger window and tells me to get in.

"The Pinto's back in the shop," she says. "Just for an overnight."

"You couldn't borrow the Buick?" I say, not moving toward the car.

"Doctor Osborne offered, which was very thoughtful," Phoebe says tightly, "and in return you're being very rude."

Inside Dr. Osborne's car, all the books have been piled on the floor behind the driver's seat. I sling the butt purse in first, then pull the door shut behind me, harder than I have to. Dr. Osborne nods at me as if he knows enough not to say hello out loud.

"Charmaine hasn't seen her father in more than two weeks," Phoebe says. Her voice is too cheerful for what she's saying, which means she's nervous. "She's really looking forward to this. I was just explaining to Doctor Osborne that your father's finally stabilized. It's hard to find just the right medication."

"A tricky business," says Dr. Osborne, like he knows all about it.

I stare out the window at the row of waiting buses. I have wanted to see my father, but it doesn't feel right to be going with Dr. Osborne. I wish myself on the bus, even sitting with Tracy, even with the threat of Cecil Goode, headed on our slow rural route down to the river. Instead, we take the road to Clay's Corner and then pick up a short stretch of highway to Exit 22, which takes us right into the late-afternoon sun. Phoebe and Dr. Osborne flip down their visors at exactly the same time. They say nothing, which bothers me more than the talking. It's as if they've already made themselves comfortable around each other.

We pass field after field of mid-harvest tobacco left to dry in long rows of teepees. Then we drive deep into the thoroughbred farms on the far city side of the county, where horses stand near each other, stepping gracefully, bowing to eat grass. We pass the sign for the county west of Rowland, Beacon County, and shortly after that, Phoebe points and says, "There," and we pull into a long, winding drive for one of the prettiest brick buildings I've ever seen. It sits up on a knoll. It doesn't look like a hospital at all. It looks like an old plantation home, with six white pillars out front and an overhanging roof on the side, also propped up by pillars, and when we drive through the side place, a man comes out and waits so he can park Dr. Osborne's car.

"This is a porte-cochère," Phoebe says, as the three of us watch the Toyota disappear around back of the house. All you can see, from where we stand, are green fields divided into horse pastures by white split-top fences. Every single tree too is ringed by its own tiny white fence, as if lassoed there, so that the horses can't scratch themselves on the tree bark the way they like to. These kinds of horse farms probably hire a man just to go around scratching horses all day, whenever one of them has an itch.

"Where do you want me, Phoebe?" Dr. Osborne asks, extra politely.

"There's the nicest lobby," she says, pressing a button by the heavy wooden door. When a buzzer sounds, she pushes open the door and we enter what looks like a rich person's living room, with brown leather sofas and an oriental carpet. Part of the room is a reception area, with a woman in glasses sitting behind a low counter. Next to the reception area, double doors are propped open onto a long, brightly lit hallway, where a nurse in blue waves to Phoebe.

"I'm sorry about the wait," Phoebe says to Dr. Osborne. "Charmaine, I'll go in first then come get you."

Dr. Osborne and I take seats at the opposite end of a long leather sofa. He's wearing his cross of nails, which dangles between his knees as he leans forward to pick through the brochures on the coffee table. *Residential Recovery. Mood Disorders. Manic Depression. Abundant Living.* He offers me the one on manic depression. It has the theater masks on the front of it, the happy and sad faces, and at first I think that's why he chose it and that we might be about to start talking about his series of spiritual scenes. But what he says, as I hold the flyer, is "The treatment has come a long way."

I've never heard of manic depression, but I know what both words mean. Dr. Osborne's eyes are on me, though, so I don't open the pamphlet.

"How're you two holding up down there at the river?" he asks.

"Fine."

"Your mom's got a lot on her plate."

I stare down at the pamphlet, at the masks with the empty eyes. I do not want to look at this man while he tells me things about my own mother like he knows her better than I do. Or about my father. Manic depression.

Dr. Osborne sighs and sits back. "I've been thinking about my next play, Charmaine. Seth and I are going to perform some David and Absalom material in November, and then maybe I'll get started writing another script. Maybe you and your mother could be my Ruth and Naomi."

I don't like the way he says "my" Ruth and Naomi, like the characters and the people who play them all belong to him.

"My father could write the script," I say. "He's a very good writer."

"I've read some of his work in *The Good Word*," says Dr. Osborne.

"You've known him for a long time," I say, testing. "You're friends with him."

"We grew up together," Dr. Osborne says.

I don't care for the way Dr. Osborne neither confirms nor denies anything I say.

"What are you a doctor of?" I ask him.

Dr. Osborne matches his hands fingertip to fingertip. "I have a doctorate of education," he says, "which I acquired in another life." He's speaking like there's an important mystery behind what he's not saying, like he enjoys the fact that he knows it and I don't.

"And now you teach at the seminary," I say.

"I do."

"And direct plays," I say.

"And direct plays."

"And help people out," I say.

Dr. Osborne presses his palms together and narrows his eyes at me. They are a dim blue, with pleated skin at the outer edges. "It's true that I don't mind helping out when someone needs it. I feel called to that service, actually."

I place the *Manic Depression* pamphlet back on the coffee table, and he spies the pen marks on my thumb. The earliest ones have faded, but altogether they make three rows of tracks that go from the heel of my thumb to the tip of it. I take my pen from the butt purse and start a fourth row at the bottom of my palm. *Inhabit me, O Lord God.* I'm still forgetting most of the time, but I'm also remembering the forgetting, since I can't ignore my own hands.

"What's that you're keeping track of?" Dr. Osborne says.

"It's between me and my dad," I say, tucking my hand underneath my leg. "And me and God."

"You must miss your father," says Dr. Osborne. "Seth's father has to be out on the road fundraising while they're on furlough. He misses his father, too."

"So you asked Seth to be in a play," I say, "since his father's away fundraising. And you're asking me to be in a play, and my mother too, since my father's in"—I check the pamphlet on the table, the one with the picture of the outside of this same house on the front—"residential recovery."

"I believe the play was your idea," Dr. Osborne says.

"My father is a man after God's own heart."

"So people say."

"People say you should have gotten married."

Dr. Osborne sits up straight, and the cross of nails slaps back onto his chest. He tilts his head to the side, which makes him look curious and unkind.

"My grandmother has your number," I tell him.

"Hah," Dr. Osborne says, opening his mouth wide. But it's not really a laugh. Over in the corner, the receptionist looks up. "Daze Peake," he says, with some defeat. "Hah."

I'd like to rip her name right out of that mouth.

"Don't talk to me about her," I say. "Or my father. You're not friends with him. And don't talk to me about my mother, either. You've never even known a woman. Nobody needs your help." Then I am on my feet and across the lobby before he can get out another word.

"Hold on a sec," says the woman behind the desk, but I keep on going, right through the double doors and down the long, bright hallway to the old winding staircase at the end. I sprint up the steps, my breasts jiggling painfully. At the top I slow down. No one's following me. Another hallway, identical to the one on the first floor, takes me back toward the front of the house. From somewhere comes a sound of muffled crying, deep and hopeless, without any highs and lows. A sound that seems like it could go on forever.

At the end of the hall I push open more double doors to a huge, gleaming white room. The floorboards, the walls, the window casings—all white. Even the baby grand piano is white lacquer. All the sofas and chairs—and the room seems full of sofas and chairs—have white slipcovers. It's big and blank and dazzling. Like heaven, maybe. Through deep windows the sun blazes as it sets. It's so quiet in here that everything you can see and hear separates into itself. The low, distant crying. The shushing sound of Phoebe, crossing her stockinged legs where she sits on one of the sofas along the wall. In all this white her blue shirt is a blast of color. The light brown sports coat of the man beside her only seems dingy, like a shadow.

"That's her," Phoebe says to him, and the man gets to his feet. He is tall, with a loose neck cinched in by a tight collar and tie.

"Charmaine, I'm Doctor Phillips," he says.

"Where's my father?"

"I told her she'd be seeing him," Phoebe says to the doctor.

"I understand," says the doctor. "Unfortunately he's not up for anything like that today."

"I don't need him to do anything, though. There's nothing he has to be up for."

"We'll try again Monday," Phoebe says.

I stand in front of the sofa, my back to the windows, and the room takes on a lavender cast. The ceilings are very high. It feels like I might have landed on another planet, the way the girl in the book does when she tries to rescue her father by traveling via the wrinkle in time. She gets accidentally sent through the "Dark Thing," which may or may not be a black hole, and she finds herself squeezed into a flat, two-dimensional atmosphere on a planet where she can barely breathe. Somewhere far away, the person crying goes on and on.

"We're making some medication adjustments," the doctor says. "Do you know what a seizure is?"

"He had a seizure this afternoon," says Phoebe, speaking at the same time as the doctor.

"He was responding well to a medicine we call Haldol, and

today we had a setback," says the doctor. "We're trying something new, but it will take a while for him to even out."

"Maybe he shouldn't be taking any medicine," I say. "He says it doesn't feel right. He says he can't hear the voice of God. And you're making him cry."

"I hear the crying, too," says the doctor. "But that's not your father."

I know, in my stomach, that it is.

"Charmaine," says the doctor. "Will you imagine something for me?"

I nod because I want to hear what he'll say next, not because I have any intention of imagining anything I don't want to. Not in this crazy white room.

"What if most of your life you understood yourself to be one kind of thing. A cat, say. Every time you looked in the mirror, you'd see a cat. You cleaned yourself like a cat, acted like a cat—everything. Being a cat felt normal."

"Like Titus," Phoebe chimes in, as if I need an example of a cat.

"And then one day someone told you there was something wrong with your eyes. Nothing that couldn't be fixed, though, and when you had them fixed and you looked in the mirror, you didn't see a cat anymore. You saw a dog. And you'd always been a dog, only you hadn't been able to see it. So now you know that feeling like a cat wasn't real, even if it seemed that way. Or you might feel that the new thing you see in the mirror is wrong, because it's not how you know yourself. So that what's accurate, like how you're really a dog, feels inaccurate at first, because you have known yourself to be a cat."

I look at Phoebe, but she is watching the doctor, her mouth half open in a wary-looking underbite.

"It might take you some time to adjust," the doctor goes on. "You might even feel some grief over the loss of what you thought you were. Over the cat. In time, you might feel some regret, maybe, for things you did that you would not have done had you understood you were not a cat. Catlike decisions you made that wouldn't be appropriate for dogs. And if there was medication that could help you feel more like the thing you really are, then you might want to try it. Am I making sense?"

"Your father's had a nervous breakdown," Phoebe says, like she's summing up what the doctor means. "The medication calmed him down, then it gave him a seizure, so now they have to find something else."

"*Nervous breakdown* is really not a term we use anymore," says the doctor.

"Manic depression," I offer.

The doctor is pleased with this. He smiles at me like I, myself, am a cat, or a dog, who has started using human speech. "Close enough," he says. "Smart girl. Come again on Monday. I'm confident he'll be feeling a lot better."

Phoebe lifts her hands into the air by her face, like she gives up, then lets them fall to her thighs with a slap. "Okay," she says to the room in general. She pushes herself to her feet, and we follow the doctor into the hall. There, the crying gets louder again. It sounds like a man saying "No, oh no." I lag behind Phoebe and the doctor, and when I reach a door where the sound seems to be coming from, I try the handle as quietly as I can. Then I try it harder.

"Charmaine," Phoebe says, spinning on her heel.

Then I'm knocking on the door, banging on it. The crying stops for a second, then picks up again under the sounds of my fist. There's a voice too. A murmur over the crying. "You locked him in?" I say.

"That's not your father," says the doctor. "It's another patient, seeing another doctor. And it's not locked, it's just latched."

"It is locked," I say, gripping the handle. "Dad," I say into the door. Then I get down on my hands and knees and speak into the inch of space underneath it. "Dad, open the door."

"It's not him," says the doctor, striding toward me.

"Charmaine, get up," says Phoebe.

"Maybe he saw us pull in," I say to Phoebe. "Maybe he saw you come in with Doctor Osborne."

"That's enough," Phoebe says. To the doctor she says, "Our car broke down again this afternoon. Charmaine, get up now."

The doctor tries to lift me from my armpits, but I wrench him off. "It's not your dad," he says again. He places one of his hands on my back. "Listen. The medication won't let him cry like that. It won't let him feel bad at all. It gives him a little break from feeling bad. From feeling much of anything, really."

I grope around in the butt purse for the letters I've torn from my freewriting notebook, and I find my pen, and I fold the pages in half and write *Dad* on the outside and slide them under the door, not even thinking that I should write his name instead—David Peake. Then while I have my pen out, I make another hatch mark on my hand and I pray again, without ceasing, all the way down the stairs, then back down the bright hallway on the first floor, then while we wait, the three of us, under the porte-cochère for Dr. Osborne's car.

I pray most of the way home, too, trying to replace the sound of crying with the words in my head. Dr. Osborne says nothing to Phoebe about our interaction in the lobby. He just asks how my father is, how *David* is, in his low voice meant for the front seat only.

Phoebe stares out over the fields. I get through the prayer three times before she answers.

"It's hard to say," is what she finally says. Then she takes a deep breath. "It certainly does him a world of good to see Charmaine," which stops me cold. My prayer, my heart.

"I'm sure it does," says Dr. Osborne, just a moment later than he should.

From the back seat I follow Phoebe's gaze out over all the horse farms, which could really be one big horse farm that goes on and on, for all I know. Half the sun is still burning on the horizon, large and pink but watchable now, as the sun rarely is. I wonder if Phoebe believes it really would have done my father a world of good to have seen me, or if she knows for certain it would have made no difference at all. I can't imagine who the lie is for, unless maybe it's for Phoebe herself. And I wonder if lying comes easily to her or if she has to talk herself into believing what she says, like I do, and then work hard at ways to make sure it comes true.

CHAPTER 11

I N ENGLISH, MRS. TEADERMAN demonstrates how-to speeches by conducting an experiment. It starts with Friday's freewriting assignment, a how-to paragraph for making a peanut butter sandwich. It seems easy enough when Mrs. Teaderman sets out a jar of peanut butter, a plate, a knife, and a loaf of bread on the demonstration table.

"Who wants to read their how-to while I follow directions?" she says.

The first boy tells her to put the peanut butter on the bread, and as if she doesn't understand, Mrs. Teaderman sets the whole closed jar on the loaf of bread that's still in its sealed plastic bag.

"No," says the boy. "You know what I mean."

"Use the knife," says a girl in the first row.

"That wasn't in the how-to," says Mrs. Teaderman.

The second boy has used the word *spread* for the peanut butter, but he has not told her to open the jar, or to take out the bread. At this point, students are scribbling on their paragraphs, adding instructions about packaging and the knife. It's tricky, because while "Make a peanut butter sandwich" is too general, as soon as you start getting specific with the details, there are more and more details to miss.

I am staring at an empty page, trying to decide if I should scrabble together a how-to or skip it to begin another letter to my father. Who may or may not be in better shape for visitors when we try again on Monday. Next to me, Kelly-Lynn has rushed through her paragraph and is hissing the words to the cheers she's memorizing for tryouts.

People keep reading their how-tos, but not one results in a successful sandwich. Mrs. Teaderman beams at the frustration in the room. She has perfectly illustrated her point that what we choose for our speech might be obvious to us but completely unfamiliar to the rest of the class. Maybe Jeff Burns, and she gestures to a quiet, tall boy at the back, will tell us how he helps his dad change the oil in a car, and she, for one, wouldn't even know where to find the dipstick. She wouldn't, she says, even know how to pop her trunk open if Mr. Teaderman wasn't around to help.

I watch my blank paper as if the right how-to words might appear on their own. How to make a peanut butter sandwich. How to know if your father will be okay. How to make sure the light of the Lord shines through you to someone else when you're not sure you can even feel it yourself.

After school I find myself standing on my own front doorstep again, Mrs. Catterson admitting me into my own home. Today she has pulled her hair back in a clip and wears no makeup. Her face looks small.

"Come on in and make yourself at home," she says, then claps a hand over her mouth. "I always say that. You know what I mean. Seth's still with Doctor Osborne practicing something theatrical. You know, top secret."

I nod politely, thinking that Seth and Dr. Osborne can have each other and their stupid play.

"I'm sure Seth wouldn't mind if you spent a little time in his room while I finish the kitchen floor," Mrs. Catterson says. "Maybe you have some things up there you'd like to check in with. I trust you'll show Seth's belongings the same regard he's shown yours?"

"Okay," I say, wondering what kind of regard he's shown my things.

Upstairs, parts of my room look the same, like the yellow walls and Phoebe's white childhood bed. But the floor is bare, the white sheer at the window is gone, and the white bedspread is gone, too. Instead there's a navy blanket on the bed and a bed sheet in a brighter blue strung across the window on a tension rod. In the corner is a trumpet on a metal stand, and my desk is covered with Seth's homeschooling workbooks.

I close the door, and there's the mirror on the back. I have not been alone with my full-length reflection since we moved. I lift up my shirt, then my bra. In just two weeks, my breasts look even bigger and rounder. Just as heavy as they feel.

I try not to see my hair. I'm afraid I will lose my will to let it grow long. As for my skin, Phoebe says I need to be more consistent with the soap and hot water and witch hazel and to keep my hands off my face. She doesn't believe that I'm already doing everything she tells me and it doesn't make any difference, since every time she extracts, I end up breaking out more.

I put my clothes back together and check for my wooden box under the bed. It isn't there. It's not on the bookshelf either. Everything I usually keep on my shelves has been collected in a crate and crammed into the corner of the room, and now the shelves hold Seth's copies of *The Chronicles of Narnia*, his Hardy Boys series, his Bibles, and his dictionary. There's also a copy of *A Wrinkle in Time*, which I know is not my own private book, but Seth has already taken over my room, and it doesn't seem fair that he has *A Wrinkle in Time*, too.

When I open the door to the closet, the inside smells different. Like something I should recognize but don't. It might be a pee smell, but I cannot believe that Seth, no matter how annoying he is, pees into my closet with his own clothes hanging right there. But boys do weird things with their pee, like Cecil's friends at school with the lockers. Pee makes me think about penises, and then I am thinking how Seth's is here with him, at all times, in my room. With its pee and other lust-related activities. It all gives me a weird feeling at the back of my neck.

I find my box on the top shelf of the closet, pushed in deep, next to the wall. I'm standing on the desk chair, stretching hard, trying to pull the box out from under a spare set of sheets, when my knee brushes something stiff and flat at the back of Seth's hanging clothes. He's turned a sweatshirt into a sack, cinching the drawstring waist all the way closed. Inside is a bunch of paper, maybe a script, bound with a big clamp. There's a file folder too and a smaller manila envelope.

"Charmaine?" Mrs. Catterson calls from the foot of the stairs. "You doing all right up there?"

"I'm looking for my box," I say, which is true. What I am also doing is grabbing the manila envelope out of the neck of Seth's sweatshirt with one hand and reaching for my box with the other. I plop myself onto the desk chair and tuck the envelope firmly under my legs just as Mrs. Catterson opens the door and pops her head in. "Found it!" I say, lifting the box in her direction.

"You know, I wondered about that. I wasn't sure what you used it for, so I put it away so nothing would happen to it. Accidentally. What sort of things do you keep in there?"

I raise the lid to show her, even though I would rather not. The first thing I notice is that my things aren't taking up space in a way I understand, as if they've been handled and returned. This makes me feel a little better about hiding the envelope I'm sitting on. I hold up Daze's bone fountain pen from Niagara Falls. Then I offer Mrs. Catterson the plastic baggy with the shaving of wood. "It's supposed to be from the cross," I say, "but it might be just a symbol."

Mrs. Catterson takes it and turns it over in the fading light.

Next I hand her the postcard of Lot's wife.

"A pillar of salt," says Mrs. Catterson. "The perils of disobedience." On some words, Mrs. Catterson's voice gets thin and breaks into two wavering notes, like she's trying to make a chord. Or like she has to cough, but she never does.

I flip open the notebook with my prayer, then flip it closed. I root around in the box for a pen and make another hatch mark on my thumb, quickly, before Mrs. Catterson sees. *Inhabit me, O Lord God.* "There's mostly just some other stuff I've saved," I say.

Mrs. Catterson sits down on the end of the bed. Even though she is a long, willowy woman without much fat, her hips spread out in a bony way, straining her stretchy pants. I don't know what Daze would call her body type. "I just want you to know that I appreciate your being friends with Seth," she says. "He doesn't have friends here yet. And he misses Africa."

"We're not really friends," I say, feeling guilty.

"Oh, I think you are. You're both such bright children. I'm pretty sure Seth considers you his friend."

"Did he tell you that?"

Mrs. Catterson smiles. "That's not exactly the kind of thing boys go around saying, dear. To their mothers." She scoots backward, farther onto the bed, lifts both her feet, and shows me the bottoms of her socks, which have leather patches sewn on them in the shape of soles. Shoe-socks. She twitches her toes toward each other and away, like a girl. "I'm guessing it's hard on you not having your own room right now. On your mother too."

"We're fine," I say. "It's good to be a part of the county. My father says it's a mission field in our midst. Like Ghana."

"Well, not exactly like Ghana," says Mrs. Catterson.

"Anywhere can be a mission field," I say.

Mrs. Catterson unclips her hair, runs her fingers through it, then clips it back again. Under her eyes, the skin puffs out in soft, purple half-moons. She gestures to the marks on my thumb. "Are you counting the days until your father comes back?"

"Yes," I say. I try to start the prayer again, but the question bothers me.

"When do you think that might be?"

I tell myself there's nothing wrong with Mrs. Catterson asking, but it feels bad that I don't have an answer. It makes me want to crack open my rib cage and say, "See? See? The secret is I don't know any more than you do." Which doesn't make that much sense and which feels all wrapped up in other things I don't know what to do with, like the crying at the residential recovery place that wasn't even him, or riding in Dr. Osborne's messy back seat.

"Mister Catterson and I have often discussed psychiatric care," says Mrs. Catterson. "What the Bible might have to say about tinkering with the human brain. Whether that might be outside of God's design for us or maybe a new capacity the Lord has given us, through the intellect, to take better care of ourselves. Like pasteurization. In a way."

"No one's tinkering with his brain," I say.

"*Tinkering*'s probably the wrong word. I just mean that studying your father might help other people like him."

"What do you mean, 'like him'?" I say. "There isn't anybody else like him. Every person is one of a kind." I can hear myself breathing now, each breath bigger and more frantic, fighting its way through my shrinking throat. I am either going to cry or pass out or burst through my skin.

Mrs. Catterson scoots to the edge of the bed and plants her feet on the floor.

"My father is a man after God's own heart," I say, and when I look up, Mrs. Catterson is nodding.

"Honey," she says. "Honey, of course. I didn't mean to upset you." She stands up in front of my chair and reaches her arms out like she wants to hug me, but I am not going to stand up. I can still feel the envelope under me, and whatever's in it, no matter what, is going to be mine. She has to stoop over to hug me, and when she's done I stay very still while she leaves the room and pulls the door almost but not completely shut behind her. I listen to the shoe-socks on the stairs, whose creaking is a sound so familiar that I would not have even noticed it before we moved out. Then I hear another sound I would not have said I cared about, that of the traffic at the intersection of Main Street and East, the steady slowing down and speeding up of engines at the two-way stop. At the edge of a black hole, time slows down. And if you could make it through a black hole to the other side, which you can't, time might even reverse, and if I could make time reverse I'd go back and stay right here in my room, knowing that Phoebe and my father are somewhere else in the house doing whatever it was they used to do that I didn't pay enough attention to. Phoebe rolling her clean pantyhose into balls, maybe, or my father staying up all night, walking the streets of East Winder, receiving prophecy, and then coming home to record it for *The Good Word*. I want this so badly that I understand how they came up with the term *homesick,* though I don't know if anyone has ever felt that way sitting in a room that is still, technically, her own. In social studies last year we studied immigrants, how in Europe during the war countries invaded other countries and took them over, with the invaders living in people's houses and driving their cars and, our teacher said, much worse, with a look on her face that could only mean she was talking about rape, which Phoebe says is the worst possible thing that can happen to a woman. I always thought the people in the invaded countries would feel mostly anger about how unfair it was, and vengeful, especially if they had been raped. But what I never imagined is how sad they might feel. I would not have said that sadness could keep you sitting motionless in a chair, in a room that used to be yours, listening to things that you didn't even know you missed. Things you wouldn't have even said were yours to hear until after you discovered that they are not necessarily yours at all.

Even though it's only five o'clock when Seth gets back from practicing with Dr. Osborne, it's nearly dark from a rainstorm. Through a crack in the bed-sheet curtain, I see the electric cross on the water tower flicker on, and I have missed that too. My rear end is numb from sitting. I lift the top off my box again, with all the things in there that mean nothing to anyone but me, and I deposit the manila envelope inside. I don't even try to cover it with anything else. I just close the lid, drag the chair back to Seth's desk, and head downstairs.

"What were you doing up there?" Seth asks when I enter the kitchen. He's already seated at the table, Mrs. Catterson pouring him a glass of juice, like he's a little kid.

I hold up the box. "Just taking back something that was already mine."

"You better not have touched my stuff."

"Seth," says Mrs. Catterson.

"I saw your trumpet," I say, "but I didn't touch it. I don't even know how to play." When Mrs. Catterson ducks into the pantry, I whisper, "Your stuff smells bad."

"It does not."

"Does not what?" says Mrs. Catterson, shuffling back into the room in her shoe-socks.

"Why did you let her into my room?"

"Why am I getting sass?" says Mrs. Catterson. "Is that what you'd like me to discuss with your father when he gets back?"

"Thank you for letting me spend time in your room," I say to Seth in my nicest voice.

Across the table, my table, he glowers at me. I think about the fact that I might be the closest thing to a friend he has, this boy who spends the whole day here alone with his mother, doing homeschool things and waiting for his father to get back from fundraising trips. But knowing I should feel bad for him makes me, at this moment, hate him even more.

"How about a 'You're welcome, Charmaine,'" says Mrs. Catterson.

"You're welcome," Seth mumbles, but whispers, "not welcome, not welcome, not welcome," when Mrs. Catterson slips out again.

Phoebe picks me up in the Pinto, which is repaired for now but coughing blue smoke. When she slows down to shift gears, as she always does, we stall in the middle of Main Street. Once she gets the engine going again, she tells me she's been thinking hard about our visit to the recovery center together, how good it is that I'm getting the chance to see the situation for myself. "I really can't shield you any longer from what your father's going through," she says.

There's this thing that happens with her voice, like she can't help being pleased to have something important to say. Even if the important thing is something bad for everyone.

"I know what he's going through," I say, and then there's the thing in my voice that responds to the thing in hers. That makes her say things like: "Right; there isn't much you don't know these days, is there?"

The lit-up cross still shows in the passenger-side mirror, smaller and smaller in the distance, and I focus on it while I roll down the window. The air smells like wet leaves.

"Must you?" Phoebe says.

I don't answer and she sighs, then rolls down her window too. The air has a chill for this early in September, and soon

I am cold, but I won't roll my window back up because that would be admitting I shouldn't have rolled it down in the first place. I wrap my arms over my chest, careful not to wince in front of her.

"Had enough?" Phoebe says, rolling up her window. "Colder than you thought, isn't it?"

"It feels great," I say, and lean my head out into the air.

"You're going to make yourself sick," Phoebe says, and we ride in silence for more than a mile. Then she knocks her elbow into mine and says, "Hey."

"What?"

"Remember how I used to come into your bedroom and tickle you at night? Remember how you and I used to be best friends?"

I tuck my elbow into me as close as I can. We're approaching the gas station Tracy Payne lives behind. It's still open, and tonight there's a truck at the pump that hides most of the cinder-block house in back. I like that Phoebe doesn't know I've been over to Tracy's. I like that she has no idea about any of the three county people God laid on my heart for Operation Outreach. That she doesn't even know there is such a thing.

"I know your father's written to you about not hearing the voice of God," Phoebe says.

The rain has picked up and I am getting wet, but I don't want to be sealed up in the car with Phoebe, snaking down to the river at twenty miles per hour, when she's talking about my father.

"You want to know what I want to know?" She hits the steering wheel with the heels of both hands, then grabs it hard. "What I want to know is, when is it my time to question something? When do I get to say, 'The voice of God told me to do this,' or 'The voice of God told me to do that'? When do I get a break from my responsibilities to figure out what's the voice of God and what's a chemical imbalance in my brain?"

"What's stopping you?"

"What's stopping me?" She sighs. She's been slumping and now she draws herself up, braces herself against the wheel. "I don't like the spirit of your question. Your attitude. But the question in itself isn't a bad one. But even taking myself out of the whole equation . . . let's just say, for example, that I don't get to wonder the same things your father does. That I, as the Apostle Paul himself suggests, have been put on this earth just to listen to and believe anything my husband, your father, as the head of this household, says about God. Are we really supposed to overhaul our lives again and again based on communication no one else is privy to and for no other reason I am given to understand?"

It gives me a bad feeling to hear Phoebe talk this way. "God told Abraham to kill Isaac," I say. "Abraham was just supposed to obey. He didn't have to understand."

Our headlights catch the edge of the short gravel drive to the cabin, and we turn in. "You forgot to leave the light on," Phoebe says. "Again." She cuts the engine and I roll up the window. "Hold on a sec," she says. It's dark enough down here that you can't really see the rain, but you can hear it murmuring against the windshield.

"Honestly, Charmaine, I try. I don't hear the voice of God directly, but I read the Bible. I pray. I don't usually insist on understanding. At times I have even allowed myself to feel special, like maybe God chose me to be with a person who hears the voice of God because I had some rare capacity, even a spiritual gift, to accept mysteries—like Mary, when she found out she was pregnant. I liked that God told your father to marry me. I felt important when God gave your father revelations. And then the fasting starts up. And I don't know what to make of it, but your father's an exceptional man, 'a man after God's own heart,' as your grandmother likes to say. And whatever else may be wrong with him, I believe he's sincere. And if God tells him to fast, who am I to say he shouldn't? And he gives me the history of fasting and all the cultures that fast, and each time he goes off on a fast, I pray for strength. Because he always comes back with who-knows-what new idea. And I have done my level best to help this man run his life—and ours—by a voice he admits he can't hear anymore now that they've slowed down his brain to what the doctors all agree is a normal pace. So what was he hearing all those years his brain was racing? Like someone whispering in his ear, he used to say. That's what I'd like to know. Because other people, other Christian people I could name, thought it was pretty strange for God to tell someone with a family to quit an honest pay-check. What if we'd had an emergency? What if you'd con-tracted leukemia?"

"I didn't, though," I say.

"And the things he tells you. Hearing the voice of God, not hearing the voice of God. There are some things you simply should not share with children."

"You share a lot," I say. "You share and share and share."

"Oh, you think so?" She reaches up and turns the rearview mirror to her face. "There's plenty I keep to myself these days. You might be surprised." Something about the way she moves her chin to the side and blinks at her dim reflection, like she's keeping a secret with it, is new, and my heart lodges somewhere in my neck, thumping hard.

"About Doctor Osborne?" I say.

She adjusts the mirror to its original position, frowning. The darkness is lighter now, greenish, and there's a moving shadow of the rain on Phoebe's face. The drops hit the windshield, stick, and spread out a little, more like big dollops of pudding than like water. You can just barely see the shape each one makes when it hits the glass, before it disappears into the rest of the wetness. When she finally speaks she sounds less shocked and outraged than I expected.

"Morris, Doctor Osborne, is a brother in Christ, and there's nothing wrong with a little support from a brother in Christ."

"What about support from brothers in Christ who aren't bachelors?" I say. "What about sisters in Christ?"

"Bachelors," she says. "That sounds just like Daze. Doctor Osborne is a very brilliant man, Charmaine, with a Ph.D. Do you know what that is? We talked when he drove us home, and there is nothing in the world to hide about it. Doctor Osborne is a man of God, and I am a woman of God."

"A defensive woman of God," I say.

"That mouth of yours will get you into trouble."

I try to imagine Mrs. Catterson and Seth talking to each other this way, even when they're mad. The loneliest thing about it is that there's no way out, once it starts. I have to say the next mean thing or I feel like I will disappear.

The rain is letting up, and I reach for the door handle.

"I'm not finished with you," Phoebe says.

I try to let everything drain out of my face the way Kelly-Lynn does, all the irritation and bad attitude, but it's hard. The irritation and bad attitude keep me from feeling scared, and it's a fight to keep a bland, bored expression. It's like I'm in water, and underneath are all the feelings, like bars of soap that want to bob up and break the surface. Only there are hundreds of them, and I only have two hands.

"What's the matter with your face?" Phoebe says.

I blink at her and count the blinks: one, two, three. I tell myself that each of her words is like a single bird in a migrating flock that will soon be gone.

"You want to know what Doctor Osborne and I talked about? We talked about how there's more than one way to look at things. You can look at things like in biblical times, where God speaks to people right in their heads and tells them to do things like part the Red Sea or build an ark or slaughter their own children. Or live on faith alone. Or maybe—and yes, Doctor Osborne suggested this to me, so what?—maybe you can take the idea that God gave us the Bible for rules and our brains to figure out how to use the rules."

"Okay," I say, "but God gives everyone brains. What happens when one person figures something out one way and another person figures the same thing out another way? How do you know who's right if they're both using their God-given brains?"

Phoebe pinches the bridge of her nose like she has a headache. "My point," she says, "the point I started to make, is that I am your mother. And the Abraham thing? You can't tell me your feelings wouldn't be hurt if I tried to sacrifice you. Things are different now, that's all. Like divorce. We can look at it and say, What did divorce mean during biblical times, and what does it mean during these times?"

The word *divorce* hangs in the air between us, delicate as a bubble. If I touch it, it will burst and cover everything.

"Are you listening?" she asks. "What did I just say?"

"Things are different now," I recite in a singsong voice. It's the unbearable voice of Little Marcy, the child narrator of Bible stories on a record I used to listen to before falling asleep. Only my Little Marcy voice is poisonous.

Phoebe sucks in her breath. "I wish you could tell me what I ever did to you that you talk to me that way. When I most need you. Seriously, Charmaine. Families in crisis have to stick together."

"Isn't Daddy your family?"

"We're all family. Even Daze is our family, if just by marriage."

"She's my family by more than marriage. I'm her blood kin."

"Listen to you. 'Kin.' You're picking up the way they talk down here. My point is about support."

"My point," I say, "is that you're the one talking about divorce, to another man, when your husband's in the hospital. Is that what you mean by support?"

Then she slaps me. I don't see it coming, and her hand catches me full on the face. "When did you become such a little viper?" she says.

The world stops for two seconds and then starts up again. I don't feel like crying, not even a little. I feel calm. It's easy to keep a blank expression now, and I wonder if this is how Kelly-Lynn feels all the time.

Phoebe recovers fast. "I'm sorry." She claps her hands over her own face. "I'm so sorry."

"Can I get out of the car, now?"

"Yeah," she says, which is a word she never uses or lets me use. She believes in "Let your yes be yes and your no, no."

A couple of fat drops catch me on the way in to the cabin. Phoebe stays in the car, and in the dark I fumble with my key and let myself in. It feels too late to start my homework, which I haven't been keeping up with very well, anyway. I can't even remember anything about school at this point, despite the fact that I spent the first eight hours of my day there. Titus is not inside. I see, with panic, that I have forgotten to leave the window over the sink open for him. I wrench it open now and call out. The only answer is the soft rushing of the river. I open the rest of the windows in the trailer and turn all the lights on so that he'll know we're home.

In the tiny bathroom I stand in the shower to change into my nightclothes. I brush my teeth, wipe my nose and chin with witch hazel, and touch my reddened cheek. My eyes peer out from behind my face, serious and unfamiliar.

Back in the main part of the cabin, Phoebe has already spread the narrow tweed couch with my sheets, pillow, and a blanket, which I usually do myself. She's standing by the kitchen sink, looking out into the night and holding a plastic cup of water. Her face is wet.

"I forgot to leave the window open for Titus," I say.

"He'll be okay," she says. She drains her cup then fills it again at the tap. "I don't expect you to understand this. But I can't remember the last time your father showed the tiniest bit of interest in anything I had to say. He's never heard a gol-rammed thing over the voice of God. So it felt good to talk to Morris. Doctor Osborne. I'm sorry about that. That in itself is probably not okay to feel. Not when I'm a married woman. And if you don't mind, I would really appreciate it if you didn't tell your grandmother."

Phoebe downs the rest of her water and upends the cup in the drain. I crawl under the covers.

"I know the two of you are close," she says. "I know you tell her more than you tell me."

"I won't tell her," I say.

"I'm coming apart," Phoebe says. "I'm very sorry I raised a hand to you, but I feel like I'm coming apart at the seams."

Instead of washing up in the bathroom, instead of pulling the curtains and changing into her nightclothes in front of me in the way I hate, she climbs the built-in ladder to the loft, clothes and all.

And because for once she hasn't asked me for a good-night hug, hasn't told me she loves me and waited for me to say it back, I feel like I could tell her, right now, that I love her. And I almost want to tell her. And to ask her to please not get a divorce. And not to come apart. And to say that it would make me feel bad, it would make me feel terrible, if she tried to sacrifice me. All of this swells up in me to say, but I don't know what that would mean at a time like this, what else she might expect from me, so I keep it all to myself and turn out the light and dream that I'm a child again.

CHAPTER 12

IN THE MORNING, TITUS has still not come home. The rain continues slow and heavy, and I pretend to be asleep until Phoebe drives off for her Saturday errands in town. Then I pull on the homemade Levi's and a dirty shirt and head outside. He's probably holed up somewhere dry, under someone's house or car. He might even be in one of those caves in the palisades, where my father has told me bats cling to the ceilings like furry, upside-down carpeting. You can get bitten by a bat and not even know it because their teeth are thinner than needles. Bats carry rabies, and Titus may or may not have had his rabies booster last year, because he was an indoor cat.

I check the river first. Rain soaks through my clothes right away and trickles down my scalp. But the wetter I get, the warmer it feels. When I step out onto our wooden dock, it creaks, pulling against the ropes that hold it to the stake my father sank deep into the garden. Today the river is a rushing brown froth, chopping up higher than usual against the edges of the bank, depositing things in the scrub and the low-hanging limbs of trees—twigs, a plastic bag, leaves. Nothing that looks like a dead cat, thankfully. I try not to look at the bridge high above, though my father says cats survive falls better than most animals. Something about how loose their bones are.

"Titus," I call, but in the rain the sound seems to die two feet in front of my face. I cup my hands to make a megaphone. "Kitty, kitty."

I hike back across the weedy lawn and start down the river road in the opposite direction of the bridge. If I were a Catholic, I could pray to a specific saint, maybe even a saint of lost cats. I wipe at the pen marks on my thumb. The earliest of them have already faded to pale blue. I am not good at prayer without ceasing, but I can hardly think how else to pray anymore, without suggesting to God that there might be things that are more important to me than him. Like my father coming home, like finding Titus, like everything going back to the way it was before. Maybe what I should be praying is for God to change my heart so that he really is more important than the other things, the same way he was more important to Abraham than Isaac was. Because when Abraham proved it by raising the knife to sacrifice Isaac, God didn't take Isaac away after all. So I pray for that, quickly, before I start to worry about my ulterior motive. Then I pray for my three Operation Outreach people, that I'll have better progress to share when I do see my father, so that he won't despair of his vision for the county. Then I pray *Inhabit me, O Lord God* and try to muster up some perseverance, because with more than fifty hatch marks on my hand for effort, I still don't feel inhabited, and even though I know it is sinful to pray with expectation, I definitely didn't expect things to get harder the harder I tried. I wish there was a medicine I could take that would do the opposite of what they're doing to my father—speed my brain up instead of slowing it down. Then maybe I could hear God's voice, or at least keep on praying while I did everything else. I rub my hands against my jeans, scrubbing off the ink marks as best I can to make a clean space for starting over.

The rain blows across the road in sheets. Even the inside of my ears are wet now, and I'm not warm anymore. Titus could be anywhere. He could be up a tree, and there are hundreds of trees. I call for him a couple more times, then turn in the other direction, back past the trailer-cabin and downriver, calling and looking, looking and calling, until I reach the base of the bridge. The concrete foot is twice as tall as I am, bigger than the whole trailer-cabin. Underneath my palms, its surface is cool and rough. I feel, more than I have ever felt the presence of God, the presence of this bridge, running through every distant point of it like a current, then right down my spine. It's not hard to understand why people are drawn to it, why they might even want to jump. It's not hard to imagine how, for the second before you let go, you could feel like you were one with the bridge and nothing bad would happen. I close my eyes and whisper *Inhabit me, O Lord God* over and over, but it feels like I am talking to the bridge instead.

Back in the trailer-cabin I peel off my wet clothes and slip into my nightgown. The rain beats hard against the tin roof. It has soaked through the towel under the window I've left open for Titus. Phoebe has taped up our "house rules" onto the tiny refrigerator door, and the edges of the paper are curling away from the wall.

I've forgotten all about the envelope from Seth's closet. It's right where I left it, inside my wooden box, and when I lift the flap, a short stack of pictures spills out. I'm thinking maybe they'll be naked pictures, but I can't even make out anything in the first one. There's red and brown and black, and some stringy things, and where the flash hits it, it shines like something wet. The next picture is of the same thing, only from farther away. Now you can see it's on pavement somewhere, and the black stuff might be oil. But it's not oil, it's blood. With shreds of red cloth mixed in. The next picture is from even farther back, so you can see, below the mess, a pair of legs in jeans, lying sideways on the pavement. The cloth is part of a shirt. It's a person. Now, where the face should be, I see upper teeth. A closed eye. There is no lower jaw anymore at all, and I don't know how I didn't see the eye and teeth first thing, because there they are in the first picture, the close-up, when I look again.

Besides a deer, once, the only dead thing I've ever seen is a mouse Titus brought me. The mouse looked like a tiny gray shoe, and the possibility that it might recover and begin moving made it seem extra still. The picture wouldn't be so bad if you couldn't tell the thing had been a person, but you can. And now I see something else in the picture, on the pavement near a black boot, and I'm leaning with my nose close to the photograph when I figure out it's a torn-off thumb, and I barely make it to the sink before I throw up.

The last photo is the naked one. It's a very pale body, a woman's, with the trunk cut open all the way down to her privates. The skin is peeled back from the middle, and the ribs are gone, and all the organs show, nestled in with each other like blind, sleeping creatures. You can't tell how old she was or how she died. Her arms and hands lie at her sides, and her legs have rotated outward just a little, and the privates are so close to the camera that you can see them right through the dark curly hair.

But what gets to me, what I am lingering over when Phoebe pulls in, are the breasts. They're still attached to the skin of the woman's chest, only the skin is stretched inside out, parted to either side of her body. The breasts are all turned around, on the underside of the skin now. I stuff the photos back into the envelope, and the envelope into the butt purse. But it's as if I've taken the dead woman into my eyes and now I can't *not* see her. It's as if, also, the heavy ache in my own breasts is connected somehow to hers—slumped out of shape onto the shoulders, half underneath the inside-out skin. Nipples pointing away from the body in opposite directions, as if ashamed to watch the excavation below.

All day it rains. Even though September is usually the driest month. After a brief, near-silent lunch, Phoebe returns to the loft to sleep. I look for Titus again, in all the same places. I try to pray, forget, try, forget, try. In the trailer-cabin, with Phoebe still sleeping, I think about starting homework and end up rereading *A Wrinkle in Time* right through to the end, again, where everyone gets back home before dinner, even though they've passed through black holes to other planets, other solar systems, maybe. Phoebe keeps sleeping. For dinner I drink two of my father's cans of tomato juice and listen to the river, which sounds faster. And closer. Before dark I head out one more time and am alarmed to see the water lapping high, our dock rocking violently, pulling the ropes taut. Before the rain, only the lowest tree branches skimmed the water, but now whole limbs dip below the surface, battered by the current.

Back in the cabin I wake Phoebe and tell her the river's rising. She yawns, scoots to the edge of the loft, then leans her head toward the window. "How far is it up the bank?" she wants to know, and I tell her I'm not sure. Maybe a couple of feet. She climbs down from the loft and heads outside, barefoot, with the flashlight. She grew up not far from the Cumberland River in Tennessee, which was a lot bigger than this one, she likes to say. From the window I watch the light move dimly through the rain, stop at the top of the bank, then return. "If it hits the top of the bank, we should probably head out of the gorge," she says as she dries off. "But I don't think the rain's going to keep up this way."

"I'm not leaving without Titus," I say.

"Titus probably knows more about the water rising than we do," she says. "From smell or something. Let's not borrow trouble. I'm wiped out, Charmaine. I don't mean to sleep all day, but I don't know when I've felt so tired." She climbs back up into the loft. "I'll check again in an hour or so."

But she doesn't check again. I do. I stay up past midnight, listening to the rain, taking the flashlight back and forth across the lawn. The rain is quieter outside than in the cabin, pattering gently on the leaves instead of drumming the roof. I can still hear the river rushing, but no matter how many times I shine the light toward the water, it illuminates nothing but rain. The ropes holding the dock groan terribly. Finally, the batteries in the flashlight die, and I have to pick my way back to the cabin in the wet pitch dark.

I mean to stay up for the rest of the night in case it floods.

Instead, I wake late in the morning, when everything's quiet and the light is gray. No rain. I cross the wet lawn to find the river a little lower, showing new broken tree limbs at the edge. It takes me a second to realize that what's missing is our dock, its ropes snapped and frayed, lying flat in the sodden grass.

"We could track it down," Phoebe says when I tell her what's happened, "or we could just let it go."

"If we found it," I say, "how would we get it back here?"

"Exactly," she says. She measures out instant coffee into her mug. It's Sunday again. Our third at the river. And it's the week I would have joined the church and maybe even been baptized if the Holy Ghost had made it clear to me that the time was right, which he hasn't. "We could go back to church," Phoebe says, "or we could take a true day of rest, like the Bible says."

"You rested yesterday," I say.

"That's true," she says. "I'll take you if you want to go. I'll pull myself together."

I picture Seth standing up front, answering all the church-joining questions. Mary-Kate and Karen too, and the blond seminary wife, all waiting for their new Bibles. "That's okay."

"I'll take you to the youth meeting later, then," she says. "And we'll see your father tomorrow night, Lord willing. Don't forget."

"I know," I say. "I won't."

I don't want to leave the pictures where Phoebe can find them, so that night I carry the butt purse to the Upper Room. The pictures, riding near my hip, feel like a secret world of their own. The mangled body on the side of the road. The woman split open. I take my place directly across from Seth in what's about to become a foot-washing circle. Every time I sneak a glance at him, the light hits his glasses as if he's moved suddenly, as if he doesn't want to be caught watching me back.

We're all in chairs tonight, beanbags piled uselessly against the wall. At Pastor Chick's instruction, we bend over to take off our shoes and socks. Foot washing is a ceremony of forgiveness, so that if there's any conflict among us, we can clear it up before Operation Outreach swings into full gear. Pastor Chick and Conley have filled a small collection of buckets in the men's room, and they stand over them, waiting, until we are all completely barefoot. Then we wait some more.

"Who will be first?" asks Pastor Chick. "Who will lead the way with their humble heart?"

We stare at the buckets, too embarrassed to look at each other. Our socks and shoes sit in sad little piles beside us. No one wants to wash feet.

"How can we accomplish Operation Outreach if we are not a unified body?" asks Pastor Chick. "If we are not willing to wash the feet of our brothers and sisters in Christ? Anyone remember John thirteen?"

I know John 13. Jesus washes the feet of his disciples. I know he says, "Unless I wash you, you have no share with me." But I keep my mouth closed.

"Maybe we're ready to bring people into this body just as it is. No purification, no cleansing, required. That would be truly remarkable, people. But if we're all that pure, to a person, then this room should already be giving the Great Revival of 1973 a run for its money. I can't see into your hearts, people. I'll just have to trust that no one's feeling too manly to wash feet. That none of our godly ladies feel it's too gross to wash feet. I can only speak for my own heart, and this heart of mine is holding a resentment. Sometimes, brother Conley, I resent your God-given musical ability."

Now that we all have somewhere to look, we look at Conley as he stands up. His eyes shift from Pastor Chick to the buckets, to the silent room, and back to Pastor Chick, who kneels, now, in front of Conley's toes. Which are enormous.

"Maybe I should sit down," says Conley, and he sits down again, the folding chair creaking underneath him.

I did not believe the Upper Room could get any quieter, but it does. It's like we're all holding our breath.

Pastor Chick holds out his hand, and Conley plants a heel, large as an apple, in the palm. "See, people? This isn't so bad." He speaks down into the bucket of soapy water as he feels around for the sponge.

Conley squeezes his eyes shut as Pastor Chick handles first one foot then the other like he has never washed anything before in his life. He even attempts to clean between toes. Conley kicks a little at this, and as water splashes everywhere, he manages a grim smile. They say a few low words of forgiveness that we can't hear.

"Thanks, brother," Conley says when Pastor Chick has finished. He rests his feet on the blue carpet, where they're soon outlined in a darker, wetter blue.

Pastor Chick stands and looks relieved. He wipes his wet hands down the front of his jeans. "See? Not the end of the world."

To give us some more time to consider our resentments, to work ourselves up to the washing of feet, Pastor Chick calls upon us individually to stand, barefoot, and share our progress with Operation Outreach. Have we prayed? Have we invited?

Have we taken advantage of all openings? The time draws near. The Main Event is Friday night.

"My people don't live here," says Mary-Kate when Pastor Chick calls on her. "But I might see them next week." She puts her hand up to her cheek, as if she's suddenly remembered her acne.

"Fair enough," says Pastor Chick. "Keep lifting them in prayer."

We sing a song and wait, again, for someone, anyone, to offer to wash another's feet. As much as I would like Pastor Chick to think highly of me, I can't bring myself to do this. Especially not the feet of Seth, no matter how much I resent him.

Pastor Chick sighs. "Ida Hughes?" he says, and one of the missionary twins stands. "I invited my people to eat lunch with me, and I led grace. And I invited them for Friday, and I invited them to prayer meeting at school, too."

"Praise God," says Pastor Chick, encouraged. After another long silence, he looks my way. "Charmaine Peake?"

I stand up in my bare feet. "I invited two of my people. From the county. I gave them the flyers. I don't know if they're coming."

"That's a good start," says Pastor Chick.

"And I try to pray all the time." I raise my hand as if to offer the new row of hatch marks as evidence, then drop it to my side. "I really try. And the third person," I take a deep breath as I remember Cecil's threats on the bus, "has been talking to me some."

"That's joy to the heart of God," says Pastor Chick.

I sit down and we all wait some more. Pastor Chick passes a hand up over his face and onto his hair. He closes his eyes tolerantly, then opens them. "Okay, people," he says with res-ignation. "Seth Catterson?"

When Seth stands up, I get ready for him to say something about his three people, something about one of them being in the hospital or being a false prophet. I get ready for every single person in this room to know he means my family. But then he stammers and glances in my direction again, and I remember the pictures in the butt purse, and I realize he is worried.

"I don't know," Seth says.

I lift the butt purse from the floor into my lap. I imagine Seth looking at the pictures, at the woman with the sad, peeled breasts. I stare at him and unzip the purse. It makes a loud sound in the quiet room. The glasses glint in my direction, and I raise my eyebrows like a dare.

"How about with the Main Event?" says Pastor Chick. "Any luck?"

"I guess," says Seth. He shifts from one bare foot to the other, then sits down hard.

I zip the purse closed, still watching him, though he keeps his head bent. I feel curious about what just happened, and when Pastor Chick signals Conley for another song, I get to my feet. The song is "God Is So Good," another one that repeats and repeats. You can make your own verses, even, to keep it going. Seth eyes me in horror as I approach him, but Pastor Chick beams. "Praise God," he says over the singing.

I choose a bucket from the middle of the circle, set it down in front of Seth, then kneel. His feet are long and thin, pale as raw lumber.

"You took something," he hisses under the music.

I clamp my hands around one of his ankles and lift, but he won't budge his foot. The room launches into another verse.

"He cares for me, he cares for me, he cares for me, he's so good to me."

Fine brown hairs sprout tentatively from Seth's upper lip. It's an embarrassing thing to see, even though it's just hair, and I feel my own upper lip curl. I hate that things are happening to Seth's body too, like we're in something together. "Why do you even have pictures like that?" I say. "What's the matter with you?"

People are watching, and Seth lifts a foot and sticks it down into the bucket. His face turns red. "They aren't for anything bad," he whispers. "They help you stop thinking things. You wouldn't know anything about it. You're a girl, so shut up."

I reach down in the bucket and splash a little water around his ankle, careful not to touch his feet in any way. I'm probably giving him a good view of my bosom, but when I check if he's looking, his eyes are squeezed miserably shut. He switches feet fast and gets water everywhere.

"Stealing's a sin," he says.

"From my own closet?"

"Not right now," he says. "It's not your closet right now."

"Tell your mom, then," I say. I have a point, and he knows it.

"Praise God, people," Pastor Chick says over the final verse. "I like the way the Lord's moving among our new seventh graders."

Seth lifts his second wet foot from the bucket and lowers it on top of his first one, as if he's cold. Or, like Noah, as if he suddenly feels his nakedness and wants to hide it.

CHAPTER 13

I DON'T REMEMBER THAT MONDAY'S the day for my how-to speech until Mrs. Teaderman calls on me.

"I'm not ready," I say, and she makes a disappointed face and gives me an extension for the end of the week, with penalties.

"I can go," says Kelly-Lynn, even though it isn't her day. She makes her way to the front and starts talking everyone through a standing back tuck—the launching, the tucking, the landing—then pushes the demonstration table to the side so she can demonstrate.

"Don't hurt yourself," says Mrs. Teaderman.

We all watch as Kelly-Lynn takes a few deep knee bends. You can see on her face that the moment where you actually jump into the air, backward, is scary.

"Do it already," says a boy in the back, and then she does.

Her knees fold up neatly and carry her over backward, and her feet land right underneath her, where they're supposed to, not even an extra step or hop. The room breaks into applause.

In activity I sit alone in the bleachers while she runs through jumps on the gym floor with the rest of the girls who have tried out for cheerleading over the weekend. They're going to announce the results right here, in front of everyone. Soon Mrs. Perry, the cheerleading coach, taps the mike and says the usual things: How everyone is very talented. How there are only a few open spots on the team. How she wishes there could be a place for everyone. She asks for a big hand for all the girls who tried out. Then she starts calling names. First are the returning cheerleaders, and when each of their names is called, Theresa, Mindy, Michelle, and the rest take a running start and flip themselves end over end the length of the gym floor, leaving twenty or so girls under the basketball hoop. Kelly-Lynn, off by herself, practices her jumps. She does another perfect standing back tuck. A few girls around her jump just as well as she does, springing high off the gym floor. They're the next ones called—Casey, Melissa, Jennifer. Under the basketball goal, the remaining girls wait. Mrs. Perry takes a little break to explain what makes a good cheerleader. There's cheering, of course, and school spirit, and tumbling, but there's also a GPA requirement and, most importantly, there's the issue of character. "Character counts," says Mrs. Perry. "Character counts more than anything."

The next girl called has very poor jumps, compared to Kelly-Lynn. She barely gets her feet under her when she lands, and when she tries to flip across the gym floor, after her name is called, she manages four cartwheels and then tumbles right out of her round-off. If this girl made the team, Kelly-Lynn must surely have made it, but she's not among the three girls who are called next. Under the goal, Kelly-Lynn jumps nervously, like the gym floor is heating up beneath her feet. When only one spot remains to be filled, all the girls except for Kelly-Lynn grasp each other's hands. Kelly-Lynn closes her eyes. "Rachel Wood," says Mrs. Perry, and Rachel Wood screams and runs down the gym floor forgetting all about how she's supposed to show off her gymnastics.

Mrs. Perry has more to say. Congratulatory words. Consoling words. But Kelly-Lynn's not waiting around. She's making her way up the bleachers to where I'm sitting, her face as still as ever. It's not until she reaches me that I can see her mouth is trembling.

"You were way better than those other girls," I say as she sits down.

"I knew it wasn't going to happen," she says.

"But they couldn't even do the standing back tuck."

She motions me to lean in close so she can whisper something, and from behind us a boy says, "The lesbians are telling secrets."

"Shut up," says Kelly-Lynn. "We're not lesbians."

"Ask Ronnie Rietz," says the boy.

Kelly-Lynn's neck begins to turn red and splotchy. I follow her gaze to a tall blond boy down on the first bleacher, surrounded by kids, including Theresa. Kelly-Lynn raises her hand for a teacher, and Mr. Rodriguez, who teaches shop, steps down from his lookout a few bleachers behind us.

I expect her to report the comment, but all she says to Mr. Rodriguez is "Can I go to the bathroom?" Then she crooks her finger at him, and when he leans in she tells him she's having monthly issues.

Mr. Rodriguez sighs and takes out his small pad of hall passes.

"She's having monthly issues, too," Kelly-Lynn says about me, and even though this will be true again soon enough, it is not true now, and it is nothing I would share. My face burns as Mr. Rodriguez tears off two passes.

We climb down the bleachers and head for the doors at the far end of the auditorium, passing near enough Ronnie Rietz that I hear one of his friends say, "Lesbian," before they bust themselves up laughing.

"Keep walking," Kelly-Lynn says through her teeth.

By the time the metal doors clang shut behind us, we're almost halfway down the hall to the bathroom, Kelly-Lynn dragging me behind her. Inside, I follow her into the handicapped stall. It smells strongly of cigarettes, and down the length of the door someone has drawn a huge cartoon penis with Magic Marker. Kelly-Lynn wipes off the toilet seat with toilet paper and then sits on it, fully clothed. "Ronnie Rietz is an asshole," she says. Her mascara is running a little underneath her left eye, and I tear off more toilet paper and hand it to her. "There was this party at his house, after cheer tryouts. You should see where he lives. Behind that horse farm? With all the buildings painted white and red? And Theresa was there, and everyone said 'Hey,' and we drank beer and watched television until more people came, then someone put on music and we danced. It was a party, you know, just regular."

I have seen a party like that once, in a movie at church about the dangers of drinking. As the night went on, the camera grew more and more shaky, to indicate drunkenness.

"So then the girls all sneak off to fix their makeup and it's just me and some guys, and one of them tells me that Ronnie

Rietz wants to talk to me. So I follow them upstairs to where Ronnie's in his dad's office, sitting behind the desk. Then it's just the two of us, and he starts talking about how none of the girls want to be my friend because I'm so pretty."

"You are pretty," I say. Even right there, with her makeup a mess from crying, it's true; she's still pretty.

"Thanks," she says. "You might be pretty, too, once your hair grows out. Anyway, I don't say anything back. He's just like every other boy. You want them to talk to you so bad, because you think it's going to be so great, but it never is. He says the girls think I lie a lot. Which I don't that much. I tell the truth a lot, too.

"So then Theresa walks in with that Mindy girl. And even though Ronnie's been doing all the talking, he tells Theresa that I have been begging him to let me suck his dick so I can figure out if I really am a lesbian."

My mouth drops open.

"I know," Kelly-Lynn says. "Theresa starts laughing, but that Mindy girl says, 'I believe it,' and then they all just look at me and I run out of the room. And no one at the party knew what was going on, but I knew they would soon, and I wasn't getting picked up until eleven o'clock. So I go out the kitchen door and hide in a bush and wait."

"What did your mom do?"

"My aunt," Kelly-Lynn says. "Rob took my mom to rehab. Again. And I would never tell Aunt Sheila because she'd probably call Ronnie Rietz's parents. Telling her would be social suicide. Not that I'm ever going to be popular anyway."

"Maybe it's not as great as you think it would be," I say. "Like talking to boys."

"Maybe."

"I'm sorry that happened," I say. And I am. We both look at the floor, with its tiny, square yellow tiles and gummy grout. "Something weird happened to me too," I hear myself say, as if what I have to share might make her feel better. I reach into the butt purse for the photos.

Like me, it takes Kelly-Lynn a moment to figure out what she's looking at. "These are real?" she says. "These are like *Faces of Death*. Have you seen *Faces of Death*?"

"No."

Kelly-Lynn studies the woman on the table for a long time, then hands the pictures back to me with a sour face. "Where did you get these?"

"Seth."

"Your boyfriend?"

"Sort of," I say. "They keep him from lusting."

"They *what*?" She blinks at me like I'm nuts. "How?" Someone enters the bathroom, and Kelly-Lynn draws her feet up onto the toilet so that if anyone looks they will think only one person is in the stall. We listen as the girl pees and flushes. "You can't have these in school," Kelly-Lynn whispers as the girl's washing her hands. "Not even in your purse."

"I didn't know where else to keep them." I take the photo with the thumb and give it one more hard look. Then I tear it in half. Then I tear the halves in half, and I keep going until it's in little pieces that I drop into the toilet, where they form a crust on top of the water.

Kelly-Lynn presses the lever, and the toilet gives a halfhearted swirl. The crust lowers, rotates, but remains intact. I try it again, holding down the handle, and even though the second flush is more enthusiastic, photo pieces pop back up as the bowl refills.

Kelly-Lynn pulls a purple lighter out of her purse. "My mother's," she says, rolling her eyes. "I'm trying to make her quit. I'm sure she's smoking like a chimney in rehab anyway." We square off on either side of the toilet. She flicks the lighter, and I let it lick at the corners of the remaining three pictures, which start to smoke. At the last second I save the one of the woman on the table and dip the corner of it into the toilet to put out the flame. Kelly-Lynn just raises her eyebrows. We watch the rest of the pictures burn. When the heat comes too close to my fingers, I drop it all into the toilet, and as the bell rings, Kelly-Lynn flushes again, holding down the lever until the first girls start entering the bathroom. This time everything disappears from the bowl. I tuck the picture of the woman, now with charred edges, back into the butt purse.

"Smokey," someone says from in front of the sinks. Then it falls quiet, teacher quiet, and when Kelly-Lynn and I push open the stall door, Mrs. Teaderman is waiting by the paper towel dispenser with her arms crossed.

"I am not surprised by the smoking," she says, "because it is unfortunately very common in this county. I am surprised, however, at two smart girls like you. Follow me, please."

"We weren't smoking," I say.

"Take it up with Principal Conrad," Mrs. Teaderman says. "Charmaine, especially. I find this very hard to comprehend."

In front of class Mrs. Teaderman seems graceful enough, but in the hallway she walks like a giraffe, leading with her knees and landing on her toes. Daze would say she walks like her feet hurt, which is something no woman should let on. Even so, Mrs. Teaderman is hard to keep up with. Kelly-Lynn nudges my arm. "Tell them you have a family situation," she whispers.

Principal Conrad takes Kelly-Lynn inside first, and Mrs. Teaderman goes in, too. In the long moments they're behind closed doors, I listen to the gentle metallic sliding of the filing cabinet as the secretary slips information into student files. My homeroom teacher says that our student file follows us for the rest of our lives. Like a tattoo on your forehead listing every time you got into trouble. Or marks on your hand reminding you that you've forgotten to pray. I start to open my purse for a pen to make another mark on my thumb, but then I remember the picture and keep it closed.

When Kelly-Lynn comes out, Principal Conrad and Mrs. Teaderman are still talking to her.

"I will," Kelly-Lynn is saying. She shows me her calmest face, fully recovered now from the cheerleading disappointment. "Thank you very much, Principal Conrad. Thank you, Missus Teaderman."

"No more smoking," says Mrs. Teaderman. "It's no way to deal with your problems."

"I'm done with smoking for good," says Kelly-Lynn. She speaks with such resolve that I'm convinced, even though I know she doesn't smoke in the first place.

"Charmaine?" Mrs. Teaderman says, and I stand and make my way into Principal Conrad's office.

"Peake," says Principal Conrad as I sit down. "Peake." He has my file in front of him on the desk, completely flat. Beside my file, Kelly-Lynn's file is as thick as a Bible, probably from all her transfers. "I know I know that name. Missus Teaderman?"

"I found her smoking with Kelly-Lynn."

"I wasn't smoking."

"No?" Principal Conrad and Mrs. Teaderman exchange a glance.

"Was Kelly-Lynn smoking?" Mrs. Teaderman asks.

I know Kelly-Lynn told them she was smoking, so if I say she wasn't, which is true, then I sound like a liar. But if I say she was, which isn't true, then I really am a liar, even though I sound truthful. I shrug.

"Can't remember?" says Principal Conrad. "That's funny, because it just happened." He's not speaking in an unfriendly way, just an unyielding way. The dome of his head is a pointed oval, like the top of an egg. "Want to know what she said?"

"Okay."

"Well, Miss Brooker admits she was smoking but says you weren't. Would you say that's accurate? Or would you say she's just trying to be a good friend?"

"Kind of both," I say.

"I don't understand that answer," says Principal Conrad, "but if you say you weren't smoking, and Miss Brooker says you weren't smoking, then I'm inclined to give you the benefit of the doubt. Just this once. And Miss Brooker has a lot going on at home."

"What about you?" Mrs. Teaderman says. "Anything at home we should know about?"

"No."

Mrs. Teaderman frowns at me like she knows better. Like she has read every single DO NOT READ entry in my free-writing journal. All the letters to my father.

Principal Conrad touches the fingers and thumbs of both his hands together in a sort of triangle, then lowers his head and peers through it. "Charmaine Peake, I'm going to tell you what I tell every young person who ends up in my office." He smiles briefly at Mrs. Teaderman, who is listening politely, then peers at me again through his hand triangle. "These are some tough years. For everyone. Transition years. Some educators even say these years are the hardest, but I take a different approach. A more realistic approach. I like to suggest to young people that these are the years when they begin to figure out what kinds of problems they're going to keep right on having for the rest of their lives."

It's the heaviest thing I have ever heard, and it blazes like truth. "Oh," I say.

"That's meant to be useful," Principal Conrad says. "Not discouraging." Then he slaps his desk with both hands. "Daisy Peake. I knew I knew you. Custer Peake. Oh, yes. I think I'm getting the picture. Smoking doesn't fly with your family, I well know." He turns to Mrs. Teaderman and chuckles. "Daze Peake had it banned from school board meetings years ago. In Rowland County. One-time tobacco capital of Kentucky."

Mrs. Teaderman squints thoughtfully at me.

"Charmaine, I don't really think this offense warrants a phone call home. But don't let it happen again. Missus Teaderman?" says Principal Conrad with finality.

"Principal Conrad," says Mrs. Teaderman, imitating him exactly, "thank you for your time."

"My pleasure," says Principal Conrad. "And Charmaine, you can tell your grandmother that John Conrad sends his very best."

Back in the hallway, Mrs. Teaderman stops me with a long, skinny hand. "You can talk to me, Charmaine, if you ever need to," she says. "I can be a good listener."

"You read my DO NOT READ entries."

"I absolutely did not."

"I don't care. Read all the DO NOT READ entries you want."

"I didn't," Mrs. Teaderman says. "And I won't. I'd like for you to believe me, but it's okay if you don't."

We have fallen into awkward step, Mrs. Teaderman trying to match her long legs to mine. The hall stretches on and on, blue lockers on one side and closed classroom doors on the other.

"Think about what I said," says Mrs. Teaderman as we reach the same girls' restroom where it all started. Then she pushes open the door and it swings shut behind her.

I don't bother going to the last bit of earth science, my final class of the day. And instead of heading out the side doors to the line of buses, I remember to head out front to wait for Phoebe. When the last bell rings, the cement benches around me fill up with other kids waiting for their rides. It's warmer than it's been, and I take out my English notebook and fan myself while station wagons and vans pull up one after another.

After everyone else has been picked up, I open the notebook and write my prayer once, twice, three times. I never thought of writing it out over and over, like lines on the chalkboard when you get in trouble, but I write it a few more times until another bell rings, which I didn't expect, since school's already over. I've lost track, now, of how long I've been waiting. The buses are long gone, and the sun is low, shining through a line of trees. I start a new letter to my father, telling him that Kelly-Lynn's mother is in rehab, that Kelly-Lynn comes from a broken home. Then I wish I hadn't written *broken home*, and I scribble over it. Then I go ahead and scribble over the rest of what I've written, too, and by the time Phoebe turns into the semicircle drive, I have, like an angry child, covered all of the front of a page and most of the back, even where there was no writing to hide, with a fierce black cloud of scribbling.

As she pulls up, the Pinto coughs and dies. She restarts it, and a grinding sound echoes against the building.

"I don't know what we're going to do about dinner," she says as soon as I get in. "I don't have a cent on me. We might be able to eat with your father in the dining room."

"Okay."

"Would that be agreeable to you or disagreeable? It's impolite to respond with 'okay.' People can't tell what you're thinking."

"Agreeable," I say.

"That's better," says Phoebe. "How was school?"

It is impossible to tell her about the pictures, about Kelly-Lynn, about the principal's office. There is too much I can't explain, even if I wanted to. "Fine," I say.

"Curious about anything?" she asks, drawing out the words like I might be hard of hearing. I have no idea what I should be curious about, so I look at her hair, which seems the same, and her clothes, which seem to be what she was wearing when she left this morning.

"Um, why you were late?"

"I wasn't that late. It didn't kill you to wait for a few minutes. Anything else? No? What I'd like to know, I guess, is if it ever occurs to you to ask me how my day went."

It doesn't. It has never occurred to me even that it would be a good or bad thing to ask. "How was your day?"

"Fine," says Phoebe. "Thanks for asking."

I wait to see if she is finished, and when she doesn't say anything more, I open my algebra book.

"I don't know how you can read in a moving vehicle," she says. "It makes me positively sick to my stomach."

I listen for something she might want me to answer, but there's nothing. I copy out the first algebra problem. I am not great at math, but I enjoy copying out each problem, the new, neat chance to get something right. I almost never see the problems through to their correct answers, though, and when I turn in math homework, whether I use pencil or pen, the paper is a mess.

Phoebe sighs loudly. I wedge my finger into the crack of my algebra book and wiggle it around until the space gets bigger, as if I could make myself small enough to crawl inside and disappear.

At the two-way stop, Phoebe asks me to check to the right for traffic while she looks to the left. "Am I good?" she says when her way is clear.

"No," I say, watching a red pickup crawl toward the intersection.

"Plenty of time," Phoebe says.

After the red truck, I track a boxy blue car a ways off but traveling fast.

"Am I good?" she says.

"I don't know," I say. "I can't tell."

Phoebe turns and glares at the blue car. "For heaven's sake. I could have gone. I know it's a lot to ask, Charmaine, but I need your help here."

"How do you make turns when you're driving by yourself?"

"I can't wait until you're old enough to drive," she says. "I can't wait for you to see how nerve-racking it can be."

We leave Clay's Corner and head west over the stretch of highway that leads into Beacon County.

"They're still working on your father's medication," Phoebe says after a time. "It's not the best situation. But it's good you've been writing to him. You have a very sweet side, Charmaine. Very thoughtful. One of these days I hope to see more of that thoughtfulness directed toward me."

I stare out the window at the last few tobacco farms before we hit the horse country. You can look right through the front doorways of the big black barns to where the rough, yellowing sheaves hang like hides from the roof beams. In the fields, rows of harvested stalks go back so far and straight you can't see where they end. They're as regular as breathing, and as we pass, I count four rows as I breathe in and four rows as I breathe out, which reminds me to pray.

"If you have something to say, say it out loud," Phoebe says.

"Are you mad at me?"

Phoebe frowns at the road. "Sometimes, yes, I admit it, but not right now. Believe it or not, Charmaine, the world does not revolve around you."

At the big brick mansion, we enter the same waiting room as before, only with two different women behind the reception counter. One is a young brunette and the other is elderly, a redhead like Tracy but with white roots. She breaks into a smile and a "Hi-dee."

Phoebe steers me toward the counter. "Marion, Lilly, this is Charmaine. We're seeing Doctor Phillips again. Both of us. I mean, all three of us."

"Well, that's fine," says the red-haired woman, the way older ladies say "that's fine," with *fine* meaning "wonderful."

The other woman, Lilly, leads us down the long hallway, up the staircase at the end of it, back down the upstairs hallway, and into the same white room as before. And although the doctor isn't there yet, my father is. He sits at a card table, facing the wall of windows like he's trying to make the most of the fading afternoon light. When he hears us, he looks over his left shoulder then turns back to his work as if he is used to ignoring interruptions. Then he straightens his shoulders like he's just realized who we are. He pushes back from the table, stands up, and turns around.

"Look who's here," says Lilly, encouraging him.

"Go and say hi to your father," Phoebe encourages me.

And I want to, or I feel like I should want to. But it's been three long weeks since I saw him sleeping in the hospital bed, and now he's standing there, very still, just the shape of him in front of the tall windows so that his face doesn't show, and he says nothing, and what I'm thinking is *He is here, he is here,* when of course I knew he would be here all along. And I feel all at once empty. I feel as though the way things used to be—even if it was a crazy way to live, as Phoebe says—has been drained right out of me, and I am filling up with how things are now. For the first time, I understand that things might be how they are now from now on, or that they might change again, and again even after that, until there's nothing left to recognize and no way back. This thought keeps me from breathing right. When I try to step forward, I can't. I seem to be moving my arm instead of my leg, reaching for something, but when I look, I see that I am not moving my arm at all.

"Let's all sit down and relax," says Lilly, which helps me find my legs again. All of us, three from one end of the room and my father from the windows, make our way to a white couch and two chairs in a corner near the white piano.

"It's good to see you," my father says to me. He's clean-shaven and puffy at the neck, and he does not sound nervous, and there is room—by which I mean *time*—for me to say something back to him, which is not normal. Usually my father and Phoebe talk hard at each other, over each other, filling in all the quiet spaces.

"It's good to see you," I say back. In the corner of my eye I catch Phoebe running her tongue over her bottom lip.

My father turns to her. "Mother came by."

"I know," Phoebe says.

We all keep sitting there in the white room. It's starting to feel like something that happened a long time ago, something I'm remembering. Maybe something I dreamed. I can't think of one single thing to say, but as long as I don't look at my father, or at Phoebe, I feel peaceful. And suddenly sleepy. Like time is slowing way, way down. Like we're approaching the edge of a black hole.

"I guess it's been a while." Lilly says. "But I made sure he got your letters, Charmaine."

"Thanks," I say, which comes out too loud.

"I think I hear the doctor," says Lilly, and we all turn in relief to watch Lilly make her way to the door.

Dr. Phillips wears the same light brown corduroy coat as last time. His glasses have been pushed to the middle of his forehead, like he has another set of eyes up there over his brows. "This is an event, isn't it, David?" he says, taking the white chair next to my father. "Phoebe and Charmaine both here."

"It is," my father says. "An event," he adds on. He talks like the sound of his own voice surprises him a little each time he hears it.

"I want you to be able to ask any questions you might have,

Charmaine," says Doctor Phillips. "This must all seem a little strange."

Phoebe and my father are both studying my face like they're waiting for something to land on it. A giant insect, maybe, or a lunar module.

"First, maybe you and your mother will catch us up on the news of home. Then maybe your father will tell you a little about his days here."

Phoebe has been holding her purse beside her, wedged in between her thigh and the chair. Now she leans over and places it on the floor. "Well, okay." She crosses her legs in my father's direction. "I have subbing again every day this week. The Pinto is fixed. Temporarily. We had some very strong rains, and the river rose, and we lost the dock. Nothing flooded, though. Margaret Deeds told me she appreciated your old piece on prayer and expectation. Your mother seems fine. We're all looking forward to having you back." She stops on the word *back* when my father and Doctor Phillips glance at each other.

"What?" Phoebe says.

"Let's keep going," says the doctor.

My father picks up his feet one at a time and puts them back down. He's wearing a pair of suede moccasins, and I wonder if they're the same pair Phoebe said he was making for me.

"Has something been decided?" Phoebe says.

"Not at all," says Doctor Phillips. "What else has been happening? You talked to David's mother, I believe you said? Daze?"

"I think I'm a little more interested in what's been happening here," Phoebe says, looking full-on at my father. "Last week there was a bit of a complication."

My father blinks at her slowly.

"Everything working better? The Haldol?"

"Lithium, now," says the doctor.

"I have all that written down," says Phoebe, uncrossing her legs. She straightens her posture with a little twist, and I steel myself for whatever's coming. "I just don't want there to be any communication loss here. What with all the other issues. Doctor?"

The doctor brings his glasses down from his forehead onto his nose and lays a hand over his mouth. One finger in the mustache, the rest curling toward his chin. "I understand you're concerned," he says through his fingers.

"Oh, you do? I can't tell you what a relief that is." Phoebe's voice is like a plucked wire. She shifts her whole body away from the doctor as if he's not there and beams the full wattage of her gaze on my father. "I said we were looking forward to having you back, and you looked at the doctor. Is there significance? Am I overreacting? I'm not sure I even know the difference anymore."

"Perhaps conversation about aftercare options is premature," says the doctor.

Phoebe nods quickly, and her voice changes to something almost pleasant, but I know better. "Because of Charmaine, here," she says. She gestures toward me with kind, cupped hands, all without turning from my father. "We wouldn't want Charmaine to experience anything painful."

"And because of David," says the doctor. "And also because of you. It's a complicated time. Can we back up a little?"

"Oh, let's," says Phoebe, and my stomach gets tight. I wish I could stop her, but I can't. It's like she has a fever. "Let's back up a month, to right before David came back from the

Holy Land inhabited by the Apostle Paul. Or how about a year, when the Lord told David to quit his job and live on faith alone, and, guess what, his family too! Or how about when God laid it on his heart to eradicate the pagan holiday of Christmas, and we all passed out those brochures." She reaches back to where I'm sitting and gives me an affectionate push on the knee. "What were you, Charmaine, nine? The year you wanted a Cabbage Patch doll? Remember we all went to Clay's Corner instead and handed out the brochures to shoppers about the ten reasons real Christians don't celebrate Christmas?"

I had forgotten about that Christmas, but now it comes back to me. Daze gave me the doll anyway, only she kept it for me at her place for a year so my father wouldn't know.

My father has leaned forward with his elbows on his knees, eyes closed. When he opens them they seem set deeper into his head, like he is trying to shrink into himself, away from Phoebe's voice. He opens his mouth to speak, then closes it, then opens it again. "That's true," he tells the doctor, as if holding on to facts he can confirm. "We did that."

"Of course it's true," says Phoebe, exploding. "Why would I make it up?"

"You're angry," says the doctor.

"You're a genius," says Phoebe.

"Are you coming home?" I say. My words come out like a little bleat, and my father turns his calm, unhappy eyes on me.

"Sweetheart," he says, a word he hasn't used since I was very young. We all wait for him to say something else, but whatever he might have been about to say has left him. He reaches his hand over the space between us, palm up like he's feeling the weight of the air.

"Doctor," says Phoebe, bending at the waist and reaching into her purse. She pulls out her pocket New Testament. "Are you familiar with Ephesians five:twenty-two?"

"Hold on a second," says the doctor.

"Or Colossians three:eighteen?"

My father drops his head into his palms. I hate that he doesn't say anything. I wish that he had an idea he was trying to convince us of, or a new plan. Something so that I could tell him I got it, that I was willing, and he could tell me he knew the Lord was at work in me.

"David, are you okay?" says the doctor.

"Yes," says my father, speaking straight down into the floor. "Let her go on."

"Let me," Phoebe says. "Let me?"

Outside the long windows it still seems like daytime, but when Lilly cracks the door open to flip on the light switch, the windows turn black against the bright white room. She dims the lights with a dial and closes the door again.

"How about those verses, Charmaine?" says Phoebe. "Do I need to look them up?" Some of the air's going out of her, and her voice sounds weary.

"Do you know them?" The doctor's loose neck turns toward me, a soft rudder.

"Does she know them," Phoebe says.

"Wives, submit yourselves unto your own husbands," I mumble, "as unto the Lord."

"And they say *you've* been confused," Phoebe says to my father. "I'm the one who's been confused."

"Do you still pray?" I ask him. "Have you heard the voice of God?"

My father lifts his head but leaves his body bent forward. "I still pray."

"Without ceasing?"

"No," he says. "Not anymore."

"Charmaine brings up a good point, David," says the doctor. "About the voice of God. Do you want to try to explain? You don't have to. Not right now. Are you tired?"

I hold my breath and will Phoebe not to say anything, and she doesn't.

"Can you hear this?" the doctor asks her. "I really am concerned for you."

The anger has burned out of Phoebe now, and what's left is worse. She palms her brow and lifts, and the skin above her eyes stretches upward. Then she takes her hand away and everything settles sadly into place.

"You've heard a bit of this before," the doctor says. "The voice of God has been a pretty powerful idea in your home."

Phoebe nods tiredly. "I'm guessing you're not a believer."

"Does it matter?"

"It might," she says. "I don't know."

"Phoebe." It's the first time my father has said her name, and at the sound of it she tears up.

"Has he told you about how we met?" she asks the doctor. "How the still, small voice of God whispered in his ear and told him I was to be his wife?"

"This must be very difficult for you," the doctor says.

The tears are leaking out of Phoebe's eyes now.

"Don't cry," says my father.

"How about you?" the doctor says, turning to me.

But Phoebe is crying, and Phoebe has been mad. And if I

feel something, too, if this is as difficult for me as it is for her, then she and I will be having the feelings together at the same time, like we're the same person. Which means the only thing I feel is numb.

"She takes it in," my father says to the doctor. "All of it. I never saw it before. I'm sorry."

"You see more now," says the doctor.

I think my father's talking about Phoebe, who has begun weeping silently, but when I look up, his unhappy eyes are on me.

"Are you still a prophet?" I say.

We all wait for his answer.

"I don't know," he says finally. "I don't know who I am."

"That makes two of us," says Phoebe. "At least."

I want to tell my father that I know who he is. Or who I want to believe he is. I want to believe he's like the girl's father in *A Wrinkle in Time*, a hero on a mission that has gone off course. A father who just needs a little help finding his way home. In the book it's a matter of traveling through space and time to a planet where her brother and father are held captive by an evil, throbbing brain that loses its power only in the face of love. In real life that kind of travel is impossible, unless you're somewhere near a black hole, maybe, where space and time flatten out, but even that, even navigating time and space, still seems easier than helping my real-life father find his way back to himself so he can come home.

"I love you," I say, which is how the book girl defeats the evil brain, and my father appreciates the words, I can tell, but nothing else happens. The room stays white, Phoebe keeps crying, the doctor strokes his mustache, and my father, my father says again, to us all, that he's sorry.

When we stand up to leave, my father hugs me good-bye. His body is softer than it was, and he holds me gingerly, like the burned parts under his clothes might still hurt. "I hope you never have to feel like this," he says.

"Why should she?" Phoebe asks, wiping her eyes, stepping in between us. With her hands on my shoulders, she steers me toward the door. "Because it's hereditary, you mean? I, for one, am not borrowing trouble. She's half me too." Phoebe does not say good-bye. We wait for the doctor in the hallway, and when he joins us I listen to him tell Phoebe there are things she can do for herself to get through this tough time.

"You know what?" Phoebe says. "I think you've got enough on your plate right here, professionally, without worrying about me. And I've done a lot already. In fact, I think I've done just about the best I could, and look where it's landed us. But thanks for all your help." Doctor Phillips covers his mouth with his hand again. He holds Phoebe's gaze with his own kind eyes. "I can tell you don't think I mean it," Phoebe says, "but I do. I'm not being sarcastic anymore. I just wish we'd met you before we all became so ridiculous."

The word *ridiculous* hangs in the air all the way down the hall. Then my father comes out of the white room and ambles after us. I stop and wait. When he reaches the top of the curved staircase, he holds out a pair of suede moccasins like the ones he's wearing. They have been unevenly stitched together with heavy leather cording, and the foot bed is made of cream-colored fleece. I slip a hand into each of them, and when I look up to say thank you, my father's face is scarier than anything so far. He's smiling uncertainly at me, hopefully, as if I'm the person who could tell him what's supposed to happen next.

While Phoebe handles paperwork at the front desk, I take

off my tennis shoes and slip my feet into the moccasins. I try them out a little in the lobby.

"Don't go anywhere," says Phoebe, but I do. I head outside to wait for her under the porte-cochère. In the early dark, the air has a chill. I keep walking, telling myself I'll wait for her at the end of the long drive, at the edge of the two-lane country road that leads back to the interstate. But when I reach that point and she still hasn't come outside, I turn my back on the huge house and start walking on the shoulder of the road.

There's hardly any traffic. I can feel the rough gravel through the moccasins, but not sharply enough to hurt. Beside the road runs a ditch, and on the other side of the ditch stretches the split-rail fence, and beyond the fence, two large thoroughbreds stand close together, watching me. "Hey there," I say softly. I can tell they're listening, just like I can tell with Titus. I would like to cross the ditch and climb the fence and stand beside them, if they'd let me, between their solid, comforting bodies.

Somewhere far behind me, the Pinto sputters to life. Soon Phoebe pulls up and leans out the driver's side window. "What's the idea?" she says.

I keep walking and she inches the car forward. It was dark before, but now the Pinto's headlights make the sky darker. It feels as though there's nothing in between me and the huge empty spaces over the horse farms, all that air, the atmosphere, and then everything beyond that. I see myself walking on the surface of the globe, on the underside of it, maybe, and I remember that gravity depends on how dense matter is. It's not nearly as strong on the moon as it is on our planet, and not nearly as strong on our planet as, say, on the sun or in a black hole. If I knew how to rearrange matter, all I would have to do is lift my feet in the right way and fall into all that space.

"You want to walk a little?" Phoebe says. She breathes out in exasperation over the struggling engine. "Okay. Walk. Walk your heart out. For a little bit." She slows the Pinto down to a shuddering idle and drops back, so that I'm walking just outside the light of the low beams. I keep walking as if I'm trying to get away from the light, as if God himself has told me not to turn around for any reason, or I might turn to stone. Or salt. Poor Lot's wife, her home burning behind her. Maybe she looked back because she thought a frozen eternity, facing what used to be home, would be better than a future without it. Maybe God didn't even turn her to salt as a punishment. Maybe it was her tears that did the job, and God was just warning her that he was about to burn up everything in the world that meant more to her than him, and that watching would be too much for anyone to bear.

When I stop walking, when I do look back, the residential recovery mansion no longer shows up behind me. I cross the road in front of the Pinto and get in. Once on the interstate we ride in silence for several long minutes. Phoebe breathes hard, like she is trying not to start crying again, and her breath makes a little circle of steam on the windshield. When she speaks, though, she sounds matter-of-fact. "Your mother is a fool."

I let the words sit there and wait for more.

"Not for the reasons folks might think. Not because I believed my husband was a prophet or because I followed him as the head of my household, against my own better judgment. And that's plenty to make me a fool, you better believe it."

"You're not a fool," I say, because her voice is so flat I can't stand it.

"I'm a fool because I thought I was already completely worn out," she says. "I thought I was beyond feeling hurt." She turns to me, and even though her voice has been flat, her eyes are wretched. For the second time this evening I wish one of my parents wanted something from me. "Don't forget this," she says. "Be smarter." Then she laughs, a single chop of sound. "And if I knew how to tell you to do that, I would."

The rest of the drive home I'm looking out into the darkness beyond the twin cones of our headlights, thinking of all the fields and horses, then all the tobacco barns, everything that I know is there but can't see. And high above all that, in space, black holes are pulling everything, all kinds of matter, all kinds of light and energy, into themselves. They can't ever be filled up. You could stand at the edge of one and try as hard as you wanted to; you could throw in every single piece of matter you have, hoping just to hear something land. You could stand there until you wore yourself out, or until you got mad about all the stuff you'd let go of, missing it, or you could stand there listening so hard to the silence that you'd begin to imagine you were hearing things after all.

CHAPTER 14

I GET CALLED TO THE office again Wednesday, during activity, in the middle of Kelly-Lynn telling me that her mother has checked herself out of rehab, broken up with Rob, and is relocating them to Omaha. "She's big into starting over," Kelly-Lynn says. "Maybe in my next school I'll call myself Theresa, or Charmaine."

I'm picturing Kelly-Lynn making her way down the hall of a strange new school, pretty enough to turn heads, no one knowing one single thing about her. Except the school officials with their thick file. I don't even pay attention to what Coach Doran's saying at the mike until Kelly-Lynn says, "That's you."

I'm wondering if Principal Conrad changed his mind since yesterday and I'm in trouble after all, but the secretary just calls me "hon" and tells me I should go straight home after school instead of to the Custer Peake Memorial Retirement

Center. Because my grandmother's had another stroke. As the secretary speaks, the room loses focus for a second, then comes back with raw color. She's saying that her father had two strokes and didn't die until years later, and her brother just had his first stroke and is already back at work.

"I'll say a prayer," says the secretary, and what I think back at her is *Good luck,* and I don't even care anymore that it's a fool's game to be angry at God. It's clear now that nothing is going to be the way it was. Not for my father. Not for Phoebe and my father. Not for me. Now maybe not for Daze. None of which you're even supposed to pray for anyway, not really. Only for the holy state of reception. To God's voice, God's call, God's comfort. Which is where prayer without ceasing comes in, only too bad it's impossible. Unless there happens to be something wrong with your brain.

The rest of the school day goes on around me, and then it's over. "You in trouble?" says Tracy on the bus. "I heard them calling your name."

I think about not telling her, but I can't really imagine anything anyone says making me feel worse than I already do. "My grandmother had a stroke."

"She old?"

"Kind of," I say. "Not that old."

"She bad off?"

"I don't know," I say. "She had one before."

Ravenna's behind the wheel this afternoon, and the bus is orderly. Even Cecil Goode only smirks at us on the way to his seat. "There's always next time," he calls softly in my direction as we file out of the parking lot with the other buses. We ride quietly through the county, through all the spiky fields of harvested tobacco. Then through town, where we pass everything I've always known. The United Methodist Church, the Church of God. First Community, my old elementary school. We pass the tree streets that lead up to the scrubby field where the water tower stands high on its hill, the unlit cross a faint mark against the cloudy gray sky.

The leaves are starting to change color, but only if you look hard. My father once explained to me that the reason some maple trees turn red is that the sugar they use as food gets trapped in the leaves when the days get shorter. Other colors, the yellow and orange, have been in the leaves all along, only the chlorophyll from sunlight covers them up all summer and makes them look green. So in the fall some things get trapped, like in the red sugar leaves, and other things, things that were there all along, get revealed.

Beside me, Tracy is digging into the sole of her tennis shoe with a ballpoint pen.

"Are your parents divorced?" I ask her.

She doesn't look up. All the weight in her face pulls her cheeks down toward her lips into a troubled pout.

"Did you hear?" I say.

"I'm writing it," she says, nodding at her shoe. She's making some block letters, and I see an *N* and a *T,* and when she pulls back her hand and shows me, the sole of her shoe says *I DON'T KNOW.*

We stop at the gas station, but Tracy stays put. When we reach the bottom of the gorge and approach the cabin, she stands up like she's getting ready to let me by, but then, instead, she heads down the aisle in front of me. "Going home with Charmaine," she says to Ravenna.

"Behave, then," Ravenna says.

We wait there in the ditch while the bus pulls away.

"I always wanted to see the inside of this trailer-cabin," Tracy says.

I look at the cabin as if for the first time. From the outside it doesn't look big enough for two people. The log walls look rough and splintery.

"You gonna invite me or what?"

"Would you like to come in?" I say politely.

"Okay," she says, after a little pause, like she's responding to a real invitation she has to consider first.

I open the door and poke my head in first, hoping to find Titus curled up on the passenger seat, but he's not there. "I have a cat," I tell her, "but he hasn't been home in a while."

On the stoop, she cups her hands around her mouth and hollers, "KITTY, KITTY, KITTY," so loud that the palisades boom with it. "I'll keep my eye out," she offers. "You know how cats are."

From the doorway, the RV interior is narrow and dim. Our box of shoes sits under the dinette, and even with the window open over the sink, I can smell the stale combination of leather, rubber, and feet.

"It's just like I thought," Tracy says. "Everything you need right here. Your little-bitty sink and stove and fridge. Can I see the bathroom?" I point to the accordion door on the other side of the dinette, and she edges around the table, opens the bathroom door, and stretches it closed behind her. "Can I use this little-bitty commode?" she says, her voice muffled by the door.

"Sure." I flip the dinette up against the wall so she can see how it makes the middle space bigger. I push the box of shoes up against the wall, too.

"Look at that," she says about the dinette when she's finished in the bathroom. "I never saw that before. It's just like a regular trailer in here, only more solid. I bet you can even stay during a tornado. A flood'll be your problem," she says.

"We lost our dock the other night."

"Happens," Tracy says, peering into the cab. "What would get me is no TV." She sits down on the sofa and makes a face. "This where you sleep? Hard. What about your mom?" I point to the flat cubby above the driver and passenger seats, and she lets out a low whistle. "If I had to go to the bathroom in the night I would forget and raise up and hit my head. What's your mom's job again?"

"Substitute teacher."

"And your dad's the preacher."

"He writes stuff, mainly. What God tells him to. He did, I mean."

"Did your mom leave him to bring you down here? Or did he leave her?"

I weigh both possibilities and am horrified to feel my eyes beginning to burn. But Tracy doesn't seem to notice. It is a relief to have her here, filling up all the usual thinking places in my head with her voice.

"Them other people still in your house?"

I swallow and nod, and she goes on.

"I thought my parents were divorced because Momma said they were and Daddy was living over in Clay's Corner. But last year he came home, and she decided they were still married, and now he goes back and forth. He had a baby with his girl-friend. When he's here we all pretend we don't know, but he took me to see her once. My baby sister. Her name's Tabitha, like on that old show *Bewitched*?"

"It's in the Bible too. Tabitha."

"You read the whole Bible?"

"Almost."

"Well, without TV what else are you going to do?" Tracy looks around with approval. "I can see living like this some-day. But with TV. And a phone. Everything kept neat. All your shoes in a box like that. 'House Rules,'" she begins reading from the list on the refrigerator.

"That's nothing," I say, tearing it off and crumpling it.

"You got rules and everything," she says, nodding. "Keeps everybody in line. You got anything to eat?"

In the refrigerator is a Tupperware container of powdered milk that needs to be shaken up again and a carton of eggs that Phoebe's already hard-boiled so they won't go bad. Half a loaf of wheat bread. Two damp boxes of spinach on the freezer shelf.

"No, you don't," Tracy says, looking over my shoulder. "No chips or pop or nothing. Good thing I've got some smokes."

We climb down out of the trailer-cabin and cross the lawn to the slippery bank. It's only a little damp, still, and we make our feet flat, then lower ourselves to sit halfway down, lean-ing our backs into the slope. The river is still brown from all the rain, and there's a whiff of skunk in the air. Tracy reaches into her tight jeans pocket and pulls out a narrow plastic case shaped to hold two tampons.

"Your dad didn't have a baby with someone else, did he?" she says, tapping out a cigarette instead of a tampon.

"No," I say, watching the water. It's moving, but unless there's a branch or leaf on top, it's so smooth today you can't tell.

"Then maybe he'll come back. You never know. 'Nothing's over till it's over' is what Momma has to say about it. 'Till the fat lady sings.'" Tracy parks the cigarette in the corner of her mouth, reaches into her jeans again, and extracts a pocketknife. She turns her head toward me, cheek resting on the ground. "You got cousins?"

"No."

"None? And no sisters or brothers either. That you know of. All right then." She flips open the tiny blade, gets to her feet, and stagger-steps down to the river, where she leans over and dips the knife in the current. Then she hikes back up the bank and sits cross-legged beside me. I sit up, too.

"You know what blood sisters are, right? You just give yourself a little cut on your finger." Tracy holds up her finger. "Then the other person does it. Then you take your fingers"—she parks the cigarette again and uses both hands to show me—"and mash 'em together. You bleed into each other, see? So then my blood is in your blood, and yours is in mine. And once blood's inside you, it keeps making more blood, so then we're blood kin." She holds the knife out to me, and I test the blade against the tip of my index finger. "If we're blood kin, we'll be sisters forever and have to help each other out, and you don't have any real sisters. You need more people, that's all. What if your parents get divorced? What if your granny dies on you?"

I think about Daze maybe dying and press harder, then I bear down on the knife's tip right into the soft part of my finger until a pearl of blood appears. "Here," Tracy says. She takes the knife back and presses the tip into her finger, too. "Squeeze it," she says, and we both do, blood blooming into the whorl

of our fingerprints. It's thinner than I expected. "Now here."
She holds up her finger, I hold up mine, and we press them
together. "That'll do it," she says, as we separate them again.
There's a warmth in me now, spreading out from my hand,
like our blood really could be mingling.

"Thanks," I say.

Tracy sucks her finger. "If we're going to be kin," she says,
"you got to keep that fool grin off your face."

We're still sitting there watching the river when the Pinto pulls
in, and Phoebe honks for me. I tell Tracy I have to go, and she
tells me to suit myself and taps out another cigarette.

"Who's that?" says Phoebe, as we back out of the driveway.

"A girl who stopped by," I say. "From the bus."

"I don't like you having people over when I'm not home,"
Phoebe says. "But at least you stayed outside."

"Her name's Tracy," I say. I slip my blood-kin finger into my
mouth, and there's the metal taste mixed in with salt.

Phoebe swats my hand away from my face. "They brought
your grandmother back from the hospital and moved her into
special care again. I snuck away during planning period this
afternoon to check on her. She's alert at least. She knew me."

"Which brain half was it in?" I ask, thinking of my father's
printout. "Hemisphere, I mean."

"What? I don't know." Phoebe shakes her head. She has not
trimmed her hair in weeks, and the long bob swings under her
chin. "Left, I think. It's her right side that's wonky. And her
speech."

At the Custer Peake Memorial Retirement Center, Phoebe
stops by Daze's apartment and sends me on up to special

care on the third floor. I find Daze in a hospital bed, her soft white hair around her shoulders. I've never seen her hair down before, even when I've spent the night with her. Even during the first stroke. She's rubbing one pale hand with gardenia lotion, a flower that smells sweet and sad at the same time.

"Daze," I say, and throw myself on her chest to give her a hug. She pats me on the back.

"Phoebe," she says, then I draw back and look at her.

"Charmaine," I say, laying a hand flat on my chest. She tilts her head to the right, like it's heavy. The right side of her mouth droops.

"Phoebe," she says again, narrowing her eyes with concentration. "No."

"It's okay," I say. "How are you feeling?"

"Figh."

"Can you walk?"

"No."

"Can you write?"

She looks at her right hand as if she could ask it. Then she reaches out with her left hand and grasps mine, making a bundle of my fingers with a strength that takes my breath. A noise comes from her throat that sounds like "Sorry." She is clutching my hand so hard that the tips of my fingers turn purple. There are tears in her open eyes, and I feel them in the back of my own throat. I have never seen Daze cry before. She looks trapped inside her body, and I think of the woman in the picture, the body split open, like the person inside has escaped her sinful, limited flesh. Or maybe it's the opposite. Maybe she's been torn from her body, separated forever from touching other bodies with it, which maybe was her only real comfort.

Maybe the body, like Mrs. Teaderman said about the unconscious, is both prism and prison at the same time. I squeeze
Daze's fingers back as hard as I can.

Paulette, a nurse Daze likes, pulls back the curtain and sticks
her head in. "How's my favorite patient?"

Daze moves the side of her mouth, but this time nothing
comes out.

"She's been asking after you," Paulette says to me. "I can
understand her just fine." She grabs Daze's foot. "Can't I, hon?
We start on physical therapy first thing in the morning. Don't
we, hon?"

Daze does something with her left eye, a fluttering.

"That's your grandmother trying to make a face," Paulette
says. "Physical therapy's not her favorite. Now kiss her good-
bye so you don't tire her out." I do and I feel it all. Her damp,
soft skin and the hard bone of skull just beneath it. Underneath the skull, her tired brain.

Phoebe's waiting in a chair in the hallway. "How's she looking?" she asks me. "She didn't look so hot earlier."

I think about the sunken side of Daze's face, but also about
the way her silky hair fell around her neck and shoulders, white
as the halo of a planet. "Her hair was down," I say. "It looked
soft."

"Then she's still out of commission. Ever seen your grandmother's hair any way but skinned back from her face?"

We find Daze's Buick in the parking lot out front. In the car,
Phoebe flips on the wipers, pushing a mess of wet leaves to the
left and right.

"Does Daze know you're driving her car?"

"It's only until we figure out what's wrong with the Pinto,"
says Phoebe. "Once and for all."

We pull out onto the county road, only in the direction of Clay's Corner instead of the river. "I was thinking McDonald's tonight," Phoebe says. "We eat in that same little space all the time. It's getting to me." She reaches under her legs and adjusts the seat forward to her shorter legs. "I've spoken to your father. He feels responsible. It's all been kind of a blow to Daze. His mental health. Your grandmother believed God was speaking to him, you know. For years."

"Everyone believed it."

"Not everyone," Phoebe says.

"You believed it," I say.

Phoebe sighs and puts the car in reverse. "Maybe you should think about being a lawyer someday. You like making a point. I did believe it, obviously. But now I feel kind of relieved. It was a big pill to swallow and a lot to keep up with." As she speaks, she is trying to pull the Buick out onto the highway. "Am I good?" she says, and even though I don't want to, I check for her.

"You're good," I say. I feel myself speaking, breathing, through a tight throat. "Do you even love him anymore?" I ask, and the words sound as squeezed as they feel. I can't shake the impression that Phoebe is weighing her options.

"Your father and I committed to each other before God," she says, "which is not to be taken lightly. Modern times or no. 'Cleave,' it says in the Bible. Do you understand the meaning of that word?"

"What about Doctor Osborne?"

Phoebe sighs. "Once and for all, Charmaine, I am not entertaining suitors. Doctor Osborne is a nice person who takes an interest in people. The way he's helping out with Seth, too, with Mister Catterson on the road. Boys need their fathers."

"Girls need their fathers, too."

"Girls need their mothers more," Phoebe says. "One of these days you're going to figure that out."

The words hit me like a warning, and I turn my face toward the window. Outside, the colors of the sky are crashing into themselves, bright pink and orange layers of cloud lit from underneath by the low sun. I have never set foot outside Kentucky, and I don't understand yet that this is a unique trick of latitude and landscape, that our evening skies hold their place among the world's most breathtaking. If you'd asked me, I would have said the sky was probably like that everywhere. I would have told you that's just the way the sky was.

Phoebe's poking around on the armrest in the door. Everything on the Buick is electronic. "Where's the window button?" she says, then, "I can't believe we're driving all the way to Clay's Corner for McDonald's, which we can't even afford. I must be out of my gourd. Look. I believe the man should be the head of the home, like Christ is the head of the church, like it says in Ephesians. But when something goes wrong with the head, I mean the head of the church or your father's head, then all of a sudden you're looking back over your life, wondering how long you've been talking yourself into things. Know who I'd like to run a few things by?"

She waits until I say "Who?"

"The late, great Custer Peake, that's who. All your father ever heard growing up was Custer Peake this, Custer Peake that. Tried seminary, but your father? Not exactly built for standing up in front of people. Not going to be Billy Graham and son, not going to bring back the Great Revival." She moves her hands from the bottom of the steering wheel to the top and frowns. "The Great Revival," she says again. "Can you believe it didn't even cross my mind to pray for myself and see whether or not the Lord was calling me to get married? I was Phoebe Savage. And I gave it up like it was nothing. All because I'd been chosen by the only son of the great Custer Peake."

We're pulling into the McDonald's parking lot. Kelly-Lynn says this is where the high school kids hang out on weekend nights, orbiting the building along the drive-thru path, adding alcohol to their Cokes. At the counter, Phoebe orders two plain hamburgers and one small fries. She informs the girl behind the register, who couldn't care less, that we will both be drinking water.

"I'll be hungry," I say, without any hope. She reminds me, as I knew she would, of the half-dozen hard-boiled eggs in our minifridge. If I'm still hungry when we get home, I can enjoy one of them.

"Maybe I'll get a job at McDonald's," I say as we sit down. "I could bring home dinner."

"If you're looking for something to do, you can learn to plan our meals at home. Now that it looks like we could be there indefinitely."

The word *indefinitely* batters at my ear. Five short syllables. Like a woodpecker. Over so fast I might have imagined the sound.

"Because here's what we need to talk about. Your father has decided to move into a halfway house in Lexington, when the time comes. Do you know what a halfway house is?"

It could not possibly be other than the obvious. A place for people who are ready to leave a hospital but not ready to come home. Or who are not ever coming home and need time to make other plans. A place for people caught between what their lives used to be and what their lives might become. "Until when?"

"Until I don't know. Indefinitely, I said. Your father is either not himself right now, or he's more himself than he's been in a long time. Either way, he's not the person we've been living with. It might be very difficult, even if he did come home."

"But you said he was hard to live with before," I say, "so if he's not that person anymore, isn't that a good thing? You complained about everything, and now everything you complained about is gone."

"Don't talk with your mouth full."

"You're just letting this happen," I say. "You didn't even put on lipstick last night. You got mad. You cried. Why would he even want to come home?"

"You think it's that easy? You think all it takes is lipstick? Why don't you make him want to come home, yourself? What kind of man has a child, a precious little daughter, and then doesn't come home to her as soon as he possibly can?"

I swallow hard and feel the bite of burger go all the way down. In the plate-glass window, Phoebe and I are two unhappy people, talking, mirrored back to each other against the fading daylight. Out of nowhere, the prayer comes back. *Inhabit me, O Lord God.* I don't try to stop it, but I don't try to keep it going, either.

"I mean, seriously, Charmaine. I'm not saying he can help it, I'm just saying don't blame me. If anyone's giving up, here, it's your father."

I shake my head so violently it's like something up there comes undone and shifts around. I feel dizzy.

"Think about Titus, Charmaine. Think what if you were out somewhere with him, downtown in some city, and someone asked you to set him down on the sidewalk and just walk away."

I do think of Titus as she says this. I think of how he likes for me to pick him up and sink my hand into his fat belly and how afraid I am that he is dead and how much I wish he would come back. If someone asked me to leave Titus on the sidewalk somewhere there is no way I would ever, ever do that. But then I remember Tracy's dog, Corky, and how mean he is, snarling and biting hard enough to hurt. "I wouldn't leave Titus on the sidewalk," I say, "but I might leave Corky."

"Who?"

"No one would leave Titus anywhere. He's a good kitty."

"Yes, they would," Phoebe says, "and that is the point. If they weren't well. It's not about the cat. If it's a good cat or not. This has nothing to do with you. Believe it or not, the world doesn't revolve around you. Truth be told? It has nothing to do with me either."

But I'm studying Phoebe's face, the way her chapped, bare lips form around each word. The way they close over a bite of hamburger, containing it while she chews. I've never watched anyone eat this closely before, not even her, though it is something I must have been seeing for years. Suddenly the way the shapes of the food move around under her cheek looks grotesque. And after she swallows I can see her tongue running across her teeth, just behind her lips, seeking any remaining food. One of her eyes is smaller than the other, too, just a little, and it seems awful the way she eats only an inch of one French fry at a time, dipping each next segment into the soft mound of ketchup. The yellow overhead light makes her skin look like raw chicken. Now she is reaching out to tap my shoulder.

"What?" I say.

"Are you okay? I just asked you if you were okay."

"Fine." But I am not okay. I understand now that Phoebe is less appealing than any other person in the universe, and that I am just like her, or at least fully one-half of me is just like her. And all the times I want to get away from her, her hands, her feelings, my father must feel the same way, and he must feel that way about me too, or at least one-half of me. And now I think that if my father really has been crazy, then maybe it's been because of Phoebe and me, because of how unbearable the two of us are, and if he isn't coming home, it is because how unbearable we are is even more obvious now that he's thinking straight.

"Why are you looking at me like that?" Phoebe asks as I put down the remaining half of my hamburger. "You better eat some of these fries before I polish them off."

"I'm not hungry."

"I knew it," Phoebe says, pulling my food toward her. I watch it go. "And you thought we needed to order more."

CHAPTER 15

ON FRIDAY, IN ENGLISH, a pale, twitching girl gives a how-to speech on selecting the proper pet based on your home situation. Dogs need a stay-at-home mom just like toddlers do. And a yard. Raise your hand if you have a dog. Cats are a good choice if your parents are busy or if you live in an apartment. And they're usually softer too. Raise your hand if you have a cat. I raise my hand and try to believe that Titus is alive, picking his way through the scrub around the river, surviving on rodents and birds. And then I'm wondering about the halfway house my father will go to, whether or not the people who live there are allowed to have their own pets, or if there's one pet that everyone shares, and what the best kind of pet for that home situation might be.

When the girl is finished, Mrs. Teaderman calls my name.

"What?" I say, and the class laughs like I'm making a joke.

But Mrs. Teaderman gives me a troubled look, and I remember that today is the day of my extension. Then she is calling on me to stand up in front and deliver a how-to speech that I have not written or even thought about at all, since visiting my father kicked off the beginning of this horrible week.

"We're waiting, Miss Peake," says Mrs. Teaderman in a frosty voice. "We were also waiting on Monday, and we are unprepared to wait any longer."

Next to me, Kelly-Lynn gives me her alarmed face, which is just a barely perceptible widening of the eyes.

"You have two choices," says Mrs. Teaderman. "You may stand in front of the class and talk about something you know how to do and receive at least partial credit for this assignment, or you may remain in your seat and accept a zero."

My face feels hot, like it might be swelling, but I get to my feet.

"I thought so," says Mrs. Teaderman, a woman who seems to have lost all patience for me since I elected not to confide in her. And since I stopped finishing my homework. And, this week, even participating in freewriting.

I make my way up the row of desks and stand in front of the demonstration table.

"Do you have any props for us?" Mrs. Teaderman asks, and when I shake my head she says, "No props," as if she expected as much.

The faces of all the kids in class turn from Mrs. Teaderman to me in one motion, sunflowers following the light. I'm waiting, though I'm not sure for what.

"My speech," I begin, but the words sound feeble. "My speech is about," I say, too loud. I let my head fall back and scan the ceiling like there might be a good topic written there.

And then it comes to me. I blink a few times, for courage, and lower my head until I can see the whole class, and I pretend-look at each of them the way Conley does in the Upper Room. "How to pray," I say.

Someone at the back of the room titters. A boy at the front says, "Dear God, amen," and then the rest of the class cracks up.

"Quiet," says Mrs. Teaderman.

The clock over the door says ten minutes to two. How-to speeches have to last from between five and seven minutes.

"'Dear God, amen' is what a lot of people think when they think about prayer," I start off when the laughing dies down. "It's the start and the finish. And you can put whatever you want in between. If you have a grandmother who's sick, you can pray that she gets better; if your dad needs a job, you can pray he finds one. If you're worried about getting fat"—here I glance over at Kelly-Lynn, listening with her best detached expression—"you can ask him to help you not eat. But if you do that, if you ask for something specific, you have to take the answer you get. Maybe your dad's going to start writing bad checks instead of getting a job. Maybe your grandmother's going to die."

Over the door, the clock says nine minutes before two.

"There's no way a five-to-seven-minute speech could cover everything you could pray about," I say to the class.

"Topic selection is an important part of the speech-making process," says Mrs. Teaderman.

"Okay," I say. "That's one way to pray, the way a lot of people do it. But you don't have to pray like that. Just like you don't really have to close your eyes." I close my eyes, point to them, then open them again and check the clock. "Or get down on your knees." I drop to my knees, and while I'm down there, I press my palms together. "Or make praying hands."

"This is a 'how-not-to' speech," says a boy in the front row. Kevin something.

I get back to my feet. The clock hands haven't moved. I take a deep breath. "Another way to pray," I say, "a better way, is to keep yourself doing it all the time. Even when you're doing other things. My dad taught me. It's from the New Testament, and it's called 'prayer without ceasing.'" Two of the girls who sit by the wall are smirking at each other. In the second row, another girl's mouth hangs open, like she's trying to breathe through allergies. Kelly-Lynn has lifted one skeptical eyebrow. I haven't told anyone about prayer without ceasing. It has seemed like a secret tie to my father, a rope strung between us, only he's dropped his end.

The clock reads seven minutes before two.

"So here's what you do," I say. "First you breathe in as far as you can." I stop and breathe in and then let it out quietly, so it will seem like I haven't let it out yet. "So when you breathe in, you think in your head, *Inhabit me.*" The word *inhabit* does a number on the smirking girls, who break out in giggles.

"Girls," says Mrs. Teaderman. "I'm sorry, Charmaine, but would you mind repeating that?"

"You breathe in and think, *Inhabit me.* But it doesn't have to be that. You can make up your own words, as long as they're the same every time. Then you breathe out and think, *O Lord God.*"

In the front row, Kevin takes several ragged breaths in and out and tries to speak while breathing. "Inhabit me. Inhabit me!"

Kelly-Lynn has arranged her face in its finest blankness, as if she is present in body only, but her real life, her exciting one, is happening somewhere else far away.

The speech has gone on more than five minutes now, and I figure we've all had enough. I move a few steps toward my seat before Mrs. Teaderman says, "I think we're ready for your conclusion."

I turn back to the class. I explain as quickly as I can that if they practice saying those phrases to themselves at the same time they breathe, pretty soon the words will go through their heads automatically, even if they're not thinking them on purpose. I say it like it's as easy as that. As wanting to. "And in conclusion," I say, "that means you're praying without ceasing" — *thatmeansyou'reprayingwithoutceasing.*

"And so?" asks Mrs. Teaderman from somewhere behind me. "Can you bring us to the final result?"

If there's a difference between the conclusion and the final result, I don't remember it, but I keep talking. "The final result is an attitude of reception," I say. "Which means you're always ready for the Lord to draw near."

"And then?" says Mrs. Teaderman.

"And then, I don't know." I check the ceiling again and then I *do* know. When I look back at the class this time, I meet everybody's eyes, one by one, no pretending. "If he's near, he can show you things," I say. "Things you want to understand, like if you have a calling. But if he's near, he's also going to know — even if you've been careful not to ask for anything in particular — what's more important to you than he is. And if something's more important to you than he is, then you are not a person after his own heart. And if you're not a person after his own heart, when you screw up you're going to feel his justice, which you deserve, instead of his mercy, which you don't." I am surprised to find myself pointing out at the class, just like my grandfather points in the famous revival picture.

"Well, okay," says Mrs. Teaderman in a wrapping-things-up voice. But I'm not finished.

"Because you're going to screw up," I say. "No matter how hard you try to follow the Bible, to pray without ceasing, or whatever, you're never going to get it all the way right. Not even with the New Testament, which is supposed to show you how to live once and for all. Like a how-to speech. But the New Testament is pretty much the worst how-to speech in the world. If the New Testament tried to tell you how to make a sandwich, then your sandwich would never, ever turn out. And when you end up with what you deserve, when God starts taking things away, the Holy Ghost is supposed to be the comforter." I find the pet-speech girl in the second row, looking confused. "Pets are a lot better," I tell her. "A lot more comforting."

The class is silent. The pet-speech girl nods vigorously, and the girl next to her with the open allergy mouth looks stunned. Mrs. Teaderman brings the fingertips of both hands to her temples, as though her head aches.

"Any successful speech," she says, speaking with her eyes closed, "is followed by a Q and A." In the first row, Kevin is already waving his hand. Mrs. Teaderman opens her eyes. "Kevin, make this appropriate."

"Are you a Jesus freak?" is Kevin's question. It's actually a question everyone in the Youth Group has been prepared for by Pastor Chick, a question everyone in East Winder, probably, has been preparing for since birth. A "Did you know him?" kind of question like the one posed to Peter after Golgotha. We're supposed to offer a proud "yes" and give thanks for the opportunity to take a stand. But I just take a deep breath and hold it as a clean, cold wave of godlessness rushes through me.

"No," I say finally. "Not anymore." I listen hard in case a cock starts crowing somewhere, but there's just Mrs. Teaderman saying, "Enough," to Kevin, who has raised his hand again, and "Thank you, Charmaine," to me.

"You're crazy," Kelly-Lynn says when I get to my seat. But she's smiling with half her mouth, like she can't help herself. The class is still whispering about my speech while Kevin is walking to the front for his turn. But all he does is imitate Mrs. Teaderman's peanut-butter-sandwich example with grilled cheese, and all he's brought in is a couple of slices of bread from the cafeteria, and he's so nervous that he drops his one prop on the floor, and everyone laughs at him, too. By the time he's finished, the class has forgotten all about my prayer speech, except Mrs. Teaderman, who hands me the grading sheet as I file out the door. The speech counts for a quarter of my grade for the term, and when I unfold the paper in the hallway, it has a big A- in red at the top.

I always thought that godlessness would feel like being trapped in a huge, hopeless sore throat, filled with the ache of despair, with sides too steep and slippery to climb out of. Instead it's a sharp, clean opening, like a crevasse in rock, an emptiness where all the effort used to be. The feeling has a nervous edge, and I catch myself laughing out loud about nothing I can name as I walk to the bus.

Anything, it seems, can be said. On the bus, when Cecil Goode shuffles past Tracy and me and tells me it's my lucky day, I say, "Sure it is," just to let him know I don't believe he means it.

Tracy jabs me with her elbow as Cecil stops behind our seat. "You asking for it?" His delivery is careful, right down the straight, strong line of his nose.

"Move on by, Cecil," Tracy says. "You nuts?" she says to me, blue eyes wide.

"He's full of talk." I've never in my life said someone was full of talk.

Behind us, Cecil heaves himself into his seat.

"What?" says Tracy under her breath. "You want to, now?"

I shrug. The part of me that has feared what might happen feels defiant. And then there's the part of me that thinks about it sometimes, when I have to cross my legs until my blood feels like static electricity. This, I realize with a tiny shock, must be lust. The girl version.

The sky looks gray and heavy, and as we make our way through the county toward East Winder, a few drops of rain splatter the dirty window near my face. Even with the sub driving, the bus stays quiet, like we're all breathing in the same thick air that could put us to sleep. When we hit Main Street, Tracy points past me to the orange brick of First Community. The marquee reads MAIN EVENT: FRIDAY NIGHT, SCAVENGER HUNT AND YOUTH LOCK-IN in its bowed-out tin letters.

"I'm coming to that thing," she says, "where we go around and ask people for stuff."

I have almost forgotten about Operation Outreach, which seems to be moving right along without my prayer to prop it up. Without my father's vision too, probably.

"A church party in East Winder," she says. "God's own Holy Land." Then quietly, still looking past me, she says, "I know where your dad's at. My mom heard it. I had a aunt that went crazy. Started off eating chalk and ended up chewing off her fingernails in Eastern State."

I consider saying he's not crazy, then I think, *What difference does it make?* I explain about the chemical imbalance in his brain, how they're fixing it with medicine. But who's to say that chemical imbalance and crazy aren't the same thing? What if chemical imbalance is actually what crazy means?

"When's he coming home?" she says.

"He's not," I say. "He's going someplace else." Even in the sluggish bus air, my voice sounds clean, like a thin, clear transmission from some other world, where you say anything you want and just ride cleanly above all the words. "He thought he wasn't crazy his whole life, but now he thinks he was, and so that makes everything he did before maybe crazy, so he's not doing anything he did before. Like live with us."

"That's a man for you," Tracy says, nodding. "Crazy or no. That's how they do."

Which is one way of looking at it. But if my father were like other men, then he would have gotten someone pregnant, like Tracy's dad did, or he'd have had a midlife crisis and gone bankrupt, like Kelly-Lynn's dad. Or gone to jail like Theresa's dad. Or even just gone from not crazy to crazy, because what I never heard of was anyone moving the other direction, coming back from crazy that you didn't even know was crazy at the time and turning everything upside down by being normal.

Tracy studies my face. "You get to stay in the trailer-cabin, then," she says finally. "You get to keep riding this bus."

"I guess I do."

It's raining heavily now. The wettest September in recent history, everyone says. We've passed the elementary school and the water tower and crested the hill on the way out of town, and now we're driving through spongy, depressed-looking fields as far as you can see. A wet brown leaf blows against the window and sticks there. Not a maple leaf with a pretty pattern, but a plain old oval-shaped leaf, and I study its veins and I listen to the bus tires hiss and then I realize that Cecil Goode hasn't said anything more the whole ride home, not to me or any other girl, about sitting on his lap. I peek back at him, and he's staring out at the wet fields, too.

Then we're at his stop, and the sub is bending over to fix the ramp. Before Cecil is halfway down the aisle, I'm on my feet and pushing past Tracy.

"Where you going?" she says, moving her legs for me to get by, but I don't answer.

"You get off here?" the sub asks when I reach the front, and I mumble that I have to see my granny, and he doesn't know any better. I scoot on down the wet, raw plywood ramp after Cecil Goode and stand there in the mud, rain pelting my head while the bus lurches into gear and pulls away. Cecil stops and pivots slowly on the shorter of his short legs.

"You lost?"

I look away across the road at four buildings I've only seen as we drive past. The two mobile homes and two outbuildings. There's a big propane tank in the yard, a light blue bullet speckled with rust.

"You following me?"

I hear him, but the clean feeling gives me the sense that I've stepped out of time again, like I'm observing myself from a long way off, from the future, maybe. "Which one do you live in?" I ask.

He jerks his head toward the smaller mobile home, the one parked right up against the hillside underneath where the limestone starts to go bald, the one that looks like it's been spray-painted brown. The only car in the yard is an old station wagon up on cinder blocks. But Cecil doesn't cross the road toward the trailer. Instead, he turns toward the river side of the road, where there aren't any buildings for half a mile either way.

As I follow him, the rain begins to let up. This high, we can hear the bus whining down through the switchbacks below, and farther below that, the river rushing swift and brown on the floor of the gorge. Then those sounds disappear under the big sound of a train, so close up here that it ricochets right through my body. Soon it edges out onto the bridge.

Cecil's gait is slow enough over the grass that I could easily catch up with him, but I keep myself back a ways. He takes a big stride on his longer leg and then kind of swings the other one up with it. I think how his whole life is like this, every movement something he has to try to do. He disappears with a dip in the land, and when I get to the drop-off, he's sitting on a large overturned tree underneath another tree, and he's using the metal claw to fish out his cigarette pack from his shirt pocket.

He bends his head to the pack and finds the end of a cigarette with his lips. "There's a lighter in my jeans," he says. "Make yourself useful." And I can just hear his voice, underneath the heavy sound of the train, soft and purposeful as a touch.

I move closer and look down into his hair, which is darker where it's damp. There's a fine copper stubble on his jaw. A "ginger," Daze would call him. He smells like cigarettes already, but also like my father, which means, I think, that they use the same shaving cream or soap.

I have never touched a boy's pants before when a boy is in them. The stitching around the pocket feels stiff and familiar, just like the stitching on my own jeans. I find the lighter with my thumb and forefinger and extract it. It's beat-up metal, not plastic, with a gold-and-black star labeled u.s. ARMY.

"No hurry," Cecil Goode says, and then I abuse my thumb against the lever until it catches, and I hold the tiny flame to the end of his cigarette, hoping I'm doing it right. He inhales deeply, watches the train for a moment, exhales, then turns back to me. "You want one?" he says, the cigarette moving up and down.

"No, thanks."

"What'd you get off the bus for, then?"

I have expected him to know, somehow, from his insinuations, and now I peer down uncertainly at the river. There are a lot of things I could say to him that would be true.

"You always say it's my day, and then nothing happens," I say, "and you should stop saying it or do something about it. I can take it. I can take what's coming."

"Girl, what are you yammering about?" he says. Like he hasn't been warning me for weeks.

"And also, God laid you on my heart one time."

"He what?"

"Charmaine," I say. "My name's Charmaine."

"I don't care what your name is," he says. Then he laughs and blows smoke out of the corner of his mouth. "You wanna sit on Cecil's lap like the big girls do?" For the first time I can remember, he smiles. He has very straight, very white teeth.

So white and straight they might not be real. Everything about his face and head is square, like magazine pictures of men.

"You're handsome," I say, before I can stop myself.

Cecil Goode throws back his head and laughs again. "You sound like my granny," he says. "You're handsome," he mimics in an old-lady voice. He's not being mean, though. The ash on his cigarette is about an inch long now and creeping toward his mouth, and he leans forward and clicks something with his tongue and the ash falls to the wet grass. "What?" he says. "Don't tell me you want to be my girl."

I shake my head. I could not in a million years explain what it is that I want from this boy, only that it holds me here. His eyes are the lightest brown. Yellow almost. Golden. They call him "Child of God," but he might be an angel. The big male biblical kind. An archangel like Michael. Or Gabriel.

"You could show me your tits," he says. "I wouldn't mind that."

The suggestion sends a sweet, scary throb through my body. Below my womanhood, down my legs. I glance again toward the road, but we're over the knoll and out of sight. When I turn back to him, he's frowning. "What," he says. "You after this?" He ducks his head toward where his right sleeve is always tied in a knot. "How about you see what's under the sleeve if you show me your tits?"

If anyone had asked me what was underneath the tied sleeve, I would have guessed "a stump." Like the smooth, short thigh of Lt. Col. Evans at the Custer Peake Memorial Retirement Center. Now I'm not sure.

"Does it hurt?"

"What—this?" He nods again toward the sleeve. "Ain't nothing but a thing."

"What happened?"

"What's it to you?"

I give him a careful shrug. High above, the end of the train disappears into the trees on top of the opposite cliff. Then the sound disappears, too.

"I just come out this way," he says finally. "Like them pill babies but without the pills. Me, I'm just lucky." He sighs and spits the cigarette from his mouth. "That stuff on the bus? Just messing with you. You don't have to do nothing. You're just a kid."

"I'm thirteen."

"Like I said."

"I'll show you," I say, and as I say it, I know that this is it. This is what I want. This feeling that's so wonderful and so wrong at the same time that if you're not married, you're supposed to do whatever you have to to make it go away. Like look at split-open women. And I can picture her right now, but the picture doesn't make anything go away at all. It just opens the door to a sadness that's already there anyway, right alongside the rest.

"All right, then, show me," Cecil says, as if it's all the same to him. "But first light me another smoke."

I slide a cigarette out from his pack and place it between his lips. This time I manage the lighter a little better. As I'm unzipping my sweatshirt, the branches above me move a little in the wind, and water from the leaves douses my head and shoulders. Cecil ducks to keep his cigarette from going out, and when he raises his head, I'm ready. I peel up my shirt, and when I get to my bra, I hook my fingers under the bottom and peel that up, too, because I don't want him to see how tight it is, how the frayed material won't even clean up white anymore. My breasts are still painfully swollen, heavy as gourds. There's a raw, red groove beneath them from the bra's elastic band.

Cecil takes a long look. "You got tits, all right."

The breeze picks up, and this time when the water shatters down from the leaves it feels gentle on my hot skin. My nipples get tight.

"Hey-hey," Cecil says.

It begins to rain again, lightly. I don't know if I should be watching him watch me, so I watch the river instead. Even this high I can see the rain pocking its surface. After a few seconds I carefully lower my bra and shirt.

"Anything of mine you want to see?" asks Cecil. He's closer in under the tree than I am, and it's catching most of the shower. I step toward him, and he nods at his tied right sleeve, then at his crotch. I'm standing near enough now that I can feel his breath, which starts warm, then evaporates into the rest of the cool, wet air. Then we're so close that neither of us can see anything but each other's eyes, and his are more and more golden, like they're lit from inside, the closer you get. For a moment I am full of him and he is full of me. Which is how I always imagined it might feel to be, for once, inhabited by God.

Then my hand is moving toward his jeans, and I'm thinking, *That's my hand, and this is me doing this,* and when I touch him all I can think again is how his jeans feel, like something I already know. Underneath them his penis feels solid. It might be pushing back against me. I'm moving my other hand up to his right shoulder, over the tied sleeve, when a car approaches and slows down.

Cecil lifts his head, listening. "I got to get up," he says.

Car wheels crunch on the gravel across the road, next to where he lives, and I'm about to move my hands, help him up maybe, when he says, "Get your hands off me," in a disgusted way that makes me feel suddenly, horribly alone.

"Wait," I say. I keep both hands where they are.

He hits my arm with the claw, then opens it and tries to pinch me, but I just take my hand from his crotch and grab the claw's metal stem. I can't believe how easy it is. With one hand on his shoulder and the other on the claw, I'm holding him down, and I don't even realize it until he says, "Bitch." Then I can feel the way he's straining to get up. He can't get leverage from his legs, though, and he's at the wrong angle to get any strength from his torso. I'm standing over him. The slightest pressure keeps him right where he is. "Let me up," he says.

I just want him to look at me again, and he does, but it's hate now, all mixed in with the way we both know I'm keeping him down. I see it, whether I want to or not, and I keep on seeing it as I hold him there another long moment. When I let go, all the clean godless feeling is gone. My insides fill up with black vomit, and I clap my hands over my mouth.

As he struggles to get himself up from the fallen tree, he doesn't look at me, and I know better than to help. "I didn't mean to," I whisper into my hands, and I wish it were true, but it's not. A car door slams, and Cecil starts his labored way up the hill without looking back.

CHAPTER 16

THE NEXT DAY IS Saturday, the day of the Main Event. The weather, cloudy but dry, cooperates. We stop to pick up Tracy, and Phoebe peppers her with questions the whole way into town.

"How long have you lived on the river road, Tracy? Where do you and your parents go to church, Tracy? What are your favorite subjects in school, Tracy? How many brothers and sisters do you have, Tracy?"

And Tracy, sitting behind me in the back seat of the Buick, answers them all like a movie star in the spotlight. She tells Phoebe about her mother and her granny and her older sister with a baby.

"Where do your sister and her husband live, Tracy?"

"She doesn't have a husband," Tracy says.

"It's not an inquisition," I say.

"I'm just trying to get to know your friend, Charmaine. Tracy, Charmaine may have told you that I am a substitute teacher. And as such, I have become fascinated by the way children choose playmates."

"Children?" I say. "Playmates?"

"It's hard to say anything right around Charmaine," says Phoebe. "I am forever using the wrong words."

"My mother says, one single working woman to another, her hat's off to you," says Tracy.

Phoebe frowns sideways at me. "Single?"

"I mean while your husband's away," Tracy says. "I showed her where you-all lived, and she said if you-all need anything from the store, like snacks, or anything from the garden, you should ask her. We got more fall squash coming in than we know what to do with. My mother gets real sick of canning."

"My mother used to can," says Phoebe. "I'd almost forgotten. Maybe your mother can give me a refresher. One single working woman to another, as the case may be."

As soon as Phoebe drops us off at church, Tracy lays a heavy hand on my back and keeps it there. "Are you and Cecil going together now, or what?" she says.

And just like that, his name heats up a secret core of shame and longing I never even knew existed before yesterday. I shut my eyes against the warmth. "No," I say. "Nothing happened."

"You turning a whole lotta red over nothing."

"Nothing much, I mean."

"Okay," she says. "I hear you. Nothing much." And when I open my eyes again, she winks at me.

We join about a hundred other kids on the back steps, all standing around waiting for Pastor Chick to come out. Some kids are Operation Outreach recruits from school or maybe from other churches. Mary-Kate and Karen are, predictably, huddled together near the church door. They eye Tracy and whisper to each other. Seth is tossing a NERF football around in the paved drive with a few other boys. I point him out as the one who's living in my house, and Tracy says, "Skinny."

A low, loud black car turns into the lot and pulls slowly through the kids, who part on either side of it in wonder. Painted on its hood is an enormous silver bird. "That's a Trans Am," Tracy says.

When the passenger door opens, none other than Kelly-Lynn steps out. She closes the car door without a word to the driver and stands there in her ironed jeans, searching the group until she finds me and makes a beeline.

"I like your car," says Tracy when Kelly-Lynn reaches us.

"So does my mom. Just ask her, she'll tell you all about it." Which is exactly the kind of talk Tracy enjoys. We all watch Kelly-Lynn's mom ease the car around the circular drive. When she turns back onto Main Street, she gives it the gas and makes the tires squeal. "Outta sight, outta mind," Kelly-Lynn says, rolling her eyes. "The school informed her that I was smoking, and so last night she went through my book bag and found the flyer for this and decided a church thing would do me some good." She looks at me pointedly. "Wonder how that happened?"

"Sorry," I say, marveling again at the tenacity of Operation Outreach. Kelly-Lynn just shrugs.

The church door opens, and Pastor Chick joins the swarm of kids. The boys throw themselves at him, slapping his back, punching his arms. "You're a tough bunch," he says, jabbing into the air, slapping a few backs of his own. Then he steps up on the curb and raises his voice. "Welcome, people," he calls out, and everyone quiets down. "And a very warm welcome to our special guests. We're glad you're here. People, none of you were around in 1973, though maybe one or two of you were a twinkle in your parents' eyes. But lo those many years ago, the spirit of the Lord worked a revival miracle in this town. Some folks showed up to celebrate Jesus Christ, and some showed up, maybe like a few of yourselves, to see what all the fuss was about. Well, people, tonight we've got a little bit of everything. Some fuss and some fun. This scavenger hunt we've cooked up will have you roaming East Winder like a pack of foraging coyotes, then racing back to the water tower, where it all went down in the first place, for some righteous fellowship. And prizes, people. Did I say prizes? And people, I'm not even going to mention the food. Or the games. Or the crazy things that happen after you've been locked into the seminary gym for hours in the middle of the night with hours left to go."

When he pauses for breath, everyone whoops.

"Listen to them," Tracy says.

Kelly-Lynn checks her watch.

"And now," says Pastor Chick, pointing to Conley, who drumrolls on the church door behind him, "I have here in my hand"—Pastor Chick brandishes a sheaf of papers—"the lists for our scavenger hunt." More whooping and a few "coyotes" howl. "But first, folks, I'd like for you to separate into small groups. And you know what? Since it's getting dark a little earlier these days, let's make sure there's at least one godly young man in each group. We don't want to send our godly young ladies out onto the mean streets of East Winder alone." Boys who have probably been ready to whoop again groan instead. They are totally outnumbered by godly young ladies and will most likely be separated. "In fact," Pastor Chick says, "why don't you godly young ladies get yourselves into groups of three or four, and I'll assign you a godly young man to keep and protect."

Tracy clamps one arm around me and the other one around Kelly-Lynn. "Hope he doesn't give us that farty guy who lives in your house," she says, and right then I get a bad feeling.

"Your boyfriend?" says Kelly-Lynn, looking at me meaningfully.

"Not exactly," I say. "Not at all, actually."

"She's got a new boyfriend now," says Tracy to Kelly-Lynn.

"I don't have any boyfriends," I say.

Pastor Chick, passing nearby, points to us. "Before the evening is over, I want to meet your friends, Charmaine Peake."

"Did we do something wrong?" Tracy says, and Pastor Chick chuckles and moves on. But soon he's back, papers in one hand, box of garbage bags in the other, Seth scowling behind him.

"Just look at this extraordinary group," Pastor Chick says. "With my man Seth, we have a grand protector. And with my good lady Charmaine, we have someone, I'll wager, who knows the mean streets of East Winder like the back of her hand. Charmaine, how's your grandmother?"

"A little better," I say hopefully, but a quick, sharp ache rises in my throat.

Pastor Chick extends a respectful hand first to Tracy and then to Kelly-Lynn.

"You two have fine instincts," Pastor Chick says. "I can tell by the company you keep. Who's going to refuse a group of young people this special when they come knocking in the name of the Lord?" He hands Kelly-Lynn a sheet of paper with the list of items. He hands Tracy a garbage bag. He reminds us to stick to households with the porch light on and to take only one item from each. And not to do anything that might be unfair, like go to our own homes. He looks from Seth to me then back. "You know what I mean," he says.

"You mean Charmaine's home," Tracy says, and Seth looks at the ground.

We're supposed to make a note of who we get things from and if it's anything they might want back. "We don't want an angry East Winder mob scene," says Pastor Chick. And we're all supposed to meet under the water tower, he tells us, before the seminary carillon chimes nine.

Seth is pretending to gaze out over the parking lot while really glancing sidelong at Kelly-Lynn. When he gets back around to her again, she's looking right at him.

"Take a picture," I say. "It'll last longer."

"I hear you enjoy photographs," Kelly-Lynn says sweetly.

Tracy narrows her eyes, and when Kelly-Lynn whispers in her ear, Seth flushes pink from his collar to his hair.

"People," yells Pastor Chick from the top step of the church. "Have you formulated a strategy? Because in ten seconds I'm setting you scavengers loose on this unsuspecting town. Are. You. Ready?"

The crowd of kids, each group studying its list, gives off an anemic "Yes."

"Convince me," says Pastor Chick.

"Yes," everyone yells.

"Ten, nine, eight . . ." Pastor Chick counts.

"'Light of the world' lightbulb?" reads Kelly-Lynn, running down the list with her finger. "What is that, just a regular light-bulb?"

". . . seven, six, five . . ." says Pastor Chick.

"'Give to Caesar' bicentennial quarter," says Kelly-Lynn, rolling her eyes again. "'The street of the city was gold' button. Now we're going to take somebody's button."

"We can get one from Doctor Osborne," says Seth. "He keeps a box for costumes."

". . . two, one!" Pastor Chick calls out, and we trail after the rest of the kids thronging out of the parking lot in their groups of four.

The crowd teems down the middle of Main Street in one direction, all getting in each other's way. Like lemmings, Phoebe would say. I lead our group the other way, up Main toward the single blinking light. Beyond the light are the tree streets, and beyond them the water tower. There aren't as many houses on this side of town, only twenty or so, including Dr. Osborne's, but if we can complete the list in this general area, we'll finish ahead of everyone.

The first place we try belongs to Mrs. Renfrew, a friend of Daze's. She comes to the door in a housedress and with her hair in curlers. "How's your grandmother, dear?" she asks me. "Don't shatter this lightbulb and cut your sweet little hands." From her purse, she gives us each a piece of stale gum, and we all work our jaws with it until she closes the door. Then I spit mine into the storm drain, and so does everyone else.

"This is lame," Kelly-Lynn says, crossing "light of the world" lightbulb from the list.

"We forgot to ask if she wants it back," says Tracy.

"You should always return people's property anyway," says Seth. To me.

A bald man I've seen around town answers the next door. "Who is it?" his wife calls from somewhere behind him, and he says, "I don't know. No, wait. It's the Peake girl. Do I have that right? How's your father?"

Everyone looks at me.

"Fine," I say, training my eyes on the man's waxy-looking head.

"You must be looking forward to him coming home."

I want to tell him it's none of his business, but then he probably wouldn't want to give us an "ark of gopher wood" wooden spoon. "Yes," I say. "Do you have a wooden spoon?"

"You kids coming from the church tonight?" says his wife, popping her head over the man's shoulder. "Oh, hi there. Charmaine Peake, right? How's your father? How's your grandmother? And Seth Catterson? I don't know you other two girls. We read about this in the bulletin. What fun!"

"We're after a wooden spoon," says Tracy, moving things along.

The woman draws her mouth in regretfully. "I have one, but it never leaves my kitchen. It was my great-grandmother's, if you can believe it."

"Then how about anything else on this list," Kelly-Lynn says and thrusts out the paper.

The man looks it over. "'Give to Caesar,' ha. A bicentennial quarter?" He jingles some change in his pocket and pulls out a handful, slowly turning over each quarter while we wait. "Nope. Nope. Nope. Tell you what," says the man. "I'll go through my change drawer and look for one of those quarters, and you kids stop by again."

We head back down their walk. A gentle, chilly wind rustles the few leaves underfoot. It's still light out, but not for long. Lamps start to come on in the windows as we pass. More porch lights too. It's supposed to be a full moon, but you can't see it for the low clouds.

"How come you said you're looking forward to your dad coming home, when he's not?" Seth says.

"Why don't you worry about your own dad coming home?" I say. It comes from the meanness that I'm figuring out might always be inside me, ready to go.

"That's different," says Seth. "He's fundraising. He's just on the road. He's not moving in somewhere else."

"On the road," says Kelly-Lynn as we proceed down the street. "That's code for getting a divorce."

Seth stops in the middle of the sidewalk. "My parents are missionaries. They are not getting divorced."

"Charmaine's parents aren't, either," Tracy says.

"I never said they were," says Seth. "What I said was her father's not coming home. He has to stay locked up."

"He's not locked up," I say, feeling the depressing way meanness only makes more of itself. *Beget* is the word, like in the Bible. Meanness begets meanness.

"He's not exactly free to go," Seth says. "He's crazy."

"Some might say it's crazy to keep pictures of dead people," Kelly-Lynn says. If I said it, it would sound like another mean thing, but she makes it sound natural, almost friendly.

"It's not crazy," Seth says. "It's just a way not to think about stuff."

"I saw *Faces of Death* at my dad's girlfriend's house," Tracy says.

"Did it help you not think about stuff?" Kelly-Lynn says.

"I never even tried not to think about anything," says Tracy. "Why would I?"

"Seth's talking about lust," I say. "He lusts after girls, which is a sin. So then he looks at sickening pictures to make him stop thinking about the things he wants to do to girls."

"I don't want to do anything," Seth says, his voice hitting a shrill note. Even in the fading light I can see his neck turning red again.

"What if it backfires and you start wanting to do stuff more?" Kelly-Lynn asks. "Like to that woman on the table."

"What table?" says Tracy. "What woman?"

We are now standing on the sidewalk in front of Dr. Osborne's house. He lives in the only Sears-catalog bungalow in town, Phoebe has told me, which his father built from a kit. We don't even see him sitting there on the swing, behind the post, until he emerges from the shadow to stand at the top of the porch steps.

"Doctor Osborne, tell them," Seth says. "About looking at pictures to control your thoughts."

Dr. Osborne fingers the cross of nails hanging against his chest. "Ah," he says. "Scavenger hunt, unless I miss my guess. Charmaine Peake, how's your mother?"

"All people do in this town is ask after your family," says Tracy.

"She took the pictures," Seth says, indicating me with a flick of his head that makes his glasses glint in the porch light.

Dr. Osborne turns an ear to us like he didn't quite hear. Interested. Polite. "Pictures?" he repeats. "Who took pictures?"

"Stole them," Seth says.

"Tell me about these pictures," says Dr. Osborne. He looks from Seth to me, then back to Seth.

"What do you mean, tell you about them?" Seth says. "The pictures." His voice is tight and high, shrill again. There's no question for me now where he got the photographs, no matter how much Dr. Osborne pretends.

"Don't have a conniption," says Tracy.

"They sound important," says Dr. Osborne. "Have all of you seen these pictures?"

"I have," says Kelly-Lynn.

"Maybe I'd better have a look myself," says Dr. Osborne. "Charmaine, you have them, if I've followed the ins and outs here, yes?"

Seth's bottom lip pulls away from his top lip, but no sound comes out. He looks at Dr. Osborne in outrage and something like despair, and I try, from meanness, to take pleasure in it.

"I might," I say, "and I might not."

Dr. Osborne squints at me, but only with one eye. "I don't understand."

"What kind of pictures would you use to stop thinking about something?" I ask him. "Say you wanted to keep on being the man who has never known a woman. Say you wanted to stop thinking about my mother."

"I'm not sure what you're getting at, Charmaine."

"Would you look at a picture of a dead woman?" says Kelly-Lynn.

"Yes," Seth says. "And other dead people. You know," he says. "Tell them." It's as if he still thinks Dr. Osborne might not understand, as if he can't imagine any other reason for what the man's saying. Or not saying.

Dr. Osborne looks away from Seth and smiles at Tracy and Kelly-Lynn in a frozen way. "I don't believe I caught either of your names," he says. "All right, kids, whatever you're up to tonight, I don't believe I have anything you need. Seth, this is a bit of a disappointment. Charmaine, don't you think your mother has enough on her plate these days without having to worry about you? How about you all head along now, so I won't feel like I have to call your parents."

"And say what?" I ask.

"You don't even know my parents," says Kelly-Lynn. "You don't even know my name."

"We don't even have a phone," says Tracy.

Beside me, Seth twists his mouth angrily, then opens it and takes a loud, shuddering breath. I want to keep hating him—for living in my house and for all the things he's said about my father—but he looks suddenly so much like a little kid. There's an undertow to his despair, like gravity at the core of him, and I'm close enough that it tugs at me no matter how mean either one of us can get.

I unzip the butt purse and take out the picture of the woman on the table. Under Dr. Osborne's porch light I study it again, even though it's already permanently grafted onto my brain. Tracy moves up behind me and peers over my shoulder. She lets out a low whistle. On my hand, underneath the charred edge of the picture, you can still see all the hatch marks I made, like a complicated network of pale veins. I think of how hard I tried to pray and how clean and relieved I felt to quit. I think, with a kind of heaviness, of the way Seth and even Dr. Osborne have been knocking themselves out not to think anything that might make them feel what I feel every time I think about Cecil. Lust. I think of how hard it is to keep trying to do what's impossible, how exhausting. How even their efforts have become something to hide.

"It's the only one left," I tell Dr. Osborne. "You can have it back. If you tell Seth you're sorry."

I can feel Seth staring at the side of my face, but I don't turn my head. I hold Dr. Osborne's gaze until he finally looks down at the picture, and when he looks up at me again, some of the coldness has drained out of his expression. And now suddenly I see more of him than I want to, just like with Seth. I see the boy who wanted to live at my father's house instead of his own, who grew up into a man who tries too hard to help. In all the wrong ways. A man who has never known a woman, maybe never known anyone else at all. Not really. Not well enough. Loneliness is what's in the gravity coming from the center of Dr. Osborne. I'm getting the idea that every person on earth is their own black hole, and if you get too close, you get sucked right in. Meanness can pull you close, just like love does, but once you're there, once you see what's inside, you've hit a point of no return and you've got to carry it all, dense as a brick, heavy on your heart. And it would be easier if what you saw was evil, pure and simple as a big evil brain in a book. But when you get to the point of no return, all the evil and all the meanness just turn sad. My father said I would know my calling when it happened, the calling I prayed for when I still believed in it. But I never thought a calling could be something like this, this sad, straight sight into what's at the center of people. I never thought it would be something I had no idea what to do with.

"I'm not at my best tonight, Seth," Dr. Osborne says finally. "I'm sorry."

Seth takes off his glasses and rubs them on the hem of his shirt. He backs down from Dr. Osborne's porch without looking at me, turns on his heel, and heads for the sidewalk. Kelly-Lynn follows him, but Tracy waits.

I hand the picture to Dr. Osborne like I said I would. "What happened to her?" I ask. I can't help it.

"I don't know," he admits, holding the picture with one hand, fingering the cross of nails again with the other. Then, inexplicably, he hands the picture back to me. Almost gently, like an offering. "Nothing good."

I put the picture back in my purse. The streetlamps have come on now, and Tracy and I step off the porch and join Seth and Kelly-Lynn in a soft circle of light.

"You're not crying, are you?" Tracy says to Seth.

"No."

"Creepy man," says Kelly-Lynn, holding her watch up to the streetlamp. She holds the list up, too, then folds it into quarters and hands it to me. "Maybe we just blow this off?"

High above the last house on the street and over the field beyond, the cross on top of the water tower lights up with a low electric buzz that hits my ears like something much closer, an insect in my hair. Soon the whole Youth Group of First Community will gather on the hill for a brief reenactment of my grandfather's Great Revival. We were supposed to bring people, and that's what I did. I brought some people.

I catch myself planning how to report this evening to my father—whether I will write it to him or tell him in person—before I remember that he doesn't even have a vision for the county anymore. That such a vision may only have been the sickness talking in the first place. Like so many other things that were supposed to have come from God.

"Okay," I say. "Let's blow this off." I slip the list of scavenger hunt items into the purse, next to the picture, and we all head up the street to wait under the water tower for everyone else.

Other places in town have openings in the barbed-wire fence that give access to the field and to the seminary's softball diamond on the other side of the hill. But not here at the end of Elm. Seth uses both hands to pin down the top strand of the fence, and I go first, balancing my weight in the sway of the barbed wire. Then I hold my breath and launch myself over and into the field. The weeds have been recently mowed, the cuttings pushed into knee-high piles, and once everyone else is over the fence, we step carefully over the stiff, sharp stalks. "I never thought we'd be tramping through a field this way," says Tracy. "Not for a church event. Not in town. We're going to be full of ticks."

"I hate ticks," Kelly-Lynn says, lifting her knees high.

Seth is silent, lagging behind, looking down at his feet. Every once in a while he sniffs and wipes at his face, but we all pretend not to notice. As we approach the tower, I realize that even though I've seen it almost every day of my life, I've never been this close. The huge tank sits high atop six tall, slender pillars and one thick center post. It's even higher than it seems from a distance. Between each set of pillars run crisscrossing diagonal cables, in four enormous Xs stacked one on top of another, each X at least four times as tall as I am.

Underneath the shadow of the tank, Seth sinks to the grass. He leans against one of the pillars and looks out toward town with a peeled-open expression, like the air on his face is something of a surprise. I still feel for him, but I want to get away from him, too. From the weight inside him that now I can't help but sense, real as my own. The inside of one of the pillars has a series of U-shaped metal rungs, and before I know I'm going to do it, I drop my purse and grasp onto the highest rung I can reach.

"You have about ten minutes before people start showing up," warns Kelly-Lynn, holding her watch outside the shadow of the tank.

I haul myself up and begin climbing fast, too fast to lose my nerve. Below me, Tracy steps onto the lowest rung and starts to climb, too. When I reach the top of the bottommost X, I stop and look out over East Winder. You can see the roofs of the houses on the tree streets, the steeples of the United Methodist Church and the Church of God. You can see the blinking yellow light at Main and Maple. Under my feet, Tracy's face is worried.

"What's wrong?"

"This is high," she says in a small voice.

"Stay there," I tell her, and I keep climbing. I don't feel the height yet, just the satisfaction of pulling myself up rung by rung. The breathtaking way the space opens up beneath me, deep and cool. How it gets darker, quieter, halfway to the underbelly of the tank. I keep going. With each rung I can feel the twin pull of my breasts as they resettle more and more heavily, and a tiny dull stroke of pain in my womanhood, a signal that my period will soon return, as it will keep on returning month after month for a long, long time, whether I want it to or not.

I climb as if I could outclimb everything—my body, my family, all the things I wish I didn't know and all the things I wish I couldn't see. As if I could outclimb God or reach him, two equal impossibilities. When I finally make it to the tank, I give the enormous belly a few pats, like it's a big sleeping animal. It's the most solid sound I've ever heard. There are gallons and gallons of water inside, maybe tons, and you can't hear a drop of it. My palm comes away coated with paint dust.

Tracy's still halfway down, at the top of the second huge X, edging herself up slowly. Every so often she presses herself as hard as she can against the pillar, wedges her feet into the rungs, and clings there.

"Oh, what the hell," I hear Kelly-Lynn say, just barely, from the ground. She grabs a rung, too, which makes a sound that echoes within the pillar all the way to the top. Then Seth gets to his feet and follows her. A breeze lifts my hair. It is longer now, and growing all the time. My crown in glory. From up here the streetlamps look very low, giving off their small pools of light, revealing patches of pavement and the occasional fender or hood of a parked car. You can see Dr. Osborne's street and the intersection of Main and East, too, where I used to live, where Seth lives now, and even where his window, *my* window, should be. Toward the edge of town a car's headlights wink in and out of the trees, heading south on Main Street to where it becomes the river road. From this high up, during the day, you might even be able to see Tate's Bridge hovering over the distant palisades, emerging red and rusty from the trees.

Dark as it seems under the water tower, we are not hidden. From farther down Main Street comes the police cruiser—lights flashing, siren off, speeding in our direction. Called by Dr. Osborne, possibly, but who knows? Any of the people in town could have glanced out their window.

"We're in for it," Tracy yells from below. Kelly-Lynn and Seth clamber down and drop easily to the ground, then wave to us as if we don't have our own view of the situation.

"Go ahead," I call down to Tracy, but she has wrapped her arms tightly around the pillar, as far as they'll go.

"I can't," she says. "I can't move."

The police cruiser makes quick work of Main Street, and now, trailing it, I see the flat box of Daze's Buick, slipping in and out of the light from the streetlamps like a huge, silent fish. I don't know how they reached her so quickly. I watch as Police Chief Ezra Burton parks over on Maple, where there's a gate in the fence. Moments later I watch him make his way up the hill with Phoebe on his arm, struggling through the sharp weed stalks in her good pumps and squinting up toward my place just under the huge tank.

"That's your mom," Tracy calls up to me.

Before I know it, we're both lit up from below by a huge police flashlight. I can't see anything, and when I take a hand from the rung to cover my eyes, Phoebe screams.

It's a small sound from this high up. "She's going to fall," she cries. "She's going to fall." The beam starts to swing wildly as Phoebe clutches at Chief Burton. Now others are making their way up the hill, kids from the scavenger hunt, and I won-der if this is what it looked like to my grandfather as the Great Revival accumulated person by person.

When Chief Burton fixes me again in his light, I squeeze the pillar between my knees and wave with both arms to show I'm okay, that I'm in no danger of falling. A gasp rises from the col-lection of people below.

"Your mom just got sick," Tracy calls.

"I'm fine," I yell into the light. But you can't look into a light for long. I duck my head behind the pillar and let my eyes adjust to the field behind me, where the softer glow from the cross breaks over the shadow of the tank and spills down the backside of the hill. I can see everything from up here. I can see the future, even, with a certainty I never imagined. It is the only prophetic vision I will ever have, my whole life, and maybe it comes from God and maybe it comes from some part of my own mind, inside my own skull, some part I don't even mean to use. Which maybe comes from God, too. This is an argument my father and I will have over the years, me saying that if all things come from God then it's the same as nothing coming from God, and him saying no. That no matter what, those are not the same things.

Later in the night, after we're done at the police station and barred from the lock-in, and Phoebe has deposited Kelly-Lynn and Tracy at their respective homes, with apologies to their respective mothers, I will wait for her to light into me. When she doesn't, I will find myself trying to explain, to fill up the silence with details. Daze in the hospital bed calling me the wrong name, her name. The futility of ceaseless prayer. I will keep Cecil to myself, but I will tell her about Dr. Osborne and the pictures. I will show her the dead woman on the table and watch the complicated way her face changes as she makes room for whatever this information means to her. I am thirteen, and I have already begun to leave home. But tonight I have never wanted to hold my mother's attention so close, on guard against the new possibility that, like my father has, anyone can say "no" to what's been their life so far, and even "no more" to the people in it. I thought I understood the meaning of the word *cleave*, which can be "to sever" just as much as "to cling," a perfect word that contains its opposite, but now I understand something else: that it can mean both of these things at the same time.

What Phoebe does, what she will keep doing for the rest of her life, is bring everything back to my father like a record stuck in a groove. She will blame herself, she will blame him. Late on this night, when we're pulling into the driveway of the cabin and I finally fall quiet, she blames him. She says that worse, really, than any thoughts one might want to control—lust and the rest—are the actions, even the best-intended, most godly-seeming actions, that pull others into themselves. *Vortex* is the word she finds. A vortex of selfishness, and I look into the night sky, more aware than ever of all the hidden black holes.

As the years spread out and my father goes off his medication—once, twice, again, each time a little worse—the half-way houses won't hold him, and it's Phoebe, of course, who takes him back. First, with hope, as a husband. Then with resignation, and perhaps true Christianity. This goes on long after she's had to sell the house in town. After she's put in a phone line at the river and found full-time teaching. After Daze recovers for what she calls her "third act," the shortest one yet. After I've left East Winder. When I come back to visit, I'll sit across from Phoebe at the tiny fold-out table, and we'll look out toward the river to where my father has pitched his tent. An arrangement they can both live with as long as the weather holds, as long as the bank contains the current, which it does for many years. Miraculously, my father says. She'll give me a cup of tea to take to him, and if he's manic, he'll offer prophecy, which becomes more and more confused. If he's low, and the lows get a lot lower, I can sometimes encourage him to remember old facts—the names of the trees, the length and history of the bridge, a rare species of river eel. Once in a while, spurred by the sound of his own voice, he remembers to ask me something about my life, and when I answer, he regards me with wonder. Not for my accomplishments, which are modest—a college degree I'll work hard to pay for, a series of cast-around social-work jobs until one catches fire—but because any evidence of a life other than his own has become something of a shock. A welcome-enough shock, it seems, but a tiring one. "Whatever happened to that black cat of yours?" he asks then, as the clouds part for this old memory of something I loved.

"He never came back," I say.

But before any of this happens, I am still right up under the belly of the water tank, convincing myself that it might be possible to stay there forever, or to jump or fall, to land softly or not land at all, to soar. It's the thought of going back down the way I came that turns my legs to jelly. Then Tracy is there, close under my feet, pulling herself up rung by rung. Her face is clenched with fear. Her knuckles are as white as anything I've ever seen.

"Girl, what are you *doing*?" she says, looking down to the ground then pinching her eyes shut.

"What are *you* doing?" I say. But then I know. I'm close enough now to feel the pull of her heart, which, as it turns out, is deep and generous. We are blood kin, and she will not go down without me.

The light, the ground, the growing crowd all seem impossibly far below. The metal rungs now feel flimsy and manmade, smaller in every way, growing sharper through the soles of my sneakers.

"They won't hold," says Tracy, feeling it too.

"Yes," I say, "they will." From up here it's not an easy thing to promise or to trust, but what choice do we have? We close our eyes and start to make our way down. One slow rung at a time. Believing, over and over, what we have to, as hard as we can.

Acknowledgments

For reading parts of this manuscript in one form or another along the way, many thanks to Vandana Khanna, Karri Offstein Rosenthal, Caroline Goodwin, Stephanie Harrell, Elisa Albert, Ryan Harty, Ann Packer, Ann Cummins, Cornelia Nixon, Sarah Stone, Ron Nyren, Vendela Vida, Steve Willis, Lisa Michaels, and, in memoriam, Nancy Johnson. Special thanks to Ed Schwarzschild, Jennifer Greiman, Lynne Tillman, and Tina Pohlman for their support from the book's inception. Nina Pneuman, ZZ Packer, Carrie Herschman, Brad Levison, Christine Sneed, Regina Lutz, Charlie Eckstrom, Lisa Salazar, Lee Kaplan, Leona Christie, and Dan Orozco all helped me weather the doubtful times. Finally, big thanks to Eric Simonoff, Jenna Johnson, Nina Barnett, Kate Davis, and Michelle Blankenship for invaluable insight and expertise.

Alex Lauren

Angela Pneuman, raised in Kentucky, teaches fiction writing at Stanford University. Her work has been included in *The Best American Short Stories*, the *Iowa Review*, the *Los Angeles Review*, the *Virginia Quarterly Review*, *Glimmer Train*, and elsewhere. Her widely praised story collection, *Home Remedies*, was hailed as "call[ing] to mind Alice Munro" by the *San Francisco Chronicle*. A Stegner Fellow at Stanford, she was also a Presidential Fellow at SUNY Albany and the recipient of the inaugural Alice Hoffman Prize from *Ploughshares*. She lives in Chicago and in the Bay Area of California.